DARK

HAZARD

Books by

W. R. BURNETT

SAINT JOHNSON

THE SILVER EAGLE

IRON MAN

LITTLE CÆSAR

THE GIANT SWING

DARK HAZARD

*   *
*

DARK
HAZARD

By

W. R. BURNETT

HARPER & BROTHERS PUBLISHERS

New York and London

1 9 3 3

TO
MARJORIE AND MIKE

Contents

*

*

PART ONE

CHICAGO : 1928

Chapter I

THE CLOCK ABOVE THE SWITCHBOARD STRUCK MIDNIGHT
slowly; each chime was preceded by a faint, weary, pre-
monitory whir, then the works buzzed for a moment
after the final chime and went on ticking. The night
clerk, sitting at the switchboard reading the *Examiner,*
did not look up. The striking of the clock fitted in
quietly with the audible silence which closed him in
each night. Down the lobby a radiator tapped; outside
the wind blew and fat white snowflakes struck the lobby
windows; taxicabs hooted faintly on Sheridan Road.
This was as it should be. The night clerk, reading under
a green-shaded light, felt very comfortable surrounded
by the black windy silence of a Chicago winter night.
He did not think about the dark waves of Lake Michigan pounding at the deserted wharfs and beaches; he
did not think about the forests of dim street lights
stretching for miles in all directions; he thought of
nothing except what he was reading: the Cubs were
going to train at Catalina, Mickey Walker had won an-

other fight, the nags started running at Agua Caliente Christmas Day.

The night clerk did not look like a night clerk. He was a big, light-haired man of thirty-four, with powerful, broad shoulders, a strong neck which widened out at the base, and a large face with pronounced masculine features; there were marked bony ridges above his gray eyes, and his forehead, of medium height, was very wide. He had tried to plaster his coarse blond hair into conventional smoothness, but it stuck up behind. He was dressed like a night clerk should be dressed, smartly, unobtrusively, but muscles bulged under his hand-me-down coat and his necktie was crooked. One thing kept him from being a very formidable-looking man—an air of sleepy good nature, somewhat like a tame bear.

There was a call on the switchboard—a house-call—and the night clerk grinned when he noticed the number—632. His wife calling to tell him good night; Marg perched away up above him on the sixth floor in their cozy little apartment. He could see the pillows scattered about the davenport; the tan shade on the bridge lamp, which made such a good reading-light; the little radio with its small illuminated dial. Pretty swell place, all right; mighty comfortable for Marg, and for him, too.

"Good evening, Mrs. Turner."

Marg laughed.

"Good night, Mr. Turner."

"Merry Christmas, kid."

"Is it twelve already? Merry Christmas, Jim. Sorry you're not up here with me."

"Ain't I?"

"Ain't you what? And don't say ain't."

"Ain't I sorry?"

"Think I'll go to bed, Jim. See you in the morning."

"Say, this is special tonight, kid, see? Christmas Eve.
Why don't you come down and have a cup of coffee
with me? I'll send the dinge out. It'll be all right with
Mr. Plummer. Anyway, he's on a party."

"Think it'll be all right? You don't want to get Mr.
Plummer sore at you, Jim. We're pretty well fixed here."

"Aw, come on! What can a guy say on Christmas Eve?
He'd be a chump to say anything on . . ."

"All right. I've got to put my clothes back on."

"I won't go away," Jim laughed and broke the con-
nection. Fat chance of him ever getting away; night
after night from eight in the evening till eight in the
morning. Sometimes Plummer got big-hearted and gave
him a night off, but not very often. Ordinarily a night
clerk could put up a kick about not getting a regular
night off, but not now with ten guys for every job. Hell!
there wasn't no place to go, anyway, except a movie.
Marg liked movies; she liked to cry about the deserted
kid or the gray-haired mother, that stuff; although she
was ashamed to admit it and was pretty hard-boiled
herself. Hard-boiled in a nice way, that is; she was nobody's fool and she knew what was what. Jim sighed.

Imagine a woman like Marg falling for him! Why,
she was nice and refined and had refined folks over in
Barrowville, Ohio. Her uncle had been a Methodist
preacher and her father was superintendent of the Barrowville High School for a long time. What a break for
him the day he saw Marg! She had her nose in the air
and that "Oh, what the hell!" look on her face, and
when he took off his hat and scraped his big feet, she

said, "How do you do?" in that cold voice she could put on when she wasn't pleased. Ma Mayhew had taken him in as a roomer; they were pretty hard hit when the Barrowville Iron Foundry failed; Pa lost his money and was sick and couldn't work. But Marg didn't sit down and cry like a lot of girls would have done; she took what little money she had and bought a millinery shop. And she really ran it. Marg was O.K.

Jim stirred restlessly and rustled his paper. A familiar name in the Agua Caliente entries made him slightly uncomfortable. The ponies would be running tomorrow away down there in Mexico where it was warm and a man could loaf around in his shirt sleeves, drink some good beer, and play Gonfalon across the board in the sixth, providing, of course, that a man had any money. But, hell! when a man was free. . . . Jim tossed the paper away, got up, stretched, and walked about for a minute or two.

For the first time that night he really looked about him; really, that is, focused his eyes on the too familiar lobby and took it in. It was shabbily elegant; a third-rate joint five miles north of The Loop, filled with small-timers of all varieties: an out-of-work hypnotist, a three-a-day vaudeville gal, clerks, agents, insurance salesmen, two barbers, a stenographer or two, all, or most all, as shabbily pretentious as the red-and-tan lobby, with its phony oil paintings, its lush overstuffed furniture, and its false mahogany radio.

That was where it was: Aqueduct. Gonfalon at six to one and Johnny Mueller saying: "Buck, he ain't got a chance. Buttercup'll beat him ten lengths." So he shaved his bet, hedged a little, and here come Gonfalon all out by himself and the little damn fool of a jockey riding him all over the race-track. That night he said to Johnny Mueller: "Well, how about that sixth race?" And Johnny said: "Didn't I tell you Gonfalon was much the best?" Jim laughed; them guys were all alike.

Wow! He'd never forget when Ma Mayhew found out that he was connected with the Bellport Racetrack. When she took him in as a roomer she thought he was a "workman of some kind." Marg's people thought that anybody who gambled or raced horses was in a class with gangsters. Ma told him he'd have to move, and he did. After that Marg was very nice to him, used to meet him after she had shut up shop; pretty soon she got crazy about him. Oh, Marg was swell, but she was like her own people. She thought that race-track folks were a bunch of thugs, although she had followed the ponies with him for nearly a year.

But that was enough. And here he was a night clerk at twenty-five per and room. He turned. A little man with a swarthy aquiline face and jet-black hair had come in on tip-toes. His tight-fitting dark overcoat was peppered with snow; he was holding his derby in his left hand and smiling. He was drunk.

"Ah," he said, raising his black eyebrows, "they got you talking to yourself, eh?"

Jim grinned. He didn't like the little man, but he was the Northland's best tenant; he had a "suite" on the fifth floor and was good pay; also a friend of Mr. Plummer's.

"Was I talking out loud?"

"Was you talking out loud! You was roaring, my big boy; roaring. You know, Turner, I always thought you was dumb as hell, but I didn't know you went around talking to yourself. You'll be picking them out of the air next."

Jim flushed. He'd like to step on this little mosquito; but it couldn't be done. It was snowing outside and he had exactly thirty dollars all told, and also Marg to think about. A couple of years ago he would have pushed this little mug in the face and damn the consequences.

The little man twirled his derby.

"You seem to be wrought up and angry about something, my good man," he said, raising his voice slightly. "Have I said something to hurt your feelings?" Suddenly he laughed sharply. "For Christ's sake give me my key and don't stand there like the Tribune Tower. Five seventy-six in case you don't remember; you've only been here six months."

Jim handed him the key.

"Merry Christmas to you," said the little man, bowing slightly.

Jim turned away and picked up the paper, but the little man leaned on the desk and meditated. Jim felt the blood slowly leaving his face; some day little Mr. D. Mosely Bright would catch him at the wrong time with some of his wise-cracks, and then, bang! no job. It was tough, living what Marg called "a good safe life"; a man had to swallow too much.

Jim heard the clink of a bottle on the desk and turned. Bright was offering it to him.

"Drink?"

"No, thanks."

"Well, merry Christmas, and I mean it this time. It's just my way, Turner. I get a kick out of riling people."

"All right, Mr. Bright."

"You don't like me much, do you?"

"I like you, all right."

"You haven't got guts enough to tell me you don't like me, have you?"

"I don't think that takes much guts. I don't like you or dislike you."

"Say, just for the sake of curiosity, how did you come to end up as a night clerk? You look like you ought to be shoveling coal. Can you really read and keep books?"

"Think this snow's going to keep up?"

"Give me that paper," said Bright, with sudden ferocity, pulling the *Examiner* out of Jim's hands, "and don't wise-crack me. It takes too long for you to think, anyway. I bet you been thinking that one up since last Christmas. Where do they run the Caliente entries in this damn . . ." Bright began to read the sport sheet.

The front door fanned and the little Rumanian, room 557, came in. His name was Joe Constantinesco and he was small, dark, and sleek. He worked for Mr. Bright and followed him around like a poodle. Jim thought that he was bad medicine, although he was always exaggeratedly polite, as if his main object in life was to make people think that he was a "nice fellow."

"Hello, Turner!" he said. "What a night! What a night! Snow this deep and I got on thin shoes. Oh, Merry Christmas!"

"Same to you." Jim handed Joe his key, hoping that Marg wouldn't come till these men had gone. Bright might say something to her and then he'd have to drape him around the chandelier. Joe, too, maybe.

Bright turned.

"Why didn't you let me in on it, gigolo? What's Maxie want to hand us one horse and Eddie another for?"

"Honest, I couldn't remember."

"He couldn't remember! Anyway, I'm going to bet on Cayenne. What does this umpchay know about it?"

Joe laughed.

"You bet your way; I'll bet my way."

"This is mutiny." Bright turned and started for the automatic elevator. "He used to own Gold Leaf! I used to own Man-o'-War, but I fed him too much salt water and he turned into a seahorse. Going to bed, Joe?"

"Coming right up."

The elevator door opened and Marg came out. Jim held his breath and watched, but Bright bowed slightly and held the door for her. Then Bright got into the elevator and they heard its metallic hum as it climbed upward.

Joe took off his hat and moved away from the desk deferentially.

"Good evening, Mrs. Turner."

"Good evening."

Marg had on her dark dress that Jim liked so well. She looked slim and young; she carried herself so straight that it was a pleasure to watch her walk. Jim was always proud of her, and he did not miss the gleam of respect and interest in the Rumanian's dark eyes.

Joe hesitated, then said:

"Good night, folks, and Merry Christmas. Turner, I'm going to bet my money on Gonfalon. That's the horse."

Jim smiled uneasily; he knew that Marg was looking at him. She did not like to hear him talking "horse"; it made her feel insecure. Neither of them said anything; they heard the leisurely hum of the automatic elevator. Finally Marg said:

"Well, Mr. Turner, where's this coffee?"

Jim looked blank, then laughed.

"I forgot. I got to talking to the fellows and forgot."

"Was Bright being nasty again?"

Jim looked at her with admiration; she always *knew*. You couldn't fool her.

"A little. I'd like to put his nose around on the back of his head."

"I don't like that Rumanian. He's got snake eyes. Well, what about this coffee?"

"I'll send Smoke out right away." Jim phoned the basement, where the negro, Smoke, who acted as night engineer, stayed. He got as close to the boiler as possible and cooked himself all night long. He came up out of the warm basement with swollen eyes, and shuddered when he saw the snow falling past the big lobby windows.

It was nearly one. Marg was just finishing the last of the coffee. From time to time Jim looked at her, noting for the thousandth time that her nose was fine and straight, her eyes blue and keen, her face delicate but forceful. She suited him perfectly, perfectly!

He thought she looked a little tired.

"Maybe you better go to bed, kid," he said. "It's around one."

"I guess I better. Did I tell you about Ma's letter yet?"

"No."

He knew that she knew that she hadn't; she was the least vague person he had ever met; she just didn't forget things. This was her way of leading up to a subject, unpleasant for both of them.

"Well, Pa's sick again and the doctor's pretty expensive. And since Conny left George he hasn't been any good; never was, much. Can't hold a job two months. Ma thought maybe we could bring Sonny up here and send him to school. Do you think we could manage it?"

Jim shifted uneasily. More responsibility, more ties binding him to this shabby hotel, this infernal cold weather, this twenty-five-a-week excuse for a job. But he said:

"If you think so, Marg, it's all right with me. It won't cost much more with him here. I guess we can make it."

Marg got up.

"I'm going to think it over awhile. It might be a good idea just to send Ma some more money instead. We haven't got much room here and . . ." She looked around the lobby quickly, then bending down, kissed Jim on the mouth and ran her hand over his hair. "We don't see enough of each other as it is. Wish you were coming up to keep me warm."

Jim flushed. After over a year of her company she could still arouse him by a little kiss, a pressure, a sudden, quick, significant look. He sighed.

"I wish so, too.

"Anyway, we'll have some breakfast together. Good night, Jim."

"Good night, Marg. Listen, if you want to bring

Sonny here it's all right. We'll get along. Maybe I can get a raise after while or find a better job."

"Don't worry about it. I'll take care of it."

Jim sat listening to the slow metallic hum of the ascending elevator. He was as much in love with Marg as he had ever been. Why not? Where could he find another like her?

It was funny. Everybody depended on her. She had to take the rap for a whole family; no matter who was in trouble or what the trouble was, Marg was asked to settle it. And now they wanted to wish her brother George's kid on her, just because George was a no-good and couldn't look after himself. What did he want to marry that flusie for, anyway? A man with one eye could see that Conny was no good.

He yawned and sank back into his chair by the switchboard; seven hours yet to go. A hell of a job, and no future!

For a long time he sat watching the fat, white flakes falling past the big lobby window, then he dozed.

Jim woke from his doze and glanced mechanically at the clock. Five till two. He got up, stretched, yawned, then turned to look out the window; it was still snowing and big flakes were falling down past the street lights. He felt cramped all over and walked about for a while, stamping his feet and swinging his arms. It was chilly in the lobby now. He stood thinking and scratching his head, then he went back into the little office behind the switchboard and put on a short sweater which he always wore under his coat during the dead hours. He returned to his chair.

The minutes dragged. Down the lobby the radiator tapped faintly. Outside there wasn't a sound; the wind had died down and now the flakes were falling straight past the lights, heavily and silently. Christmas. Jim looked at the tree at the far end of the lobby, with its tinsel and imitation snow; a silver star gleamed on the top. Merry Christmas! Jim laughed shortly and began to clean his finger nails; then he picked up the *Examiner* and tried to read, but he knew most of it by heart and pretty soon he threw it aside in disgust. The same old stuff: murders, suicides, traffic accidents, robberies, attacks, political exposés. Nothing else except some dull editorials and the sport sheet. Hell! He played himself a game of tit-tat-toe, then he turned and sat for a half hour watching the snowflakes.

A little after two-thirty a taxi stopped outside. There was a short argument, then the door opened and the hypnotist, known as The Great Mario (when he could find work), and Jeannie, the three-a-day gal, came in arm-in-arm, both drunk. Jim got up.

"Well, Merry Christmas, folks."

"What's merry about it?" said Jeannie, a big blonde, who was very plump and always had her clothes too tight. "Me and Ed, here, went to a party after I was through, and some big cluck spilled coffee all over my dress. Take your Merry Christmas and . . ."

"Now, Jeannie," said the hypnotist. "You haven't the proper spirit at all. Merry Christmas, Turner."

Jim put their keys on the desk. He wanted to talk to somebody, even these drunks. He was tired of the silence of the lobby, of his own society.

"Well," he said, "it's still snowing. Been snowing most all evening."

"You're right," said Jeannie, "and before we found us a taxi I got most of it down my neck. Why don't you get you a car, Ed?"

"A car's no use to a man in a place like Chicago with all this good transportation."

Jim smiled to himself. The hypnotist was a first-class fourflusher with his Astrakhan collar, his cane, and his sad, detached air. His face was long and sallow, his hair dead black; he wore a neatly-clipped mustache and his eyes were large, black, and penetrating. Bright said that he looked like John Barrymore half made up for Svengali, but that was over Jim's head.

"This good transportation!" cried Jeannie. "Do you call that galloping bathtub we was just in good transportation?"

"No, I meant the elevated."

"He likes the elevated. Why don't you come right out and say you ain't got enough money to make a down payment on a spare tire?"

Jeannie roared with laughter at her own wit, and stumbled against the desk, nearly upsetting the inkwell. The hypnotist's face was red, but he said:

"I'll admit my money is tied up."

"Tied up is right. You know this guy, Turner. He's got fish-hooks in his pockets. When he was making over a hundred a week at the Bijou over on Milwaukee Avenue he brought me home on the elevated. I took him to a night club a friend of mine was opening. My friend, she says: 'He's a swell-looking guy. Is he a spender?' 'A spender!' I says. 'Why, his money flows like asphalt.'"

Jeannie roared again and lurched against the desk. Jim grabbed the inkwell and held it till she recovered.

"If I was you," said the hypnotist, getting redder, "I'd rehearse that cheap act of mine up in my room. You've been pulling that 'asphalt' gag since Eva Tanguay was in rompers."

"Yeah? Well, at least I give my public something, songs and good patter. I don't make goo-goo eyes at a lot of morons, then stick 'em up between two chairs and walk on 'em." She shook her forefinger at the hypnotist. "Don't talk back. You've already been the cause of ruining my best dress. Now don't spoil my Christmas spirit." She gave the hypnotist a bronx cheer and started for the elevator.

The hypnotist smiled apologetically and his sharp black eyes roved, avoiding Jim's.

"She's had a drink or two. Nice as she can be when she's sober. Good night and Merry Christmas."

Jim heard them laughing in the elevator, then he went back to his chair. He sat vaguely wondering what the boss, Mr. Plummer, was going to do about The Great Mario's bill. He owed the house over a hundred dollars and he never said anything about paying. Nobody seemed to have any use for him. Joe Constantinesco said with a polite smile that he thought Jeannie was paying what bills were being paid; Bright said bluntly that The Great Mario was pimping for Jeannie. Jim sort of felt sorry for the hypnotist; he was a four-flusher, all right, but not a gay one; his face was melancholy and lined, his eyes were very sad. Jim sighed. Money was the answer. There wasn't a problem money couldn't solve. Here he was, bored to death, working a whole week for twenty-five dollars. Why, he used to think that twenty-five dollars was a piker bet; he'd often paid twice that much for a good tip. Oh, well. He picked up the phone book and began to read the names.

But he kept on thinking about the hypnotist. Everybody said that at one time he had made a lot of money with his act; that he was as big an attraction as Thurston or Houdini. Now look at him; yesing a big broad like Jeannie, who ought to be told to shut her big mouth.

Another taxi stopped outside and a taxi-driver, blue with cold, stepped into the lobby.

"Say, pal, kin I get warm a minute?"

His face was tough and weathered, but his air was apologetic.

"Sure," said Jim. "Help yourself."

The taxi-driver leaned on the desk and rolled a cigarette.

"Christ, brother, you're lucky sitting in here soaking up heat. I took a fare down to the end of Argyle. Lived right on the Lakefront. He was boiled and I had to get him in. I couldn't leave him there; he might of went to sleep and froze to death. Jees! did I get cold. That wind was blowing across the Lake sixty miles an hour and cut like a knife. Look at my hands. If I hit my fingers against the desk they'd drop off. Some cluck stole my gloves. Can you feature a guy that'll steal a taxi-driver's gloves on a night like this? Christmas Eve, too."

Jim hesitated.

"Say," he said, "I got an old pair of gloves down in

the basement you can have. They're just cotton and dirty, but they might help."

The taxi-driver glanced at Jim, uncomprehending.

"Say, you ain't from Chicago are you?"

"No. Why?"

"Just wondered. If you can spare them gloves, O.K."

Jim phoned the basement and told Smoke to bring up the extra pair of gloves. Smoke came up rubbing his eyes and moaning feebly. Jim took the gloves from him and gave them to the taxi-driver.

"Godamighty!" said Smoke, "Ah cain't even get wahm layin' up ag'in' that ole boilah. If this ain't a bittah night Ah nevah see one. What you all want with them gloves? Ah was wearin' 'em on top my othah pair. Ah 'clare Ah cain't get wahm to save me noway."

Smoke was a blue-gum from lower Georgia; he complained constantly and his face was long and black and melancholy and sagged like a hound's.

"I'm going out and throw some snowballs with them gloves," said the taxi-driver.

Smoke said nothing; he didn't even look up, but turned and went back into the basement, humming dolefully.

The taxi-driver smoked in silence for a while, trying on the gloves. Finally he said:

"Where you from, pal?"

"No place in particular. I was born in western Pennsylvania."

"I'm from lower Illinois, myself. We used to have real winters down there, but I lived in Florida for three years and I can't get used to this cold."

"I know Florida."

"Yeah? I was on the east coast. Miami Beach. That's the place. I never would of come home if my old man hadn't got in a jam. Had to look after the old woman. Well, I'll be seeing you. Got to get going." The taxi-driver pulled on the gloves and grinned. "Many thanks, pal. If I can steer you any customers, I'll do it. What's your rules on one-night stands? I get a lot of couples looking for a place to throw one."

"The boss don't like it."

"And he's right. It ruins the joint in the end. Pretty soon somebody gets bumped off, then you got the dicks watching you. So long, and say . . . Merry Christmas. That's the first time I've meant it tonight."

"Merry Christmas."

Jim woke with a violent start, then groaned. His neck was so stiff that he could hardly move it; sharp, rheumatic pains ran up and down his legs and his feet were full of pins and needles. He got up and began to stretch, then he glanced at the clock. Ten till six. No wonder he was nearly paralyzed; he had been sleeping in that damn, uncomfortable chair for over an hour. The switchboard buzzed; the woman in 267 was calling, complaining that there was no heat in the radiator and that she was freezing to death.

"I'll fix it," said Jim; then he went down into the basement. Smoke was lying flat on his back on some piled-up sacks, snoring loudly. Jim woke him and told him to fire up; it was six o'clock. Smoke got up by inches. First he dragged himself to his hands and knees, then he raised his arms and, taking off his cap, scratched his head carefully, then got slowly and creakily to his feet.

"Mistah, mistah," he said, "Ah'd like to see that old sun coming up over Georgia. Yassuh, Yassuh. This ain't no fit place for black folks, noways. Ah 'clare my bones is friz."

Jim went back to the lobby and turned off half the lights, then he washed his face with cold water and sat down to wait for morning. Two mortal hours yet.

The big radiator at the far end of the lobby began to knock faintly, then louder and louder until it was pounding like a hammer on an anvil; then gradually it subsided and started to hiss. The clock struck six, the machinery whirring faintly before each chime. Then a milk-wagon passed, its wheels creaking in the still, cold morning. Jim went over to the window. It had stopped snowing, but the sidewalks were covered and there were drifts in the street. The milk-wagon stopped near the corner and Jim saw the milkman get down with his rack of bottles and disappear into a doorway. A white vapor was rising from the nostrils of the horse.

Jim yawned and turned back to his chair before the switchboard.

Chapter II

IT WAS SEVEN O'CLOCK IN THE EVENING. JIM AND MARG were just finishing their dinner. Marg had on a new padded robe Jim had bought her for Christmas and she looked small and kiddish, he thought, all bundled up, and with her light-brown hair tucked back over her ears. They had a little Christmas tree on the card-table, all complete with tinfoil icicles, small electric lights, and cotton snow at the base. Jim beefed about the damn tree being in the way in this little room, but Marg said it was going to stay where it was till New Year's Day.

When Jim knew that he felt sentimental he always beefed. He did love that tree. He had come up from the lobby Christmas morning feeling like he was eighty years old and ready to throw up the whole business and light out. But Marg, all dressed and looking fresh, opened the door for him, shouted Merry Christmas, then kissed him, showed him the tree, and fed him a good hot breakfast with sausage and wheat cakes. In no time he was sitting back with his feet on a chair, smoking a cigarette and feeling like Rockefeller. The apartment was warm and cosy; below him he could see the snow-covered rooftops, and beyond, Lake Michigan, slaty in the bleak morning. By God! it was good to have your own money, your own home, your own woman.

Marg filled his plate again, steak and fried potatoes, then laughed at him for eating so much. He grinned.

"Got to stoke this old engine."

"It's a good thing you're making some money. It takes it to feed you."

"Say, Marg, speaking about money, what you going to do about George's kid?"

"I decided that we'd better send Ma a little more money and let her take care of him."

"Right you are."

"Of course, if you could get a better job—later, I mean—why, then maybe we could take care of Sonny. But right now it'd be too crowded."

"You know what's what, kid. I like to have you all to myself."

"Why shouldn't you? Look who I am."

"Why shouldn't I is right." Jim pushed his plate away. "Come on over. Sit on papa's knee."

"No. Drink your coffee. I know you. You've got to get to work in a little while."

"Say, it was just a . . . just a innocent invitation."

"Oh yes. I know you and your innocent invitations. Drink your coffee."

Jim laughed and lit a cigarette to go with his final cup of coffee. Then he looked at Marg for a long time.

"Kid, sometimes I have to laugh thinking what the old bunch would say if they knew I'd settled down like this."

Marg's face tightened slightly. She was a little afraid of that old bunch. Before she met Jim she had gone about with Pres Barrow, the son of the man who used

to own the iron foundry; he was a very nice fellow, sort
of prim, but likable. When he found out that she was
going places with a man from the Bellport Racetrack,
he nearly died. He would just sit and look at her and
shake his head, or he'd talk for hours about what a
bunch of dissipated, brawling brutes those race-track
men were. And he was telling the truth, Marg agreed.
They were no good; they'd end up in the poorhouse,
the jail, or prematurely in the morgue. She did not like
to hear Jim talk about the "old bunch."

"What do you care what they say?"

"I don't care. Only it would be funny. I can just
imagine Johnny Mueller walking in here and seeing me
behind the desk. He'd sure think I was crazy."

"Do you think you are?"

"No, I don't. Sometimes, maybe. But it's on account
of you, Marg. If it wasn't for you I'd be right back
where I used to be."

"A bum."

"Not always. Not always."

"I know. A feast or a famine. Diamonds or crackers
and milk."

Jim laughed.

"That's about right. I remember one time . . ." He
felt very expansive and was getting ready to tell Marg for
the hundredth time about the day when he'd been broke
at Havre de Grace, borrowed twenty from Tom Lift,
got stewed on somebody else's whisky, and bet the whole
twenty on a hundred-to-one shot which came in. But
noting Marg's troubled and disapproving expression,
he hesitated, then said, "Oh, well. I guess a man's bet-

ter off living this way." He knew that that was what Marg wanted him to say, so he said it.

She smiled, then got up to get him an ash-tray.

It was five till eight when Jim stepped out of the automatic elevator. For a little over six months he had followed an exact routine. He ate dinner at six-thirty; at a little after seven he was reading the evening paper; and at a quarter till eight he got ready to go on duty. Marg always helped him comb his hair, always selected his necktie and approved or vetoed the condition of his finger nails. Left to himself, he would never have passed the rigid inspection of the boss, Mr. Plummer, who had been a clerk in a big hotel for fifteen years and was fanatical on the subject; as it was, Jim looked as neat and unobtrusive as was possible for a man of his size and character.

Mr. Plummer smiled when he saw Jim, ran his eyes over him professionally, then said:

"Good evening, Turner. Come in the office, I want to see you a minute. Miss Dolby will stay till we get through with our talk."

Miss Dolby, a tall, thin, blonde girl, who operated the switchboard in the daytime, said nothing, nor did she turn; but she was swearing under her breath, as she had a heavy date and was anxious to get away. Anyway, she didn't like Jim; thought he was a big lout, always talking about that snooty wife of his, never even looking at another woman. Why, a girl just didn't exist as far as he was concerned; he was the most distant and impersonal fellow she had ever seen. Of course that was a pretty good attitude in a romantic man, you know, one of them Arrow-collar boys, but what did a big bumpkin like him have to get snooty about? The switchboard began to buzz; four calls at once. Miss Dolby viciously chewed her gum and in a bitter-sweet voice said:

"Just a minute, please. Just a minute, please."

Mr. Plummer offered Jim a cigarette and they sat down. The boss was a sleek, finical little man with sparse light hair combed in a flat pompadour, a thin colorless face, and near-sighted blue eyes which were magnified and distorted by the thick lenses of his nose-glasses. He was always dressed in black, and his clothes were always fanatically brushed and pressed. He was affable, attentive, friendly in a professional way, but behind this hotel-clerk front he was excessively indifferent and cold, completely absorbed in the difficulties and triumphs of Mr. Plummer.

He had hired Jim for two reasons: first because he very evidently needed a job and would not be too particular about his pay or his quarters; second, because he considered Jim's wife "a lady," and gentility down at the heel was very attractive to him. Besides, he had had a lot of trouble with the wife of Jim's predecessor, who had been caught making a little money on the side while her husband worked.

"Turner," he said, "it will soon be nineteen twenty-nine, a new year, and the Northland is going to turn over a new leaf. But we're not going to wait till the first; we start now."

Mr. Plummer annoyed Jim a little with his precise diction and his somewhat oratorical manner when stating the simplest facts, and he wanted to say "So what?" but he held his tongue and puffed on his cigarette.

"No more credit. That's our new policy. Not that we ever did extend much; but you know we've got some bad accounts on our books even as it is. That's over. The tenants pay their weekly or monthly bills, as the case may be, or they go out."

"I understand."

"Now, our worst account is Edward Schultz, the hypnotist. The Great Mario! Strutting around with his cane and all, and trying to borrow breakfast money from poor Miss Dolby. You deal with him tonight. Tell him that he must pay one-third of what he owes, or out he goes. I mean it. Don't let him go to his room tonight. If he doesn't pay at the desk, plug the keyhole of his room. Above all, don't let him have any of his luggage. Is that clear?"

"I guess so." Jim laughed. "But you don't mean to tell me you want me to turn a guy out in the snow?"

"I don't care where you turn him out. I'm not responsible for the weather. He pays or out he goes. Is that clear? We'll make an example of him and then maybe some of those who owe us a week's rent or a little more will see the light."

"You're the boss." Jim didn't say that this all went against the grain. He was used to a different atmosphere. The people he knew didn't worry about money; they threw it around and when it was all gone, they borrowed or won more and that was that. He couldn't imagine any of the people he had known turning a guy out in the snow for a board bill. They'd laugh it off.

Mr. Plummer got up.

"Schultz owes one hundred and thirty-four dollars and sixty-three cents. Tell him he must pay, say, forty-five dollars. Is that clear?"

Jim nodded and got up.

"All right," said Mr. Plummer, "and don't be lenient with him. I mean, talk to him like you meant business, Turner. You know, you're a pretty easy-going fellow. You'll never get any place in the world with that attitude. Look after number one; in this case, your job. All right, Turner. I hope you had a nice Christmas."

Jim went back to the desk, smiling. He was picturing to himself what Johnny Mueller and Tom Lift would say if they knew he'd let a little squirt like Mr. Plummer talk like that to him without a word or even a laugh. Oh, well; live and learn. You never knew how you'd end up. He might be a nickel-grinder himself when he was fifty.

"Well," said Miss Dolby, taking off the ear phones and putting on her fur coat, "I see you finally got through with your conference. Did you decide the future policy of the great Northland Hotel or . . ."

She stopped suddenly, and innocently began to rouge her lips, staring into her vanity-case mirror. Mr. Plummer was coming out of the office with his coat and hat on. He stopped to light a cigar, then he nodded, crossed the lobby, and went out.

"Shrimp!" said Miss Dolby. "He knows I'm in a hurry. I told him. He's got his car out in front. Wouldn't you think he'd at least take me over to the L station?"

Jim coughed but said nothing.

"You know," said Miss Dolby, "you're always reading about the boss falling for his secretary and all that.

I'd like to see the secretary that bird would fall for.
A lizard has got more temperament."

"Do you want him to fall for you?" asked Jim, merely
to be polite; he thought that Miss Dolby was a bore.

"Him? I should say not. But he might open up a
little, anyway. Know what he give me for Christmas?
A candy cane."

Jim leaned on the counter to laugh. Shrugging, Miss
Dolby went out. Jim watched her thin legs crossing the
lobby. The first few days he'd worked there she had
made herself very agreeable to him; now she hardly
seemed to know that he was about. Did she think he'd
fall for her? Good Lord! He had passed up better ones
than her out of laziness long before he was married. He
sighed and, picking up a newspaper, sat down; but the
hotel was busy at this time of night and the switchboard kept buzzing, the front door fanning; and there
was a parade of messenger-boys, special-delivery men,
and visitors. Jim put his paper aside for the dead hours.

Bright and Joe Constantinesco came in about ten
o'clock. The hotel had quieted down and Jim was looking through a magazine somebody had left on the desk.

"Look," said Bright, "he can read. No; he's looking
at the pictures."

"Well," said Joe, "whether he can read or not, he
knows his horses. Gonfalon really paid off."

"I still think Cayenne was the best," said Bright. "He
was just bored. You know when a horse is bored he
won't run. You've got to entertain a horse or he gets
fed up with living. Sometimes they commit suicide.
Isn't that right, Turner?"

"It must be, if you say so." Jim put their keys on the desk. He couldn't help feeling a glow of triumph. Bright had bet on Cayenne and he had run last. Let him talk; he could talk his head off; but Jim knew that the loss rankled. Bright wasn't so smart.

"Got any more tips?" Bright inquired. "You know, Turner, you might make a good thing out of this. Get out a tip-sheet. You might hit a couple of more lucky guesses and make a reputation for yourself. A man has to be right only once to be a prophet."

Jim smiled.

"I'm no tout. I used to pay for my tips when I thought they was worth it."

"He used to pay for his tips, Joe. Can't you tell he's a man of affairs?"

"Anyway," said Joe, "I won six hundred dollars."

Bright lit a cigar and leaned on the desk. His small dark eyes were shining with malice. He was used to impressing people, being the big-shot, getting special consideration; it was very apparent to him that Jim was not at all impressed. It was getting good when you couldn't impress a lousy night clerk; a twenty-five-per man!

"Why don't you pay up?" said Bright, with a nasty laugh. "What do you think Turner here's handing out info for, his health? Slip him some coin; he needs it."

"It was just a friendly tip," said Joe. "I know, see? I know. Right, Turner?"

"Sure it's right. And I don't need money. I got plenty." Jim's face was getting red and the look of sleepy good nature was slowly fading.

"Joe always was a piker, Mr. Turner," said Bright;

"you know, he gets his mitts on a little dough and you can't pry him loose. He works for me, I'll have to admit that, but I'm not proud of it. If I could do without him, I would." Bright took out his billfold and laid a twenty-dollar bill on the counter. "But I feel responsible for his debts. Know what I mean? So there, Turner. There's something on account."

There was a short silence, then Jim leaned forward:

"If I wasn't getting paid for being nice to mugs like you, I'd tell you what you could do with that twenty, Mr. Bright."

"Don't worry about that," said Bright, his eyes shining. "Tell me. Tell me."

"Wait a minute, wait a minute," said Joe, edging forward, but the door opened and two nurses who lived in 304 came in, talking and laughing. Jim turned to get their keys.

Joe took Bright by the arm.

"What do you say we go upstairs, boss?"

Bright turned without a word, crossed the lobby with Joe, and got into the automatic elevator. Joe waited and finally, taking off his hat, said:

"Are you ladies going up now?"

"Yes, thanks," said one of the nurses, and started for the elevator; the other nurse was looking at her mail. She grabbed it up in a hurry and ran across the lobby, crying: "Wait for baby."

Jim turned back to the switchboard; 656 was calling. Somebody in 556 was making a terrible racket and wouldn't he make them stop? He would. It was Eddie Cramer and his wife fighting as usual; Eddie was an insurance agent with an eye for easy-going ladies; his wife was extremely jealous. They spent their evenings fighting; once the missus had thrown an iron ash-tray through one of the windows. Jim rang them up. Eddie answered the phone.

"This is the night clerk," said Jim. "Mr. Cramer, you've got to cut down that noise a little."

"O.K., Turner. Mabel's just having one of her tantrums."

Jim forgot all about Mr. Bright, thinking about Marg. Since he had started working at the Northland they hadn't had one quarrel; not one. Before that, Marg had been pretty unpleasant off and on; especially one time at Saratoga when he had bet eight hundred dollars on one race and lost. But he couldn't imagine her throwing things; Marg was "a lady." She thought Mabel Cramer was terrible and would hardly speak to her in the lobby.

At eleven o'clock Joe Constantinesco came down into the lobby and stood at the desk, smoking a cigar. Jim looked up from his magazine. Joe grinned.

"I hope you don't pay no attention to the boss, Turner."

"The boss?"

"Mosey, you know. Bright. Lord, he better never hear me calling him Mosey. I got to get over that habit. He's an Irishman, see? Goes to mass every Sunday morning."

"Yeah; I've seen him go out. Always wondered where he was going that time of the morning."

"His name's Daniel Mosely Bright. He says Dan is a horse's name. So he calls himself D. Mosely, see?

Some smart guy said he looked like his name ought to be Mosey, so that's how he got it hung on him. Don't let it slip. He'd chew the wall-paper off."

"What's his idea, ribbing me all the time?"

Joe hesitated.

"Well, that's his way. He likes to stir people up. But I don't know. He's kind of got it in for you. Know why?"

"No."

"I ain't sure. But I think it's because you don't 'Mr. Bright' him all over the place. He rates it, see, and he expects it. The guy that used to have your job did everything but kiss his hand. The boss is a big man in this town. He's got the cleaning-and-dyeing business in the palm of his hand. He's got a big house out in Evanston, and plenty dough. But he can't stand his wife and never goes home only to see the brats. That's what he calls 'em. He likes it here. Nobody knows where to look for him, so he ain't pestered all the time."

"Well," said Jim, "I don't mind a little kidding. But he gets nasty."

"Take it, take it. He may be your friend yet. And if he is, that means something. Look at me. I used to work in a fruit store. Hell! now I'm in the money. By the way . . ." Joe took a sealed envelope out of his pocket and put it on the desk. "There's some dough. I bet a ten spot on Gonfalon for you. He closed at six to one."

"What are you trying to do, kid me?" Jim shoved the envelope back.

"Hey, don't be that way. I was going to give it to you when I came in, but the boss got heavy, so I didn't.

The boss don't know nothing about this and he never will unless you tell him. Don't be a chump. Any guy can use sixty bucks."

Sixty bucks! Two weeks and a half's work. Jim scratched his head and meditated.

"I'd of lost that hundred sure if I hadn't heard what you said about Gonfalon. Take it, take it."

Jim took it. He'd give it to Marg and she could send it to Ma; that would be a big help. Of course Marg would have to be told all about it and would probably lecture him, afraid he'd get started back at his old ways. But Ma could sure use it.

"Thanks."

"Sure. And if you know any more hot ones, let me know. I'll bet ten for you every time."

Jim was pleased. He knew a good deal about the ponies and might be able to hand Joe some hot ones; of course he'd miss much oftener than he'd hit, but it wouldn't cost him anything and Joe seemed to have plenty of money. By God! it would feel pretty good to have a thick roll on your hip for a change. Just suppose that . . .

A big man in a heavy ulster stepped up to the desk briskly. His face was dark and partly hidden by a slouch hat pulled low.

"Yes?" said Jim.

"Good evening," said the man, who spoke with a slight foreign accent. "I'd like to see Mr. D. M. Bright. Will you tell me his number so I can go up?"

Joe turned his back to the desk and leaned against it, puffing at a cigar.

"I think he's in," said Jim, a little uncertainly, remembering what Joe had said about Bright not liking to be bothered; "I'll see if I can get him on the phone for you."

"Never mind that," said the man. "Just give me his room number. Fourth floor, I think he told me."

Joe turned.

"Looking for Mr. Bright? He ain't here. He went to New York, I think, for a week or two."

"Yeah? I seen him yesterday."

"Mr. Bright ain't here," said Joe, calmly. "I room right next door to him and I know."

The big man hesitated, then he leaned on the counter and said to Jim:

"What was that number? Four something, wasn't it?"

Jim said nothing; he sat fooling with the switchboard. He thought it was his play to keep out of this; it was up to Joe, whose icy calmness warned him that something was wrong. Jim turned. The man was looking at him, and Jim saw the expression of his face change from stolid determination to surprise, to fear. Joe was standing very close to him, holding the cigar in his left hand; his right hand was out of sight below the desk.

"I tell you Mr. Bright ain't here," said Joe.

"All right," said the big man, moving away from Joe cautiously. "If you room right next to him you ought to know."

He turned and went out quickly; they heard a car start off with a roar. Joe said nothing. Jim picked up his magazine and began to look at the pictures.

"Say," said Joe, finally, "it's kind of dull in here. Why don't you turn that radio on for a while?"

The lobby radio was controlled from behind the desk. Jim twisted the dial till he got WGN, which had good dance music at this hour. The band was playing softly and a baritone was singing:

> "Two by two,
> They go marching through:
> The sweethearts on parade.
> I can't help sigh,
> As they pass me by:
> The sweethearts on parade. . . ."

"Nice band," said Joe, nodding.

The lobby was deserted now; Jim had shut off the radio. It was quarter-past twelve. Outside, the night was cold and clear; the snow was as dry as powder; there was no wind. A tenant had told Jim that the thermometer at the drug store round the corner was registering eight below, so he had made Smoke fire up. The lobby was warm and stuffy; the radiator at the far end was hissing and sending up steam; all the front windows were frosted over.

One of the barbers who lived at the Northland had given Jim a comic magazine; he sat laughing over it. From time to time he glanced up at the frost-incrusted windows. Then he sighed with satisfaction. It wasn't bad on a night like this to be in a warm place with very little to do except sit; it must be pretty raw out; the barber told him that a customer of his had had his ears frost-bitten walking five blocks. Boy, that was real cold weather. Jim sat whistling softly and slowly turning the pages of the magazine. But of a sudden he remembered the hypnotist and his feeling of contentment vanished. Good Lord! What a nice job Plummer had wished on him. But then, maybe if Schultz didn't have the money he could borrow it from Jeannie; she was working steady. All the same, the pictures in the magazine were no longer very funny and in a moment Jim got up, lit a cigarette, and stretched his legs.

Just before twelve-thirty the hypnotist came in. He walked up to the desk and smiled at Jim, but Jim could see that it was an effort. His long, sallow face was blue with cold; he had the collar of his shabby overcoat turned up nearly to his ears.

Jim stood tapping on the desk with a pencil, unable to make up his mind to say anything. The hypnotist took off his coat and carefully draped it over his arm.

"Lord, it feels good in here. They tell me it's ten below out. Has Jeannie come in yet?"

"She came in around eleven, I think."

"That's funny. She said . . . well, it doesn't matter. Any mail? No? Well, I really wasn't expecting any. Nobody writes to me any more." He leaned on the counter, staring into space. He looked tired and discouraged. "I went down to Keith's tonight. They got a faker down there everybody's raving about. Terrible. He does a clairvoyant act, and then some hypnotizing. A boy four years old could see through his stuff. His helper, out in the audience, uses a code I discarded when I was twenty-five years old. And he's no more a mesmerist than you are. All fake. Of course I faked up my act, too. You have to. It makes it run smooth. But I can really mesmerize. For instance, I could put you out like a light. Jeannie's easy. All I have to do is come up behind her quick and snap my fingers. But who cares? All fake nowadays, all fake."

"Say," said Jim, a little uneasy, "don't work none of your stuff on me. I have a hard time staying awake as it is."

The hypnotist laughed shortly.

"Don't worry. I'm too tired right now to put a flea to sleep. It's all will-power, understand? My will has to be stronger than yours. A hypnotist needs vitality. He must have it. He must be stronger than others; all others. Understand?" Schultz's black eyes flashed. Jim was a little startled. The hypnotist looked crazy as a loon when he opened his eyes wide and stared steadily.

"Hey!" said Jim, "never mind that stuff."

The hypnotist lowered his eyes and shrugged.

"I'll be frank with you, Turner. I know a man ought to keep up his front, but with you it doesn't matter. You're not like the rest. I can't get an engagement to save my life. They say I'm too old; I'm passé! What a joke! Is a man passé at forty-three? A man should be doing his best work at that age. But I can't convince them. They merely shrug and say that The Great Mario doesn't mean a thing to anybody any more. Anyway, who gives a damn about hypnotizing? It used to be a great act for the boobs, but they've got smarter." The hypnotist hesitated and coughed. He thought that Jim looked uncomprehending. "I'm merely telling you what the booking-agents say, the swine. All swine. No refinement, no breeding, no courtesy, no education. Just swine."

The hypnotist hesitated, then offered Jim a cigar; but Jim declined it, cleared his throat, and said, hurriedly:

"Mr. Schultz, I got bad news for you."

"What is it? Something happen to Jeannie? I know. She moved out."

"No," said Jim, very much surprised, "she didn't."

"What is it, then?"

Rubbing his hands together nervously and avoiding the hypnotist's eyes, Jim explained to him the new policy of the Northland Hotel. The hypnotist puffed on his cigar and stared at the carpet. When Jim was through he said:

"When does this start?"

"Right now."

"Tonight, you mean?"

"Yep."

The hypnotist laughed.

"Turner, I've got exactly forty-six cents to my name."

Jim cleared his throat.

"Well, Mr. Schultz, I'm sorry. But that's my orders."

"You don't mean to tell me. . . . Why, say, it's ten below zero! Where could I go?"

"I'm just telling you what Mr. Plummer told me. It ain't my fault."

The hypnotist seemed shaken. He ran his hand over his face, staring.

"What must I pay?"

"Forty-five dollars, Mr. Plummer said."

"I haven't got it. I can't get it. So what do I do? You must be joking, Turner. Why, a man would freeze on a night like this."

"Couldn't you borrow it? I thought maybe . . ."

"Let me go up to my room and think it over. I'll call you in fifteen minutes."

"I'm sorry, Mr. Schultz, but . . ."

"I can't go to my room?"

"No. Mr. Plummer said I was to plug your door if you didn't pay."

"Would you do it?"

"Well, I . . ."

"I know. Like everybody else, you've got your own troubles. You've got no money, and a wife to keep. You don't need to explain. It all narrows down to one thing—money. Is that right, Turner? If you've got it, fine; if you haven't, everybody looks down on you and calls you names. . . ." The hypnotist leaned on the counter and stared off across the lobby. For a long time he puffed on his cigar, then he turned. "It's funny how things turn out. Everything at once. You'd think things could be spread out a little more. A man can stand a little hammering if he gets some rest in between but . . . Say, may I go up and see Jeannie?"

"Well . . ."

"Oh, never mind. What about my luggage? I've got everything I own in my luggage."

"You can't touch that, Mr. Plummer says."

"Nice fellow, Mr. Plummer. Well, get Jeannie for me. I'll talk to her. Tell her it's important."

Jim rang Jeannie's room. He knew that she had gone up hours ago, but she didn't answer. He rang at intervals for a quarter of an hour, then he gave it up. The hypnotist paced up and down the lobby, looking very pale and worried.

"That's funny," said Jim.

There was a long silence; Jim heard the clock ticking loudly overhead. Finally the hypnotist said:

"Any new tenants?"

Jim looked up in surprise.

"Why . . . yes. I registered a man tonight. About eight-thirty."

"Tall fellow with light hair?"

"Yes. About thirty-five."

"Don't ring Jeannie any more." The hypnotist leaned on the desk. He looked sick.

Jim felt so sorry for him that he turned away and picked up his magazine. If the man had showed fight it would have been different; but he was whipped; you could see it in the sagging lines of his face.

"Well, what do I do now?" he asked at last. "I don't suppose you'd let me stay here in the lobby till morning."

Jim didn't reply. He stood staring at the hypnotist for a moment, then he said in a loud voice:

"Oh, hell! Go on up to your room. I'll fix you up. I got a little extra money. Only, for God's sake try and get your hands on something, because I won't be able to do you any good next time. I'll put forty-five in the till for you; and you owe me, not the house. Now go to bed."

"Say, Turner, I . . ."

"Go on. You give me the willies. See if you can't scare up some money tomorrow."

"I got some things I might pawn."

"All right. Good night."

"Mighty white of you, Turner."

Jim didn't say anything. He was already calling himself a sucker. What a chance he had to get any of that dough back; and Ma needed it almost as bad as the hypnotist.

The hypnotist hesitated, then turned and walked to the elevator, but after a moment he came back, took something from his pocket and put it on the counter. Jim looked up. It was a black automatic.

The hypnotist smiled slightly.

"Well, Turner," he said, "you've done your good deed for the day. I'm going to make you a present of this."

Jim took the gun and slipped it into the till under the desk. He didn't feel like such a sucker now. Schultz looked like just the kind of man who would get in a jam and shoot himself.

"Did you ever get that low?" asked the hypnotist.

"Not me. I like living too much. I been in some pretty tight ones, too. Never say die."

"I wish I could feel that way. Good night."

It was a dead night. All the tenants were in by one-thirty. Outside, the city was quiet; people were staying in because of the cold; a lone taxicab passed the hotel at long intervals. Yawning, Jim went to look out the big window at the left of the lobby entrance; the glass was cold as ice to the touch and was half covered by an intricate and sparkling pattern of frost. He might have been looking out at a suddenly deserted city. The streets were white and still; there was not a footprint in the snow; as far as he could see all the windows were dark; under the street lamps the snow glittered like mica. Damn! a man might just as well be at the North Pole. After a moment he turned and went back behind the desk, where he sat dozing and reading alternately . . . where had all the snow gone? Why, good Lord! that was funny! Palm trees were leaning over a white beach; the water was blue, the air mild. Well, he couldn't explain it, but here he was back in Florida. A man who looked like Johnny Mueller but had wild black eyes kept yelling at him; he said that if he didn't stay away from that switchboard they'd never let him race horses again or even bet. "You'll be ruled off," the man kept saying, "like that fellow, Schultz." He heard a crowd roaring and the man cried, "Gonfalon wins; here's your money, tout; here's your money." But Schultz came up and began to complain that he'd been ruled off; Schultz had a gun in his hand, and Jim suddenly realized that Schultz and Mueller were the same. Now wasn't that funny? But Schultz turned away; there was an argument some place, a loud argument . . . niggers . . .

Jim woke with a start. He heard scuffling and the sound of voices. A high-pitched negro voice was repeating over and over the same phrase: "Ah said no dice! Ah said no dice!" Jim was bewildered for a moment, then he saw that the basement door was open about six inches.

"Sounds like a crap game," he said, aloud, still puzzled.

He went hurriedly into the basement. A big buck in overalls had Smoke backed up against the boiler-room wall, trying to choke him. Smoke was yelling "Ah said no dice! Ah said no dice!" A small negro in a ragged overcoat was looking on indifferently. In the struggle some one had struck the electric-light bulb which hung by a long cord and it was swinging wildly, throwing grotesque shadows over the walls.

"Hey!" Jim shouted.

The big buck jumped back from Smoke, pulled off his hat, and then looked frantically about for a way out. But Jim was blocking the doorway. The little negro laughed at the antics of the buck, then turned a solemn face toward Jim. Smoke said:

"Jest killing a little time, Mistah Turnah. Jest a little friendly game. We wasn't even betting. Ah 'clare we wasn't."

"The game didn't look none too friendly to me," said Jim, with a laugh. "But you've got to stop this damn yelling. Who's your friends, Smoke?"

Smoke cleared his throat.

"This big boy heah is Harry. He wuks at the Sherwood Ahms, right back of us 'cross the alley. He's a night engineer. This little one is a friend of Harry's."

"Yassuh," said Harry, rolling his eyes. "Ah jest came ovah to bah a wrench, yassuh and we kinda gets to talking . . ."

"That's right, that's right," said the little negro.

"Well," said Jim, "if you're going to shoot crap you'll have to shoot quiet. No more yelling."

They looked at him, stunned. Smoke had expected to be fired; the other two had expected to be kicked out into the alley.

"Kin we sure enough shoot, Mr. Turnah?" asked Smoke, still unbelieving.

"Sure," said Jim, "if you'll quit your damn yelling.

I don't know anything about it, see? If Mr. Plummer
ever catches you, don't blame me."

"Nossuh, nossuh."

"Ah be dawg," said the little negro, "if Harry wasn't
a picture, yassuh. Did you see him retch for his hat,
mistah? That boy cain't run a lick 'less he retches for
his hat." The little negro bent down to laugh. "He
was sure enough marking time with them big feet."

"Git out, niggah," said Harry.

They stood shifting about, self-conscious and embarrassed, waiting for Jim to go. But he didn't go. He just
stood there in the doorway. Finally Smoke knelt down,
took a crumpled dollar bill from his pocket, and put
it on the cement floor.

"Fo' bits of that's mine," said Harry, kneeling down
also. "And don't give me no mo' a that 'no dice' stuff."

"Ahm shooting that fo' bits out," said Smoke. "A
man kin call 'no dice' when he pleases. Ain't that so,
Mistah Turnah?"

"Sure. But he's got to call it before they stop rolling."

"He nevah did," said Harry. "He saw that old bad
news and calls out, 'No dice.' But Ah let it pass this
time. Go on, niggah."

Jim leaned against the door jamb, watching the game.
In a few minutes he came over closer. Smoke had got
hot and Harry was groaning. The little negro cried:

"Ah'll take half. Le' me take half."

Smoke made five straight passes. Harry groaned
loudly and said:

"Ah 'clare Ah ought to take them dice away from

you, niggah. Ah 'clare you did it to me that time when you yelled 'No dice.' "

"Ahm hot, boiling ovah," said Smoke. "Shoot two dollahs."

Jim knelt down.

"I'll take half," he said.

Twenty-five minutes later Jim got slowly to his feet, brushed off his knees, and said: "Well, that's my contribution. Better fire up a little, Smoke. Good night." He had lost sixteen dollars.

When he had shut the door behind him, Harry said:

"Bam! That white man knows his dice, but they sure was rollin' bad."

The little negro cut in.

"Did you see how he handled them bones? Man! he kin make 'em do eve'thing but talk."

"Yeah," said Harry, "and theah's that ole lucky Smoke, cain't even hold a pair of dice propah, lets 'em fall out of his hand; but they reads seven. Man, oh, man!"

Jim sat down with a sigh and picked up his magazine. Marg was right. He didn't have an ounce of sense. Sixty dollars piddled away for nothing, and a dollar besides. Sixty or six hundred, it was all the same, he'd never saved a dime in his life, and probably never would.

Above his head the clock slowly struck two.

Chapter III

IT WAS PLEASANT SITTING IN THE MOVIE THEATER WITH Marg. The seats were overstuffed and very comfortable, especially as he was used to a stiff wooden chair. The theater was dimly lighted and warm, and on the screen a race-track picture was unfolding, scene after scene of a familiar locale, rail-birds sitting on the fences of the back stretch, gamblers trying to keep the odds up, swipes walking the blanketed horses round and round, cynical little jockeys. Swell! But the heroine was awful; a damned bore that ought to be squelched, always doing something noble or else complicating matters for the overworked hero; and the leading gambler was a riot. Going about in riding-pants, or dressed up like them swells he used to see at Palm Beach, with slick hair and one of them mustaches that looked like a dirty lip. Jim forgot the picture for a moment, thinking about the big gamblers he knew—Marty Gross, a little bowlegged man whose upper front teeth were all gold and whose Adam's apple quivered when he was excited; or Tex Sanders, six feet three, who spent all his spare time chewing tobacco and spitting at a crack to test his accuracy. Wouldn't they get a wallop out of this riding-pants gambler with his cigarette-holder?

Jim sat up suddenly. The big race was on.

"Look at that baby come down the stretch," he said to Marg. "Take him through, you chump. You could drive a team of horses past that horse on the rail. Jees! he done it, he done it!"

Marg took him by the arm and shook him.

"Jim! Not so loud!"

"Say," said Jim, "I thought that guy with the mustache had the jockey fixed. He rode that horse a good race. How come?"

"The girl rode him," said Marg. "Wait and see."

"The girl . . . !" Jim began; then he snorted with disgust. It sure enough was the girl; she was sitting up on the horse, smiling now, with her cap off; a fat guy was putting a horseshoe wreath over her head. "Good Christ!" he exploded. "And they expect you to swallow stuff like that! A girl riding a horse in the Kentucky Derby! Wow!"

"You're too literal-minded," said Marg, laughing. "That's so the public will like it."

"Let's get out of here."

Marg was still laughing at him, but she put on her coat and followed him up the aisle. He was growling, but she took him by the arm and said, jokingly:

"That's the thanks I get for telling you there was a racing picture over here."

"No, listen Marg, I appreciate it, but, look, why don't they get somebody that knows something about it to make a racing picture? I'd like to take Johnny Mueller to see that. He'd drop dead when he found out the girl rode the . . ."

"Never mind. Let's stop in at Steve's and get some

salami. I haven't got anything in the house to fix you a lunch with tonight."

"Salami? Swell. It makes good sandwiches. Say, Marg, let's get some oysters so we can have oyster stew. I like oyster stew on cold nights."

"Well, they're pretty expensive now, Jim. I got my dinner all planned, anyway."

"Good Lord! Can't we even have some oysters once in a while!"

"The picture show cost sixty cents. You don't get paid till Saturday."

"All right, Marg. You're the boss. If it wasn't for you we'd eat big till Wednesday, then starve the rest of the week. But sometime I want oysters."

Marg didn't say anything. She was already planning to surprise him.

It was dark when they came out of the theater. All the electric signs were blazing along Broadway and the windows of the L trains running high overhead were lighted. It was warmer and the snow was melting slowly, leaving here and there shiny black patches of asphalt in the streets. Automobiles went by with tire chains clanking; crowds of pedestrians were crossing Broadway and Lawrence, and the motormen of the surface cars were clanging their bells and cursing. They walked down Lawrence to the combination grocery and delicatessen under the L station; newsboys were running about, selling the evening editions; trains rumbled overhead; everybody was hurrying home.

Jim bought a paper, giving the boy a dime and telling him to keep the change. Marg laughed and said:

"Still a big shot."

Jim smiled.

"Marg, I swear I can't get used to pinching dimes."

Marg gripped his arm.

"I probably wouldn't love you if you could."

"Do you love me, Marg?"

"No. I just pretend."

The delicatessen was warm and smelled rankly of strong cheese and pickle brine. Marg went to the counter to make her purchases and Jim tipped back his hat and leaned against the wall to read the paper. Another murder, another suicide, a revolution in Central America, a train wreck in Missouri; column after column of boring trash. Jim turned to the sport page with relief. By God! they beat Wanderlust in the U. S. Grant Hotel Stake. How come? Almost left at the post. Why, Wanderlust broke like a shot out of those new stalls. You never could tell. It's a good thing he was in Chicago and practically a pauper; if he'd been at Caliente he'd've sure shot the works on that big chestnut horse. Who won? Melba Downey, the Australian mare Jimmy Borden brought over. Wasn't worth her feed last year. Forty-six dollars and seventy-five cents for a two-dollar ticket. Did Jimmy clean up or not? Smart boy, Jimmy. Used to win race after race with a three-legged horse that couldn't move hardly after the race was over; humane societies used to get after him. What was that big horse's name? Seagoer II; looked like a milk-wagon horse.

Marg came up with her arms full of packages. He didn't look up.

"Here, James," she said. "I'm no squaw."

"Didn't see you," said Jim, taking the packages. "Say, Marg, Jimmy Borden won the big race yesterday with that Australian mare of his. I wouldn't have give him seventy-five dollars for her last winter."

Marg opened the door for him. A cynical little newsboy with an impudent dark face cried:

"Look at Santa Claus."

"Hello, pal!" Jim grinned. He knew the kid and was always slipping him dimes. The kid was a joker, and when business was dull went around yelling: "Extra! Extra! Jack Dempsey appointed ambassador to England," or, "Extra! Extra! Lake Michigan on fire," and laughing at all the fall-guys who turned their heads.

"Got you loaded up, ain't they, mister?"

"You tell it."

Jim laughed it off, but all the same he felt like a damn fool walking down Lawrence Avenue with his arms full of packages.

He walked along in silence for a while, thinking about Jimmy Borden's mare and resenting the bundles, certain that the young unmarried fellows were laughing at him and taking him for a chump. Finally he said:

"Seems to me you bought an awful lot of stuff. Funny we couldn't have a half-pint of oysters if we could buy all this stuff."

"It's things I needed. Coffee and flour and sugar and potatoes and things like that."

"Yeah, and them potatoes weigh a ton."

"Want me to help, weakling?"

He said nothing, but stared straight ahead, very indignant. When finally he turned to look at Marg she wasn't there; she had darted over to a lighted window full of the latest lingerie. Jim cursed briefly and slowed his pace. In a moment Marg caught up with him.

"They've got the loveliest things in there. But too expensive for me."

Jim grunted.

"I can't buy silk underwear on what I get. But there was a time when I could buy silk underwear, plenty of it."

"You probably did, too."

"Me? I wouldn't wear silk underwear if I was as rich as Sam Insull."

"No. I mean for women."

"Me? Not on your life."

Marg hardly ever mentioned his past; didn't seem at all curious about it. Once in a while she made a joke about it, that was all. She seemed pretty innocent to him. Lord! it was a good thing she didn't have a picture of some of the flusies he'd been with.

They walked along in silence for a few blocks, turning from Lawrence Avenue into Kenmore; ahead of them they saw the big electric sign, Northland Hotel.

"What a dump that is!" said Jim, softly but forcefully. "I've seen the time I wouldn't sleep in that place."

"Yes," said Marg, laughing, "and you've seen the time it would look like a palace." She stopped for a moment under a street light to look at her watch. "It's after six, Jim. We'd better hurry."

Jim thought about the twelve-hour stretch ahead of

him and groaned inwardly. All the same, he'd had a
nice afternoon and Marg was a peach.

He had just finished shaving when Marg called:
"Jim! Come and get it."
He had been thinking about the picture and how
silly it was for them to have the girl ride the horse.
Why, a six-year-old kid would jeer at such stuff as
that! He slipped on his bathrobe, still resenting that
final scene. If he knew where Johnny was (funny he
hadn't seen any of his horses in the Caliente entries)
he'd write him a kidding letter and tell him not to
miss that picture. It would be as good as a show!
Jim and Marg lived in what was called a three-room
apartment, nobody at the Northland knew why; in
fact, most people at the Northland had no thoughts
on the subject at all, because they could afford only
one room. Jim was allowed an extra room because the
hotel was less than forty per cent full. Their apartment
consisted of a living-room and a bedroom, with a bath
in between; it was really two hotel rooms thrown together, as the living-room had an in-a-door bed. Marg
managed to cook their meals on a little electric stove,
which was fastened onto a board and the board laid
across the top of the radiator in the bedroom; they ate
from a card-table with rickety legs which they set up
in the living-room; one touch and it jiggled and spilled
the coffee into the saucer and the soup on the tablecloth.
Jim sat down, still absorbed, paying no attention to
what was on the table. Marg was getting the coffee.
Of a sudden a pleasant and familiar odor rose to his
nostrils. He looked down.

"Oyster stew!"

Marg came with the coffee.

"Well?"

"Say Marg, that's swell. I sure do appreciate it. Give us a kiss."

She kissed him, but when he tried to pull her down on his knee she pushed him away.

"Eat your soup."

"Say, this is mighty fine. Nothing better than good oyster stew on a cold night."

Marg laughed.

"I knew I'd have to get it for you sooner or later, you're such a big baby."

It was eleven o'clock. Jim had had a bad evening and was leaning on the counter, turning his grievances over and over in his mind. In the first place, when he came on duty Mr. Plummer was in a bad temper, said the hotel was run in a slovenly fashion at night; tenants had been complaining that their rooms were cold and that they had telephoned the lobby time after time and got no response. Besides, the cash-drawer was short forty-eight cents. Jim replied that he had checked it with Miss Dolby that morning, and Miss Dolby had whirled and said, bitingly:

"I suppose you mean I'd swipe forty-eight cents."

Without a word Jim had taken forty-eight cents out of his pocket and put it in the drawer. Mr. Plummer was very angry about this and made him take it out. It was merely a matter of principle, of efficiency; the forty-eight cents didn't matter. Somehow things got calmed down and after a while Mr. Plummer became affable. All the same, it rankled.

Then at nine o'clock Mr. Bright had stepped up to the desk to leave his key and had said:

"Hello, tout! How's the nags?"

Jim had flushed violently, but had said nothing; then Bright had laughed, merely laughed, but this laugh was more cutting than what he had said. When he had gone Jim cursed and called himself a coward and a trimmer; taking all kinds of insults just because of a damn piker's job.

It was too much. But in the midst of his rage he thought about the oyster stew. That was mighty nice of Marg, surprising him that way. She had no idea what he was forced to take, merely to hold his job. She stayed in her room most of the time, associated with no one in the hotel, didn't know anything about what went on. She thought he was too touchy. Maybe he was, at that. But he wasn't built to knuckle under, that was the long and short of it; never had, till he met Marg. Well, he'd have to bear it. Marg was depending on him. She didn't have it any too soft herself. Marg was good-looking and knew how to dress; she liked pretty clothes and jewelry and stuff like that; it wasn't very pleasant for her to have to get her clothes in bargain-basements and Jew stores. Marg knew a lot about hats and made her own; all she needed was a cheap frame and a couple yards of stuff; and she looked swell in the hats she made. But many times he had seen her looking wistfully into the windows of swell hat shops at hats marked from $10 to $35. He'd like to bring her home one of those hats, just to see her face light up. If he had

money, she'd have all the hats she wanted, and everything else, too.

Twenty-five a week with insults thrown in! What
a job! Laughing sardonically to himself, he began to
figure up how much that was an hour, twelve hours a
day. Less than thirty cents an hour; that was certainly
good! No wonder Marg wanted him to save the dimes.
A man making less than thirty cents an hour couldn't
afford to throw many dimes away. But it was hard to
think in dimes.

He didn't know what to do with himself; he had read
the comic magazine from cover to cover; he knew the
Caliente entries by heart and the rest of the paper didn't
interest him much. Pretty soon he turned on the radio;
Jean Goldkette's band, playing over WGN, was sooth-
ing; none of this loud banging and jazz; quiet pieces,
quietly played, and well sung by a good baritone. Jim
didn't like tenors.

The music helped; he began to relax; presently his
eyes closed and his head dropped forward.

Somebody woke him by banging on the desk. It was
Mr. Bright, and Jim could smell his breath from where
he sat. Boy, what liquor! Jim was too befuddled as yet
to be angry; he merely blinked.

"Well, Rip Van Winkle, my key, my key."

Jim got up and gave him a key, but it was the wrong
one. Bright glanced at it, then flung it against the key-
rack.

"Goddam," he cried, "if I don't have to put up with
plenty from you. Yesterday you wouldn't pay for a
C.O.D. package for me. Tonight you give me Joe's key.
What is this, anyway?"

"I've got orders about C.O.D. packages," said Jim, boiling. He flung Bright's key on the desk so hard that it bounced off onto the floor.

Bright's eyes narrowed and he stared at Jim for a long time. Finally he spoke in a sharp, nasty voice.

"Listen, tout, if you want to keep your lousy job, step around here and get me this key."

"You go to hell."

"You won't, eh?"

"You heard what I said."

Bright picked up the key.

"Consider yourself fired. I'll see Plummer in the morning."

"All right. And if I'm fired let me tell you something —I'm going to slap hell out of you."

"Do it now."

"You heard what I said. As long as I'm behind this desk you're a tenant, see, and I ain't fighting with no tenants."

"You're just yellow, you big stiff. I never saw a big guy yet that wasn't yellow."

"Get me fired and I'll show you how yellow I am."

"You are fired, boy, you are fired."

"Nuts."

Jim turned his back, picked up Joe Constantinesco's key and put it in the rack, then he sat down. He already regretted having lost his temper. What would Marg think? Bright was still leaning on the desk, his eyes gleaming with malice.

"So you won't fight, eh? All right. When does Plummer get here?"

"About eight o'clock, sometimes not till nine."

"All right. And if you want to find me I'll be over at Petersen's, getting my breakfast. I spend a lot of time over there in the morning."

"You're drunk."

"Yes, my big boy, I'm drunk. But I know what I'm doing. I know enough to know that you're yellow. And I'm going to prove it to you. You'll get the bad news in the morning. I'll be over at Petersen's if you want to see me about it."

"Aw, go to bed."

Jim's anger had evaporated. What was the use getting all het up over a drunk? Bright would go to bed and sleep it off and forget all about it. But Bright didn't seem so drunk at that; he was laughing now. Finally he turned and went out the front door instead of taking the elevator as Jim expected him to do. Twenty minutes later he came back, crossed the lobby without looking at Jim, and went up in the automatic elevator.

Jim shrugged and picked up the magazine, but he couldn't help worrying. He and Marg didn't have over twenty dollars all told. Suppose Bright did get him fired. Wouldn't that be a nice mess?

Chapter IV

MR. PLUMMER CAME AT EIGHT O'CLOCK SHARP. AS SOON as Jim saw him come in the door he knew that something was up.

"Miss Dolby isn't here yet?" Mr. Plummer demanded, curtly. "A nice set of employees I've got; a very nice set."

Without a glance at Jim he disappeared into his office. Jim began to have hope. Bright was probably just bluffing, after all. When you came to think of it, what would a rich guy like him want to make a night clerk lose his job for? It wasn't good sense. But in a moment Mr. Plummer called:

"Turner. Here."

Jim went into the office. Mr. Plummer was sitting at the little desk in the corner; a check was lying on the blotter before him.

"Turner, your usual pay day is Saturday, is that right?"

"That's right."

"Good. Today is Wednesday. I am giving you a check for the entire week."

"But what for? I can wait."

"No doubt. But your services are at an end here, Turner. I can put up with carelessness, but I won't have an employee abusing the tenants. That simply won't go at all."

"Mr. Bright?"

"Yes. You're through now. I'm sorry, but I'm very strict about such things. I'll work your spell tonight. Miss Dolby will work by herself this afternoon. Sorry, Turner."

Mr. Plummer turned away. Jim just stood there, staring stupidly at the check in his hand; he was stunned. Although his trouble with Bright had worried him, he never really believed that Bright would have him fired. That was the scummiest trick he ever heard of; pure meanness. No use kicking to Mr. Plummer, though; he could see that.

"And by the way, Turner," said Mr. Plummer, without looking up, "I'd like to have your rooms as soon as possible. Unless, of course, you want to stay on as a tenant. That can be arranged, I think."

Jim hesitated.

"I'll . . . I'll have to see my wife."

"All right."

Jim took off his coat to remove the sweater he always wore under it from two o'clock on; then he hesitated, remembered, and, shaking his head, put the coat back on. He looked around the office in a dazed way. For seven months he had been removing that sweater every morning and hanging it on the hook by the water-cooler. No more of that.

"Well . . ." he said.

"Sorry," said Mr. Plummer, mechanically.

Jim went out into the lobby. At the far end the radiator, which had kept him company for so many nights, was hissing. The mailman and Miss Dolby came in the front door at the same time. Miss Dolby ran in behind the desk, took off her hat and coat hurriedly, then went into the office to repaint her face for the morning. She started back, then said, "Oh, good morning, Mr. Plummer!"

"Good afternoon."

Miss Dolby began to explain about her L train having been held up. Jim took the letters from the mailman and glanced through them. There was one for Marg—from home, addressed in Ma's shaky handwriting. Suddenly he thought about Pa and Ma back there in Barrowville living in a little house, trying to take care of their no-good son's kid, and depending on him. It was hard to take, getting let out like this just because some smart guy wanted to show what a drag he had.

Miss Dolby came out of the office with a red face.

"Turner," she said, "why didn't you tell me the boss was here? You double-crosser!"

He shrugged, crossed the lobby and went up in the automatic elevator. What a nice surprise Marg was going to get, and the more he thought about it the more he dreaded the moment when he'd have to tell her. She would think it was his fault. Maybe she would be right, too. But he just wasn't cut out to be a hotel clerk; he couldn't manage that nice counterfeit smile and all the other little monkey tricks recommended by Mr. Plummer.

Marg met him at the door. She was wearing her little silk padded robe and she had her hair tucked back over her ears; she looked very small without her high-heeled shoes. He stammered, kissed her, then said:

"Good morning, kid."

"Morning, Jim. Got a nice breakfast for you. Is that a letter for me?"

He gave her the letter and sat down to the card-table. The coffee smelled good and the bacon was cooked to suit him. He began to eat, watching Marg out of the corners of his eyes. The apartment was all in order, all clean and tidy; Marg certainly knew how to keep house, and she liked this little dump of theirs. He saw her get up and stand looking out the window.

" 'Smatter, Marg?"

"Dad's flat on his back. Ma says she's having a hard time making things meet, with the doctor bills and . . . Oh, damn it! Every time I get up in the morning feeling good and glad to be living, something happens. George hasn't sent her one penny yet. What do you think of that?"

Jim said nothing. He put down his fork and sat looking at his plate.

"Jim, I hate to say this. I know you're doing the best you can. But don't you think I better get a job? I know hats and . . ."

Jim slammed down his napkin.

"No. I won't stand for it. I . . ." He hesitated and ran his hand over his face.

"That's silly. Lots of married women work. Nobody thinks anything about it. Listen, Jim . . ."

"I said 'no.' "

Usually he was tractable enough, but there was a mulish streak in him that was very seldom apparent.

Marg knew now that there was no use to argue with him. She temporized.

"Jim, maybe you could borrow some money—just to sort of tide us over. You know, so we could send more home till George begins to send some."

Jim remembered the sixty dollars he had fooled away and blushed heavily. There was only one thing to do —look Mr. Bright up, tell him how things were, and try to get him to speak to Mr. Plummer. That was a bitter pill, but what could he do? By rights he should beat him up, and if he had been single he would have done it long ago; but this was different. Marg was all worked up over Ma and Sonny. Suppose now he'd tell her that he'd lost his job and that they'd have to move out. That would finish her. They didn't even have enough money to go to Barrowville, even if there had been any reason for going. He knew that there was no use in trying to get his money back from the hypnotist. The hypnotist had been avoiding him ever since he had paid that bill for him.

He got up.

"Marg, maybe I can fix things. I'll be back in a little while."

"You haven't eaten your breakfast. Don't let me get you all up in the air, Jim. I always forget that you've been up all night. You never look tired."

"I never am tired. I catch a few winks at night. I'll be back pretty soon."

Miss Dolby was leaning on the desk when he came up.

"I hear you're not with us any more."

"I guess not."

"I'll be next. Shall I bounce a paper-weight off shrimp's head while I got a chance?"

"You'd just bust the paper-weight. Say, has Mr. Bright come down yet?"

"Yes. He just went out. He asked about you."

"Did he?"

Miss Dolby nodded.

"Isn't he a nasty little thing?"

"Nasty, is right."

"Say, I'm sorry, Turner. We never got along very well, but it's tough to be out of a job in this town. I often wish I was back in Superior, Wisconsin."

"Thanks."

Jim turned and went out. This was going to be a hard job, asking Mr. Bright to give him a break—a real tough job! He started off for Petersen's Restaurant, walking fast, afraid that he'd change his mind. He knew that Bright would ride him, make himself very offensive. Bright had won and would crow about it. He'd just have to take it.

The restaurant was crowded and Jim looked about him without seeing Bright, then he asked the head waiter.

"Mr. Bright? Right back here, I think."

Jim followed the head waiter back through the crowded restaurant to an inclosed booth at the rear. Bright was eating alone. The head waiter bowed and went away. Bright looked up and smiled.

"Ah," he said. "Fired, eh?"

Jim forgot all about Marg, all about Ma and George's kid and the fact that they needed money;

there was something so cutting, so unbearably arrogant in Bright's words, that he flared up instantly.

"Yes, you dirty little bastard. And now I'm going to show you what I think of you."

Jim started around the table after Bright, who quickly stood up and swung. His fist hit Jim a stunning blow on the side of the head, knocking him off balance. Bright grinned and waited, his eyes shining. Jim came after him, but Bright moved with surprising swiftness around the table and swung again, landing. Cursing, Jim reached for him, stretching across the table. But some one touched him on the shoulder and a chill, level voice said:

"Don't do that. I wouldn't do that."

Jim turned. He caught a confused glimpse of the crowded restaurant. Men were standing up, pointing; a big waiter was coming on the run. Joe Constantinesco was leaning against the booth with his hand in his pocket.

Jim was panting with rage.

"What you got there, Joe, a gun?"

"What do you think?"

"All right. Pull it out and we'll see who gets it."

"What?"

"Pull it out! Pull it out! And we'll see who gets it."

Joe shot a look at Bright, who began to laugh. People were crowding around the booth now. The big waiter came up and tried to take Jim by the collar, but Jim hit him and he fell backward, taking a chair with him.

"Wait! Wait!" cried Joe, taking hold of Jim's arm.

Bright waved his arms and shouted:

"Hold on! Hold on, everybody! It's all a mistake."

Three more waiters came up, but they hesitated when they saw the big one on the floor. Bright spoke briefly to the head waiter, who finally got the patrons back to their tables. Bright gave Joe a five-dollar-bill, which he handed to the big waiter.

"Sorry, Tommy. Didn't know it would be like this."

Tommy threw a glance at Jim.

"Big punk, eh? What a kick that bird's got."

Jim just stood there, dazed. He felt a stinging pain under his right eye. A shanty; blue and purple probably. What would he tell Marg? She hated brawls. He turned. Bright was pulling him by the sleeve.

"Sit down, Turner. Sit down."

"What for?"

"Don't be an airedale. Sit down."

Joe was holding his sides with laughter. Jim stared at him, then sat down.

"O God!" said Joe. "I'll never forget the look on Tommy's face when he caught that one with his chin. Jees! that was worth a five-spot."

"Turner," said Bright, "you're all right. You're all O.K., all wool and a yard wide. Let's have some beer."

"Say, Mr. Bright," said Jim, "this ain't no joke for me. I haven't got any job, and me and the wife have got some people back in Ohio who . . ."

"Who hasn't?" said Bright. "How much do you want?"

"What?"

"Don't be dumb. You haven't lost your job. If you want it back, I'll fix it with Plummer. If you want some money, I'll lend you some. It was just a joke, see? I had the whole thing planted. Except the firing stuff; that was O.K.; but I can fix that. Now, get it?"

"And I didn't have no gun, either," said Joe, delighted. "But, listen, Turner, you won't live long in Chicago if you try that 'pull it out; we'll see who gets it' stuff! You'll get it through the pocket, that's all."

"Well, I'll be damned!" said Jim. "You birds certainly go to a lot of trouble to get a laugh."

"That's the boss," said Joe. "That's his racket. Tell 'em about the one you pulled on Ed Boylan, boss."

"No. Let's don't drag up the past. I got better ones than that up my sleeve. Tommy, three of the best. The tall ones. Like beer, Turner?"

"You bet."

When Tommy came with three big steins of beer, Jim looked up at him and grinned.

"Sorry. I didn't know this was all in fun."

"Am I sorry, too? I won't be able to eat on the left side for a week."

"I think I got a shiner myself, but Bright give it to me."

Joe bent forward to look.

"You have, Turner, and it's a lulu."

Jim thought about Marg, but it didn't matter so much now. Everything was all right.

"Let's go," said Bright, raising his stein.

They drank, then Joe said:

"It's like this. I always said you was O.K. The boss says you're a yellow fourflusher, so that's how it all happened. By the way, boss, you can let me have that fifty, any time. The boss thought you would dog it, see?"

Jim thanked his lucky star. He had almost "dogged" it; if it hadn't been for Bright's attitude he'd've probably eaten humble pie and asked Bright to get his job back for him. What a close one!

"About that dough," said Bright, all smiles. "If you need some, say so. I'll lend you some."

"I could use about thirty dollars, Mr. Bright. But I don't know when I can pay it back. I don't get much, you see."

"I'll bet you don't. Plummer is so tight he squeaks. Here's the thirty. Pay me back when you please. That laugh was worth it."

They had some more beer. People were still staring at them. It was bad enough for a brawl to start at nine o'clock in the morning; no one could remember having seen one at that hour. But the worst of it was that now the combatants were sitting together, peaceably drinking, of all things, beer—beer in the early morning. It was too much for most of the patrons, who began questioning the waiters, then the head waiter, who shrugged and said it was all Greek to him. He thought this remark was funny, as he *was* a Greek; but nobody else seemed to.

After the fourth stein Jim began to loosen up. He told Bright all about his horse, Gold Leaf, and how he had made a great horse out of him and how he had beaten Tommy Spain.

"What made you sell him?" asked Bright, interested now.

"Oh, I went broke," said Jim. "I couldn't even scare up enough money to buy feed for my horses. I had five then, only one good one, though. So I sold him, and lost the money in two days."

"Lost it?"

"Yes. I bumped into a big faro game. I used to like faro. Used to be pretty lucky at it. But, well, I'm married now and my wife can't stand that stuff. I mean, she likes to know there's something coming in, even if it ain't much. I was broke when I met her; that is, I was working for Paul Mellen at Bellport. Cashier."

"Turner," said Joe, finally, "know anything about dog-racing?"

"Not much. Why?"

"Well," said Bright, "I got a third interest in a dog track out in California. We just wondered if you knew anything about it."

"There ain't much to know, is there? The betting is all the same. I don't know anything about conditioning dogs, if that's what you're driving at. To tell you the truth, I never had much use for dogs or dog-men. It's a gyp racket."

"I can't see how it's any worse than the horses."

Jim considered this for a long time.

"Maybe you're right," he said.

"We wasn't interested in what you knew about getting dogs ready to race. Think you could find out what it was all about in a day or two, the betting, I mean; it's the option system, see? Think you could find out if the park was run on the square and all that?"

"Why not? Sure."

Joe and Bright exchanged glances. Bright rubbed his hand over his face.

"What time is it, Joe?"

"Nearly ten."

"He'll be here in a minute. You're not going any place, are you, Turner?"

"No; not particular. I got to get back to the hotel pretty soon, though. I told the wife I'd only be gone a little while."

"You like that wife of yours, don't you?"

"I sure do."

"Well, if you've got the right one you're lucky," said Bright, with a laugh. "My wife goes in for literature. Know what I mean? She reads papers and stuff like that before a woman's club. She thinks I'm ignorant and she's right. But I know I'm ignorant. She's ignorant and thinks she's smart. Oh, to hell with that!" He sat thinking for a while, then he said: "And she sends the boy to dancing-school. Won't he be a nice specimen when he's twenty-one?"

They were on their sixth stein and Jim had begun to protest that he'd have to get back to the hotel, when the head waiter came over.

"There's a Mr. Miller up front wants to see you, Mr. Bright."

"All right. Bring him back. This is the guy we want you to meet, Turner. Him and Joe fixed up the dog-track business. He's got something to do with a mechanical-rabbit patent. Is that right, Joe?"

"He's got a third interest."

Jim lifted his stein and drank from it. He felt warm and comfortable, but things had begun to get a little vague to him; Bright's voice seemed to be coming from across the room instead of from across the table. He finished the rest of the beer, wiped the foam from his mouth with the back of his hand, then smacked his lips, and said "Ah!" A big, thin man in an ulster was leaning on the table, staring at him; the man's face was sunburnt and leathery, his eyes small and shrewd.

"Well, for Chr . . ." he began; then he hit Jim on the back and let out a yell. Bright and Joe stared at each other. But Jim said: "Johnny Mueller! What in God's name . . ." Then he jumped up and they began to pound each other.

"Buck Turner," shouted Johnny. "If I ain't glad to see you. Tom Lift told me that you'd turned decent and gone to work, but I see from the company you keep you ain't. And I'm mighty glad. I sure am. There's forty million guys to do the work in this country. Why should you horn in?"

Bright finally got them to sit down and, without waiting for an order, Tommy rushed up with four steins. Johnny lifted his stein and said:

"Here's to you, Buck, old boy. I'm damned glad I walked into this restaurant today." He turned to Bright. "There's an A-number-one, square-shooting guy sitting right there. I'll bet my bank roll on him, any day. Say, Buck, they tell me you been having a hard time. I forget who told me. Need any dough? I got plenty right now."

"No," said Jim, laughing. "I guess not. I'm doing all right."

Bright was beaming.

"Know him do you, Mueller?"

"Know him! I'll say I know him. That guy's had more ups and downs than a roller-coaster, but he always laughs it off. Get me? I seen him clean out Pat Desmond's faro game in two hours; made him turn the box over. And I've seen him matching pennies with exercise boys. It's all one to him. What you been doing, Buck?"

"I been working in a hotel."

"You've been doing what?"

"He's been working night clerk over at the Northland," said Joe.

Johnny's eyes popped, then he roared with laughter. "Him? Night clerk? That's a good one." Then he thought for a while. "Some of the boys told me you'd married some gal from Ohio and that she'd have you in a church pew in no time. She's from down around the prohibition belt, ain't she? Where the boy's vote dry solid and go out to the barn and get so drunk the cows laugh at them. Night clerk, eh? Well, it's better than selling corsets." Johnny roared with laughter and called for another stein all around.

"Mueller," said Bright, "this is the guy we're thinking about sending out to Crescent City to sort of look after things."

Jim blinked.

"Buck?" cried Johnny. "You couldn't find a better man than him. He's straight. It may cost you considerable in faro money, but you'll get a square deal."

"Wait a minute," said Jim. The world was foggier than ever now and his lips had begun to get that strange numb feeling. They sure must shoot plenty of ether into that needle beer. "Wait a minute. I ain't heard nothing about this job yet. Why didn't somebody say something to me?"

"We wasn't sure," said Bright. "What's a fair salary, Mueller? You know what we want him to do."

"Well, no matter how much you pay him, he'll never have a cent. Give him a hundred a week and his fare out to California. He'll be worth it."

Bright didn't flinch. He said:

"What do you say, Turner?"

"Well, good Lord!" said Jim. "A man would be a fool not to . . ." But he hesitated and his face fell. Marg! What would she say? A hundred dollars was a nice sum to have coming in every week, but Marg would probably put her foot down. She hated race tracks and gambling; would never associate with any of the people connected with them; thought they were all a lot of drunks and loafers, very little better than actual criminals. "I don't know," he said, avoiding their eyes. "Maybe the missus wouldn't want to go away out to California. She's got her people back in Barrowville and . . ."

"Quit stalling," Johnny interposed. "Ain't you the boss at your house?"

Jim laughed.

"Nope, I'm not."

"I like this guy," said Bright, with a laugh. "He's honest. He's the first guy I ever heard admit that he wasn't the boss. Can't you fix it with the wife, Turner? It'll mean pretty good dough and a nice little trip."

"I think maybe I can. Her folks are kind of . . . well, they could use a little dough right now. You know how it is. Her old man had a steady income from his stock in the Barrowville Iron Foundry. Not much, but enough to keep them going. It blew up."

"Everything's blown up," said Bright. "I could paper a house with the no-good stock I got. Listen, Turner, hundred-a-week jobs don't grow on trees. Seems to me you'd get mighty sick of sitting behind that desk every night."

"I do."

"He'll take the job," said Johnny. "I know this guy. He's just being polite about his wife." Johnny rubbed his hand over his face and stared at Jim. "Buck, you know you've changed some. You're fatter than you used to be. You look older . . ."

"Any man that's married looks older," said Bright. "Take a slant at my gray hair."

"He's had some dandies in his time," said Johnny, jerking his thumb at Jim. "What ever happened to that . . . what was her name . . . you know, Buck, that black-haired woman who owned Gold Center?"

"She . . ." Jim hesitated. "She was a Cuban."

"That explains everything. One time Buck was in a honkytonk in Tia Juana, talking to a broad, and this Cuban person got her dander up; just waltzed in, yelled at Buck, and threw an empty beer-bottle in his general direction. The broad ducked and the bottle went through the glass front of a mechanical piano that was playing. You should have heard the music that piano played after that. Chinese music; make your hair stand up. But everybody got a big kick out of it, so the guy that ran the place just left it that way. Whatever happened to her, Buck?"

"I hear she went to Australia."

Tommy brought more beer. Bright had begun to get drunk; Joe's slick hair was all ruffled and he kept falling asleep; the beer had no effect at all upon Johnny, who in between drinks pulled at his flask, which contained corn. Nobody would help him drink the corn and he resented this and made some cutting remarks, so Jim took a long pull.

"Friends of mine," snapped Bright, giving the lookout a shove.

"Yes, sir, Mr. Bright," said the lookout, hastily.

Joe had gone back to the hotel to sleep it off. He wasn't much of a drinker and a little alcohol made him sick. Bright was drunk and somewhat unsteady; Johnny was stone sober; and Jim was somewhere in between. He could walk, all right, but his tongue was thick and seemed to be covered with flannel.

"It's just a little joint," said Bright. "Fifty-dollar limit. But they say the wheel is straight. I've always had pretty good luck here."

They went past the little bar just behind the grilled front door and into a big gambling-room at the rear. There was a crowd around the crap table; two tables of poker and one of bridge were going; and a man with a red face and white hair was dealing blackjack. But the roulette wheel was deserted; the croupier with his green eyeshade aslant was leaning back with a bored expression on his thin, pale face.

"Roulette, that's the game," said Bright. He bought fifty dollars' worth of chips and began to play. Johnny tried to lead Jim up to the wheel, but Jim kept saying: "Gotta call my wife. It's after five o'clock. I tell you, Johnny, gotta call my wife."

"Oh, hell! we'll get you home for dinner."

"No. Gotta sober up. Gotta go to work at eight o'clock."

"Listen, Buck; we ain't going to let you go back to work at that joint. Twenty-five a week. Don't be a damn fool."

Jim kept insisting that he must phone his wife, but Johnny finally got him up to the roulette-table and shoved a stack of chips into his hand.

"Do your stuff, Buck. We'll go partners. It's a fifty-dollar limit. Go as far as you like. I'll stake you."

"Listen, Johnny, I gotta call my . . ."

"Get your money up, gentleman," said the croupier. "Here goes the wheel."

Jim pushed his hat back and considered; then, with an intent face, he put the whole stack of chips, fifty dollars, on the red. The red won. He played the red three straight times, winning. Then he switched to the black; black won.

"Look at him go," said Johnny.

Some time later all the other gambling devices were deserted. Even the blackjack dealer was watching the roulette wheel. Jim had his coat and vest off and sweat was streaming down from under his hair; his face was drawn, his eyes shining. Johnny stood next to him, his lips set in a thin line; Bright was asleep in a chair. Once, in his excitement, Johnny put his hand on Jim's shoulder. Jim turned, pushed him roughly away, and cried:

"Keep your hands off of me. Want to break my streak?"

"All right, Buck," said Johnny, meekly.

A crowd was jammed round the table, watching the wheel. The croupier spun the wheel impassively, but from time to time he looked up at Jim, cursing under his breath; this guy was sure a dog for luck. Jim won again and the croupier shoved him the chips. Somebody said:

"Who is that guy?"

Johnny turned.

"It's Buck Turner, and he'll just about bust this joint."

"Hell!" said another man, "that guy's the night clerk at the Northland."

"You mean he *was* the night clerk," said Johnny.

Jim won steadily; the croupier began to shave his bets from fifty to twenty-five, from twenty-five to ten. Jim said nothing. Finally he said:

"There's only three numbers on this board. Three, twenty-four, and thirty-three."

He had been playing red and black, odd and even, before; now he played ten each on the three numbers he had mentioned. Three won; the croupier counted out three hundred and fifty dollars. Jim played the numbers again; fifty on each. The croupier shaved the bets to ten. Thirty-three won. The croupier counted out another stack—three hundred and fifty dollars. Then he raised his hands and said:

"That's all. That's all. The boss ain't here and I can't take the responsibility."

Jim stared.

"And me right in the middle of a streak."

"If that's the middle," said the croupier, "I'd hate to see the end."

Somebody started a poker game. The crowd drifted slowly away. Johnny woke Bright up and told him that the croupier had stopped the wheel.

"How much did you win?"

"Around six thousand dollars."

Bright laughed.

"Good God! Won't that put a crimp in Benny, though. I never did like that wop."

While they were counting the money, Joe Constantinesco came in. He was still pale, but seemed sober now. He took Jim by the arm.

"Turner, your wife's having sixty fits over at the hotel. Thinks something has happened to you. I didn't tell her nothing. I just beat it over here after you."

Jim started.

"I forgot. . . . What time is it?"

"Quarter till ten."

"My God!" He stuffed money into all his pockets and started out on a run. But Johnny caught him and said: "Take it easy. I'll go with you."

"Johnny," he cried, "I got plenty of dough now. I'm going over and buy my wife a hat."

"A what?"

"A hat."

"A hat! At this time of night."

"Sure. The place over on Lawrence stays open late this time of year. Come on."

Johnny told Bright where they were going. He laughed, then said:

"Don't forget, Turner. You leave for Los Angeles Monday evening. Joe and me'll stick around here for a while. See if we can't get some of that two hundred back I dropped at the wheel."

When Mlle. Irene saw the two men looking at the hats in the show-window, she hesitated, then started to lock the door. She was afraid of a hold-up; there had been a good many of them on the North Side during the holidays and these men looked rough. But Johnny opened the door before she could lock it; they went in, and stood shifting and clearing their throats before this small, sleek, ultra-fashionable little person, who looked French but had been born Mary O'Connor.

"Yes, gentlemen?" Mlle. Irene was reassured by the expression on Jim's face. He looked so good-natured and harmless.

Jim flushed, then said in a loud voice:

"I want the most expensive hat you've got in the place for my wife."

Mlle. Irene lowered her eyes to keep from laughing.

"Yes? We have some newly-arrived Paris models. What sort of hat did you want?"

Jim looked blank, but Johnny said:

"You try 'em on. We'll see." Then he turned to Jim and smiled proudly, as if to say: "See, you big tramp, I know how to handle these things."

"Yes," said Jim, "will you be so kind as to try some on?" He thought that this was a very polite speech and began to feel easier.

Mlle. Irene dazzled him. She was perfect from her shiny black hair to her high-heeled red shoes; her hands were slim and elegant, her teeth startlingly white in her dark face, her mascaraed eyes big and blue, with enormous, almost grotesque, lashes. A faint perfume arose from her clothing, filling the little shop. Everything in the place was so dainty and fragile that Jim was afraid to move.

She tried on a hat and stood before them with her hands on her hips, smiling.

"I like that one. How much?"

"That one is . . ." Mlle. Irene hesitated for a moment. "That one is forty-two fifty."

"Shall I take it, Johnny?"

"Look at some more, chump. Don't take the first thing you see." Johnny was very lofty, and when Mlle. Irene turned to get another hat Jim stepped on his foot. "Ow!" said Johnny, and Mlle. Irene turned, startled. "Pardon?"

Jim and Johnny stared at each other for a moment, then Johnny said, "Oh, that's all right," and Jim snickered.

Mlle. Irene tried on another hat. Jim said:

"That's swell. How much?"

"This one," said Mlle. Irene, taking off the price tag, "is fifty-three dollars."

"I like this one better. Shall I take it, Johnny?"

"Sure. Take it."

"Put it in a nice box, see?" said Jim. "It's a surprise."

They stood waiting while Mlle. Irene wrapped up the hat. Jim was going to light a cigarette, but Johnny punched him in the ribs.

"Not in here, chump."

Mlle. Irene came back with a hatbox tied with ribbons.

"The box is special," she said. "Two dollars extra."

"Just fifty-five," said Jim, counting it out. "Thanks very much."

"Thank you. I hope your wife likes it. Come in again, gentlemen."

Jim and Johnny walked along in silence for several blocks; then Johnny spat out into the street and observed, quietly:

"I wouldn't kick her out of bed."

Johnny left Jim at the entrance of the Northland Hotel. It was nearly eleven o'clock. Mr. Plummer tried to stop Jim on the way in, but Jim brushed him aside and went up in the elevator. Marg would be sore as hell at him, but with nearly three thousand dollars in his pockets and a fine new hat for her, the kind he had seen her looking at, he felt very optimistic.

He unlocked the door softly and went in. Marg was lying on the davenport, with all the lights on; she had her hand over her eyes; her face was very pale. When she heard him, she jumped up and stood staring at him.

"Jim!"

"Hello, honey! What a day I've had!"

He handed her the hatbox, then he began taking money out of his pockets: tens, twenties, fifties.

"Jim, I've been half crazy, worrying about you. You've been gambling and you've lost your job. Mr. Plummer told me so. And look at your eye!"

"Oh, the hell with Mr. Plummer! I won three thousand dollars and I've got a new job; one hundred a week. And we're going to California Monday night. Look at the hat I bought you."

The color was beginning to come back into Marg's
face. She unwrapped the box and took the hat out.

"Why, Jim . . . how did you . . . It's wonderful."
She ran over to the mirror to try it on. "It fits. Oh, it's
swell and lovely, Jim."

Jim walked over to the mirror, looked at her for a
long time, then kissed her. She kissed him back; then
began to look at herself in the mirror again. He counted
out ten fifty-dollar bills and handed them to her.

"See? Five hundred dollars. Send that to Ma; that'll
keep them going for a while."

Marg took the money and stood holding it.

"What kind of a job have you got, Jim?"

"Well, it's at a dog track."

"A dog track!"

"Yes. I'm going to sort of look after things for Mr.
Bright. A hundred a week, Marg. We can send the folks
plenty."

Marg sighed and sat down.

"Well, this money is mighty good to have. But I can
see that we're going to start all over again. I was hoping
we wouldn't."

Jim sat down and stared at the floor. Marg took off
the hat and, holding it on her lap, turned it over and
over. Jim was depressed; he could see that Marg was
doubtful and was probably thinking that he was a big
fool and couldn't be depended on. He didn't want her
to think that. But suddenly Marg began to laugh.

"What you laughing at, Marg?" he asked, brighten-
ing.

"Nothing. Only I certainly wish I'd seen you buying
that hat."

PART TWO

CRESCENT CITY : 1929

Chapter I

"You know, marg," jim was saying, "you're sure a bearcat at fixing things up. This place is swell. Imagine getting a place like this for thirty a month. You sure are good."

Marg smiled, then went out into the kitchen to get dinner. Jim took off his coat and hat, and strolled out into the little garden at the rear of their small, stucco house, to look around. This was the first time in his life that he had ever had a house of his own, even a rented house, and he felt very proud and responsible; a sure-enough citizen he was now, not a hopscotcher. He lit a cigar, then shoved his hands into his pants pockets and stood looking off across the flat land surrounding the house. It was early evening and the sun had almost set; in the west the sky was a pale mauve with long horizontal golden clouds just above the horizon. Jim knew that these clouds were lying over the Pacific Ocean, which was only a mile or so off; the breeze was blowing from that direction; it was cool and smelled strongly of brine and seaweed. Far to the northeast Jim could see the sharp, irregular peaks of a mountain range, mist-blue in the evening light, nearly merging into the darkening sky. But near at hand, stretching in all directions, the land was as flat as Indiana. Toward the ocean there was marshland where frogs sang at night, and beyond that a cluster of oil-derricks, which loomed black in the dusk.

Funny place where you could see tall palms growing as natural as oak trees! Jim had never got used to the palms, nor to the great eucalyptus trees which bordered a good many of the roads, nor to the olive groves, nor to the orange and lemon trees. He had felt the same in Florida. It was like a play. A man could never consider such a place his home. At home you had snow in the winter, rain in the spring, wind in March, oranges in the grocery stores, and palms in pots. All the same, the queer blue sky and the dazzling light were fine; palms were swell, if they did look like up-ended feather dusters; and you didn't need an overcoat, except sometimes at night.

The trip out was fun. He had been West before; had been to Caliente, in Mexico, twice; but he had come a different way and besides he had played poker most of the time and drunk whisky and had scarcely looked out the window once. Coming out with Marg, it was another matter; she made him see things. She had never traveled much and she liked it. Kansas bored Jim to death with its mile after mile of dreary plains; but it awed Marg and she talked to him about how sad it must be to live all your life in a place like that. They ran into a blizzard in the middle of Kansas. They saw isolated farms lost in the immensity of the prairie, the roofs of the houses and farm buildings covered with snow, the roads hidden, rail fences half buried by the drifts, and smoke rising slowly from the chimneys in the heavy winter air. No one was out; the countryside was deserted. Occasionally they saw a lighted window.

They crossed the Raton Pass at midnight. They had gone to bed early. Marg was tired and her head ached from staring out at the snow-covered plains; she went to sleep at once. Jim dozed, waking every little while. Several times he got up to smoke, but the compartment was cold and he was glad to get back into bed. Finally he fell into a deep sleep, but Marg woke him and got into his berth.

"My ears are ringing, Jim," she said. "We must be up in the mountains."

Jim raised the blind and they lay looking out. They had never seen such moonlight; it was nearly as bright as day; trees and bluffs cast long shadows. The train was curving up through the mountains; above them towered huge, craggy slopes; they could not see the peaks; below them were deep fissures and ravines filled with the blackest shadows. Several times they saw the engine toiling up a great curved grade, its fire-box glowing red.

"Oh, this is swell!" Marg said, and Jim agreed that it was, and meant it. He had never known that he could get any kick out of mountains and moonlight, but with Marg it was different.

When they woke the next morning and raised the blinds, Marg rubbed her eyes and said:

"Good heavens! I never knew the sun could be so bright."

They were in New Mexico, a great, barren, rugged country with desolate, steep hills. The real Southwest was beginning and their eyes, used to the mild sun of the temperate zone, were dazzled by the fiery white light. They passed little huts strung along a sandy river bed. They saw ragged Mexicans lazily riding bony little horses along a dusty trail at the side of the tracks; some of them waved, some of them did not even look at the huge, transcontinental train. Marg stared at the cactus, the mesquite, the red buttes and great sandy stretches of this desert land. Once she shivered and said:

"I'd hate to get put off the train here," and Jim laughed.

Marg saw her first Indian at Albuquerque—a big fat buck Navaho who was selling beads and trinkets at the station. They had some coffee at the lunch-stand, then Marg bought a little silver-and-turquoise bracelet for Ma. When they were getting back on the train, Marg gripped Jim's arm.

"Gee! I'm glad we came!"

Marg was a good sport when she let herself go. But she was from a small town and a little afraid of things sometimes; at least that's the way it seemed to him. Chicago had been too much for her at first; she had got lost four blocks from the hotel, and she had hated the L trains which ran headlong above the rooftops and swayed and shrieked on the curves.

Marg liked security, an ordered life, the pay check at regular intervals. She was afraid of being without money; and was fanatical on the subject of bills and would owe nobody, annoying Jim sometimes by her insistence. But she was a good sport all the same. If it hadn't been for the trouble George had caused by being such a no-good, she might not have been so particular about everything.

Jim puffed contentedly on his cigar and walked about the little garden. He saw the light go on in the kitchen; he heard Marg humming to herself as she got supper ready. This was something like it.

"Marg," he called, after a while, "come here, will you?"

"I'm busy. What do you want?"

"Come here. I want to show you something."

Marg came out, looking very domestic in her apron. "What is it?"

He bent down and pointed.

"What's this stuff, Marg?"

In the middle of the little garden there was a small cement pool, dry now, surrounded by tall, slim green reeds.

"What's what? Oh! Why, that must be bamboo! It is bamboo."

"Bamboo, eh?" said Jim. "Pretty swell, ain't we, with bamboo in our back yard?"

"It's nice here. Gee! it's quiet, but it's getting cool. Let's go in. We'll eat in fifteen or twenty minutes."

Jim picked her up, whirled her around, and kissed her. After a short struggle she freed herself and gave him a push.

"Don't do that, Jim. The neighbors will think we're not married."

They both laughed and went into the kitchen arm in arm.

It was nearly seven-thirty when Jim got to the track. The ticket-booths on either side of the big entrance gate were just opening for business. Cars were driving into the huge parking-space which stretched for four blocks at the rear of the tall fence which surrounded the racing-plant.

"Got a pass for James Turner?" Jim asked one of the ticket-sellers.

"Try the next window. I don't handle passes."

Jim asked at all the windows, but there was no pass for him. He bought a ticket and went in. The flood-lights over the track had not yet been lighted, the judges' stand was in darkness, and there was little activity; but the grandstand, which surprised Jim by its size, was blazing with light. The girl ushers, dressed in blue silk trousers and jackets and wearing tall, military shakos with gleaming patent-leather tops, were already at their posts. The program-sellers were just coming from the office under the grandstand and some of them were already shouting: "Program. Buy a program. You can't tell one dog from another without a program."

"Damn big plant, all right," Jim told himself. "I had an idea they'd race dogs in a smaller place than this. I've saw horse tracks that didn't have a grandstand that big."

He walked about, looking indifferently at everything. The inclosure in front of the grandstand sloped gradually down to the rails at the track and was covered with fine gravel, nicely tamped and leveled. The track itself was dark and he couldn't see it very well, but he was pretty sure it was a quarter-mile and it seemed very small to him. He leaned on the rail to look at the starting-box; it had eight separate compartments with glass fronts. So that's where the hounds came out of? He shrugged. Looked like small stuff to him. He couldn't imagine who would want to see dogs run. A dog was a dog; no jockeys, no nothing; everything was on too small a scale for him.

Finally he went up into the grandstand and asked one of the ushers where he could find Mr. Fallon.

"He just came in," said the usher. "His office is on the mezzanine."

"On the which?"

Jim began to hate this place with its monkey-suited girl ushers, its dinky track, its mezzanine! Imagine all this fuss over a lot of dogs! It was damned silly.

"Right back through there, sir," said the usher, looking at him as if she thought he wasn't very bright.

He crossed the corridor beyond the box-seats and went into the mezzanine. He felt more at home here; the lights were lit in front of the cashiers' cages and he saw the boys getting their tickets ready for the first race. He'd sold tickets himself; this was familiar. He wondered if they got a big play on the dogs; it didn't seem possible.

He found Fallon's office and went in. A small, sharp-featured man with cold gray eyes turned to look at him. The man said nothing, but his eyes said:

"What the hell do you mean by walking in like that?"

Jim said:

"You Mr. Fallon?"

"I am. Don't you ever knock?"

Jim just looked at him. A stenographer, who had been sitting at a desk, glanced from one to the other, then got up hastily and went into the next room.

"Well, what is it?"

"I'm James Turner. Mr. Bright sent me out."

"From Chicago? All right, Turner. Don't mind me saying what I did. I've got people walking in on me all the time. I'm damn sick of it." Fallon smiled and they shook hands. "We were looking for you opening night."

"I couldn't make it. How's things?"

They sat down and Fallon gave Jim a cigar. Jim could see that Fallon was a hard customer; not that he looked tough, he didn't; but it was very apparent that he had no difficulty in taking care of number one.

"Fine. I suppose you've got an identification of some kind?"

Jim handed Fallon a letter, which he glanced at briefly, then laid on the desk.

"Having any trouble? Mr. Bright's anxious to know how things stand."

"Naturally, with the wad he's got in it. We may have a little trouble. Dog tracks always do. But we're operating under the option system, same as Tanforan at San Francisco, and we've got a couple court rulings that its not illegal. We may have a fight on our hands before we're through, but we're all used to that kind of trouble. How is Mosey?"

"Fine. How do I work?"

"I'll introduce you to Billy Diegel when he gets here.

He's got charge of the odds. You check up with him.
I'll tell Stein about you; he's got charge of the books.
You can look them over any time you like. I'll help
all I can. So make yourself at home. If you want to do
a little betting, the handicapper will give you tips. He's
pretty good."

"Do the whippets run to form as much as the horses?"

"The what? Say, don't let any of the dog-men hear
you say that." Fallon laughed shortly.

"Say what?"

"These aren't whippets; they're greyhounds. Whippets are little things, that high. Some of the greyhounds
weigh over seventy pounds. The word whippet means
fight to the dog-men."

Jim laughed.

"I'll remember. I know horse tracks, Fallon. I know
betting, but I don't know dogs."

"You'll learn."

"Must be pretty tiresome running a place like this.
No kick like the horses."

"You'll be surprised."

They talked for a while about Chicago and about
Bright, puffing on their cigars. Suddenly Jim noticed
a steady, low rumbling which seemed to fill Fallon's
big office. He listened intently but could make nothing
of it. Finally he said:

"What's that noise?"

"That's the crowd coming." Fallon looked at his
watch. "It's almost post-time for the first race. Turner,
we had eighteen thousand people here opening night.
It's almost too good to be true. I've got to go downstairs and see Eddy Clemens. I've got a box down in

the A section; just make yourself at home. Come up here after the last race."

When Fallon opened his office door the noise of the huge crowd hit them full force. The mezzanine was packed; there were long lines before each cashier's window; and people, coming from the grandstand proper, were pushing and shoving in a hurry to get their money up before the dogs went to post.

"Well?" said Fallon, with a smile. "Bright made a good investment, didn't he?"

"Looks like it."

Jim elbowed his way through the crowd, reached the wooden corridor behind the boxes after a long struggle, and finally found the A section; but the usher barred his way.

"I ain't got a ticket. Mr. Fallon told me to sit in his box."

The girl looked at him doubtfully.

"Well, go ahead. I'll ask Mr. Fallon later."

Jim found the box and sat down. It was the only empty box in the whole section. A great rumbling, indeterminate noise rose from this huge crowd which was packed from the last row of the grandstand to the guard-rails around the track.

"They must be nuts," muttered Jim.

The flood lights had been turned on now and the track was bright as day. Three huge loud-speakers were blaring a march, and, turning, Jim saw the dogs coming down the track to be paraded before the judges, each dog led by a groom. The grooms were dressed as huntsmen in red coats and black visored caps; they were preceded by a strutting drum-major, twirling a silver baton. Jim's lip curled. All this ballyhoo for a bunch of dogs!

The dogs were paraded before the judges, then led to the three-sixteenth box at the end of the first turn. The dogs were numbered from 1 to 8 and the boxmen slipped them into the boxes which corresponded to their post numbers. The grooms stood at attention till the last dog had been slipped in, then they trotted, two by two, to a gate at the head of the first turn and left the track. All this military precision irked Jim and he slumped down in his chair and muttered to himself.

Suddenly all the lights in the grandstand were switched off. Jim was both aroused and befuddled by the violent yells from the crowd. He jumped to his feet. The dogs had broken from their boxes and were chasing the electric rabbit which ran like a streak along the inside of the track. The crowd continued to roar, but Jim didn't hear the roaring. He stood, stunned, watching those dogs run. He had never seen such speed in his life. They ran in a bunch till they reached the stretch, then a big brindle dog, number one, pulled away, stretched out his neck, and it was all over.

The lights were switched on in the grandstand, the numbers of the win, place, and show dogs were hung up, and the crowd settled back into the seats; but Jim was still standing. He hated to admit it, but, compared with the dogs, the horses seemed slow. These dogs really went places. Wow! Finally he sat down. The loud-speakers were blaring out the same march and the grooms were parading the dogs back to the kennels.

A big red-faced man in the next box tore up a handful of tickets, then said:

"Good, eh? Couldn't lose, eh? A swell tip."

"Them dogs can sure run," said Jim.

The big man looked at him.

"First time?"

"Yeah. I've seen plenty of horse-races, but I never saw whip . . . I never saw greyhounds run before."

"Hell! Them dogs you saw were all hamburgers. Wait till you see the real dogs run. The real dogs begin to run about the seventh race. Look at that time. Twenty and one-fifth seconds. I could run that fast myself. They got a dog here can run the three-sixteenth in eighteen and one-fifth seconds. Dark Hazard. One of them Shy Warrior dogs. Wait till you see that baby step."

Jim offered the man a cigarette and they sat smoking.

"That's pretty fast sprinting."

"Pretty fast!" said the man. "I'll say it's pretty fast. It's a world record. You can't go wrong betting on that dog. He don't pay much; they always bet him down to even money or less; but he pays off. I saw him beat the best dogs in the world seven races out of eight at Miami, and he's only two years old at that."

"He must be worth a lot of money."

"I'll say. If he keeps on the way he's going he'll be worth a small fortune in the stud. He's in the ninth race tonight and he'll take that bunch like Grant took Richmond." The big man started to leaf through his program. "Here it is," he said. "Look at that record."

Jim took the program and read where the man was pointing.

DARK HAZARD   Cl. P. $5000   WT. 65
Bk D—Shy Warrior—Porcelain—Jan '27—Kiowa Kennels

PL	DST	TK	TM	PP	OFF	1/8	ST	FIN	ORDER OF FIN
CresC	Fut	F	28 3/5	5	1	1	1	1	Dk.Haz,JimK
Flda	3/16	F	18 2/5	6	1	–	1	1	Dk.Haz,Rd.R
Flda	Fut	F	28 3/5	5	3	1	1	1	Dk.Haz,TimW
Flda	1/4	F	22 4/5	5	2	2	2	1	Dk.Haz,GolB
Flda	5/16	F	32	5	4	3	3	2	WilJ,Dk.Haz

"Some record," said Jim. "I see he ran a quarter in twenty-two and four-fifths seconds. That's sure traveling."

"He's some pooch," said the big man. "That record was made on a five-sixteenth track, though; only one turn. The world record for the quarter on a quarter-mile track is twenty-five seconds. Well, I got to go out and lose some more money. They say Going Some is hot in the second. I hope he's hotter than that meat-hound I bet on in the first."

Jim nodded, then he took an old envelope from his pocket and wrote on it in pencil, Dark Hazard.

"I better get myself a bet on that bird in the ninth," he told himself.

Long before post time for the ninth race Jim had been converted to dog-racing as a sport. He still resented the musical-comedy ushers, the drum-major with his self-satisfied strut and his silver baton, and the dressed-up grooms with their mechanical precision of movement; but the dogs were wonderful. They ran true races, breaking from their boxes like bullets; they were always trying, and there were no jockeys to pull them and get them into pockets. Jim had had enough racing experience, however, to see that the post position of the dog made an enormous difference; a dog in the 1 box had a distinct advantage over the others, providing he could break fast; if he couldn't, it was probable that he'd be cut off at the turn. The outside box, No. 8, was also a good one, allowing the dog to get away well without interference of any kind on one side of him. The boxes in between 1 and 8 were the bad ones, particularly five and six. It was all right, though, because the dogs could be handicapped that way. Horses were handicapped by weight, but that was impossible with the dogs. He turned to the big man in the next box. The big man hadn't won a bet so far and his face was a yard long.

"Say, what about post positions? They make a big difference, don't they?"

The big man turned.

"What? Post positions? I'll say they do. The six box is the hot spot; the five is just about as bad."

"Do they draw for position? Or does the judge handicap 'em that way?"

"They spot the dogs. That dog I was telling you about, Dark Hazard, he hardly ever gets anything but the five or the six box. Sometimes they get big-hearted and give him four or seven. He never gets a smell of the outside boxes. They got him in the five tonight and a fast-breaking dog on each side of him. Trying to beat him. And they stuck that Australian dog, Round Robin, in the two box. The crowd will bet Dark Hazard down to two-to-five, see? And if he don't fall down he'll win. I'm going to try to get even on him."

"I'm going to bet him a little," said Jim. "But I never saw a horse that could win all the time, and I don't expect to see a dog that can, neither."

"Well, here I go," said the big man, taking out his

billfold and counting off a stack of bills. "Black dog be good to me."

Jim sat looking down into the inclosure, where a mob was milling. It was nearly post time for the feature race and he could feel the excitement of the crowd. There were arguments going on all around him and he heard the name Dark Hazard mentioned every minute or so. A man behind him contended loudly that Round Robin would win in a walk from the 2 box; another man shouted: "Bet you three to one Dark Hazard finishes ahead of him." The argument ran from box to box like fire before a wind. Jim was getting anxious to see this wonder-dog, but when some man shouted: "That pup's the Man-o'-War of dog tracks," he smiled to himself; a dog was just a dog, after all.

The excitement increased. Across the track the figures on the illuminated odd-board were changing rapidly. Round Robin fell from three-to-one to even money; Dark Hazard sank steadily from four-to-one to three- to-five; the dog in the 1 box, Jim King, continued at three-to-one; the rest of the dogs ranged from eight to twenty to one. Jim began to feel excited himself. They sure were playing those two dogs off the boards. Finally he took twenty-five dollars out of his pocket and left the box for the mezzanine floor, where the people from the boxes bet. It was a piker bet for him, but he decided that it was all he would risk.

As a matter of fact, he had promised Marg that he wouldn't bet at all. But he still had most of that three thousand dollars he had won at Chicago, and a twenty-five dollar bet certainly wouldn't hurt a man any. Marg didn't really care about the betting part; she was afraid that he'd gamble his salary away. She was thinking about Pa and Ma back in Barrowville and she was right to think of them. All he had to do was to be careful, and he sure was doing that, only betting twenty-five dollars.

He saw Fallon lounging against the railing at the head of the stairs with a cigar in his mouth and a self-satisfied smile on his face.

"Hello!" said Fallon; then he jerked his thumb at the money Jim had in his hand. "They got you doing it, have they?"

"It's my first bet of the evening. Say, I'm sold on dog-racing except for the monkey tricks. Them dressed-up ushers and the guys that lead the dogs out! The drum-major's the worst of all, though."

Fallon laughed.

"That, Turner, is what's known as class. The public eats it up. You won't notice it at all in a day or so; you'll get used to it. Betting on Round Robin in this race?"

"No. Dark Hazard."

"Pick him on form?"

"No; a guy down in the box told me he was hot. I'm only going to get ten tickets."

"The handicapper thinks Round Robin will walk in out of the two hole. All the dog-men are betting on him. He likes the top and he's fast as the devil. Dark Hazard's going to have plenty of interference getting out of the five hole with Timber Wolf right next to him. Timber Wolf's not only big, but clumsy, and he breaks like a shot."

"Well," said Jim, scratching his head, "maybe I better trail along with the smart money. I'll admit I don't know straight up."

"Then get your dough on Round Robin. Billy Die-gel's brother bet four hundred on him and he's smart. The one-ticket bettors are all on Dark Hazard. He's a crowd-pleaser."

Jim decided that he'd bet on Round Robin. What did that big guy know? He hadn't won a bet all eve-ning. Jim walked back into the betting-shed on the mezzanine and stood watching the odd-board. Round Robin had gone up a little; he was now two-to-one. Dark Hazard was a prohibitive favorite—two-to-five.

The last-minute bettors were pouring out into the mezzanine now and the betting-shed was in confusion. Long lines were forming before the ticket-sellers' cages, and the floor-men were walking about in the crowd, shouting: "Don't get shut out. You've only got a few minutes left. Get your money up right away, folks."

Jim hesitated. All the smart boys thought Round Robin was in; here was a chance to win a little money. Two-to-one was pretty fair odds on a smart-money favorite. Making up his mind, he added seventy-five dol-lars to the twenty-five in his hand and got in one of the lines.

When he got back to the box, the dogs were being paraded. Round Robin was a big, brindle, Australian dog, weighing seventy-eight pounds; he had his head up, barking at every step, and his tail was waving from side to side. Jim thought he looked ready to go and sank back, smiling. Good thing he'd run into Fallon.

The big man in the next box touched his arm.

"Well, what do you think of him?"

"Who?"

"Dark Hazard."

Jim had forgotten all about him.

"I got on Round Robin."

"You'll be sorry."

"I was talking to Fallon. All the smart money's on him."

The big man looked doubtful, and taking out a cigar he lit it and puffed meditatively. Finally he observed:

"Well, if the smart money's right it'll be a perfect score for the evening. I ain't won a bet." He pointed his cigar at Dark Hazard. "Slick job, ain't he?"

Jim looked at the No. 5 dog indifferently; the only dog in the race that interested him now was the dog he had his money on. And, after all, Dark Hazard didn't look like much; he walked along with his eyes on the ground, stepping daintily, with his tail down between his legs and his hind quarters sloping in exaggerated fashion. He was sleek and black as jet and looked much smaller than the other dogs, though he weighed sixty-five pounds. He looked weak and fragile compared with the huge Australian dog.

"He slinks," said Jim.

"Is that the dog I got my money on?" yelled somebody behind them; "that black, number-five dog. He looks like he's hunting a place to lay down."

"He looks to me like he's had his dinner. Hell! What does he care about a rabbit!" shouted another comedian.

Jim laughed. The big man was puffing furiously on his cigar now, looking very glum.

As soon as the lights went out the crowd began to yell; all the pent-up excitement of waiting for the start of the feature race burst out at once. Jim leaned on the rail and stared at the futurity box, which was just beyond the judges' stand and in plain sight. A bell rang loudly; the mechanical rabbit whizzed round the stretch turn, gathering speed on the straightaway; then the starter dropped his flag, the boxes flew open, and out came the dogs, flying. Round Robin's red blanket flashed first round the turn; Timber Wolf was right at his heels on the outside; Dark Hazard was last.

"Goddam!" cried the big man, sinking into his chair. "He ain't got a chance now. He'll never catch that Australian dog."

Jim smiled to himself as he saw the big Australian dog pulling away on the back stretch; all that pooch had to do now was hold on; the tickets were as good as cashed. Roar after roar rose from the crowd as the dogs flew into the back turn. Timber Wolf had dropped back; Round Robin was out by himself, but was running wide. The rest of the dogs were bunched. Jim shrugged. Not much kick to this race; it was a cinch. He turned to look at the big man, taking his eyes from the track momentarily.

"Round Robin's in, I guess," he said. But the last part of his remark was drowned by such a powerful burst of yelling, that he was startled and confused. "What the . . . My God!"

Round Robin was still in front, but he was fading fast; a black dog running low, with his nose almost to the ground, was coming like a streak on the inside rail. Zip! It was all over.

Jim sank into his chair and mopped his forehead.

There was dead silence for a moment, then the stands burst into a prolonged and violent uproar.

"Dark Hazard wins! Dark Hazard wins!"

The lights came on. The winning numbers were hung up in the timer's stand. Jim turned. He thought the big man was having a fit; finally he subsided.

"He's a dog, ain't he?" he shouted. "He can beat them bums in his sleep. Last in the stretch and runs over them coming home. Wow!"

Jim shrugged and tore up his tickets.

After the last race Jim went up to Fallon's office, where he was introduced to Billy Diegel, a short, fat little man with red cheeks and a pleasant smile. They sat smoking, waiting for Jud Stein.

Jim laughed.

"Round Robin almost won that ninth race, didn't he?"

Billy snorted.

"He run out of gas. I don't like them big dogs. When they get 'em over seventy pounds they're too big."

"Hell!" said Fallon. "No wonder he ran out of gas. That black dog knocked two-fifths of a second off the track record."

Billy shrugged.

"Bud took a nice whipping on that race. He thought Round Robin was a cinch out of the two hole."

"How about the girl-friend?"

"Don't mention it. She'll climb the wall. She shot the works on that dog of hers."

"Valery's some girl!" laughed Fallon, then he turned

to Jim. "You been around horse tracks. You ought to know her."

"Valery Wilson?" asked Jim, staring.

"Yeah. She owns Round Robin."

"She does? Is she here?"

"Yeah. She sold her horses over in Australia and raced dogs till they closed the tracks."

"Well, I'll be!"

"I think Bud Diegel's getting ready to take her on for life. Is that right, Billy?"

"I guess so. Bud never did have much sense. He'll be her fifth. I told Bud I never did like to stand in line, myself."

They all laughed.

"Valery's some girl!" said Jim, absently echoing Fallon. What would she say when she saw him? He hadn't seen her since she threw that water on the waiter in the Pullman diner; the waiter had spilled some water on her dress, so she gave him a taste of his own medicine. Nobody ever knew what she was going to do. She had been married three times before she was twenty-five years old. She was half Cuban and half cockney English and had raced horses all over the world, even in Russia. Jim thought that it would be a good idea to avoid her; she had complicated his life considerably at one time. Marg would think she was awful.

Jud Stein came in after a while, smoking a long stogie. He was a tall, thin, lanky man of fifty with a dark, weathered face and the narrowed, imperturbable eyes of a professional gambler. He had a big ledger under his arm and he put it down to shake hands with Jim. Then he said:

"Let's get on with it."

They sat down and bent over the ledger. Stein explained all the entries to Jim in a level, monotonous voice. The bookkeeping was simple; and as Jim understood the mutual system thoroughly, everything went smoothly. Jim finally nodded and got up.

Billy Diegel said:

"Get the morning odds from me. Check up on us all you please. You'll find we're pretty straight."

"Well," said Jim, "you were a little short on the third race tonight. But outside of that you're paying what you put up. That's what Bright wants. He thinks dog-racing's good in California. He don't want to make a grab game out of it. That'll kill it sure."

"And he's right," said Fallon.

"About that third race," Billy interposed: "there was a rush for that number three dog just before the starting-bell. We didn't have time to change the odds."

"We school Tuesday and Thursday mornings in case you want to come out," said Fallon.

"All right. And another thing, Bright says that a crowd likes good place money. He says to pay good place money if you have to shave the win money a little. A lot of people bet place and they get sick of this three-eighty and four-dollar stuff."

"Good idea," said Stein.

Jim looked at the clock. It was after twelve. Time to get going. He shook hands all around and started out, but the door opened, there was a loud argument in the corridor, then Valery Wilson came in, followed by Bud Diegel, a small, handsome young man, with curly dark hair, who looked more like Billy's son than his brother. Valery was loudly dressed, smelled strongly of a musky perfume, and had an amazing number of ornaments scattered over her small person—diamond rings, strands of beads, a dozen bracelets, long ear-rings and a vanity-case which glittered. She was slim and straight, with very small hands, and small, well-arched feet; her complexion was olive, her eyes dark, her nose aquiline.

"Oh, my God!" she said. "Here's my rabbit's foot. Buck Turner, are you really alive? I thought you were dead long ago."

She kissed him.

"Hey!" he said, with a laugh. "I'm a married man."

"You married!"

Jim was introduced to Bud Diegel, who was scowling and shook hands limply.

"Bud," said Valery, "invite Buck to come downtown and eat with us. We know a nice place where they have good beer. You're not really married, are you, Buck?"

"I am. Good night, everybody. Got to get home. Glad I saw you, Valery. Sorry your dog lost."

"You must have bet on him."

"I did."

"I told you he was my rabbit's foot." She came over and put her arm through his. "Don't run away, Buck. Let's go drink some beer and talk over old times. Be a sport."

"Sorry. Got to go home."

"You've really got a home to go to?"

"I have."

"You've certainly changed."

"Let him go, Valery. Can't you see he wants to go,"
said Bud Diegel, scowling.

Jim started out.

"I'll be seeing you," called Valery.

Not if I see you first, Jim was thinking. What a nice
chase she was going to lead that Diegel kid. Why, she
must be at least ten years older than he was. Valery
was a handful.

When he left the grandstand the plant was all dark
except for a few lights in the betting-shed downstairs.
It was very still and there wasn't a person in sight. He
looked at the track, which was in darkness, and thought
about that black dog sliding through on the rail at
express-train speed.

"That's a dog," he muttered, going out through the
big entrance gate. "That's a real dog."

Marg was asleep on the lounge in the living-room
when Jim got home. She had her face turned to the
wall and her knees drawn up. Jim laughed to himself,
thinking: "She ain't any bigger than a straw hat with
the rim kicked off."

He lit a cigarette, sat down, and took the night's program from his pocket, but he didn't look at it; he just
sat holding it. He felt suddenly tired and a pleasant
glow of contentment made him smile. The night was
very still; a small clock was ticking on the mantelpiece;
a bridge lamp with an amber-colored shade cast a mel-
low light over this cheerful little room. Marg surely
knew how to fix things up! Jim stretched out his legs
and began to nod. This was home, a place where a man
could shut himself off from the world when he felt

like it. He had lived as a transient, at the mercy of others, long enough. His head dropped sharply forward and he woke with a start. Marg was sitting up, looking at him.

Jim had a confused notion that the switchboard was buzzing and that he had a long dull night ahead of him. But Marg said:

"Well, it's a wonder you wouldn't wake me up. I waited for you till I couldn't keep my eyes open. How do you like it, Jim?"

"Fine. Say, Marg, I was dreaming that we was back at the Northland. I'm sure glad we're not."

"So am I. It's wonderful here. I sat out on the front porch for an hour after you left. Imagine sitting on the front porch in the middle of January. A fog came up about eight-thirty, so I had to come in. Did you have any fog at the track?"

"A little. I noticed some around the flood-lights about the third race, I think. Say, Marg, I like dog-racing. I didn't think I would. There's a lot of hokum to it that's pretty sickening at first, but that's just the trimmings. Them dogs! Talk about run. I saw a dog tonight that I'd sure like to own. I . . ."

"You what?"

Marg said this so sharply that Jim stared at her, then he laughed.

"Don't get excited. I meant I'd like to own him if I had a lot of money and was racing dogs. Why, you couldn't buy him for less than five thousand dollars. You couldn't buy him at all. He's the best there is."

"Well, I hope you're not thinking about buying any

dogs. I'd think that the trouble you had with your horses would've taught you something."

"Now don't get all worked up, kid. I just meant if. You know."

"Sure you did. Want some lunch, Jim? I've got some weenies. We could have weenie sandwiches."

"I could eat one. Say, Marg, you must come out to the track with me some night. You'd like them dogs."

"Maybe I will some night," said Marg. "Do they have big crowds?"

"Big crowds! They had eighteen thousand people opening night. They had capacity tonight. Saturday night, you know. Fallon even expects a big crowd Monday night."

They went out into the kitchen and Marg tied on her apron, then Jim picked her up and kissed her.

"I like to see you in that apron. You look . . . well, you look like this was your home."

Marg laughed.

"Is it or isn't it?"

"It sure is and I hope you stay a long time."

"I'll stay till you put me out."

Jim threw back his head and laughed. The idea of him putting Marg out was too much for him. "Say," he said, "no chance of me ever putting you out, Marg. It's the other way around."

"If that's the case, I'm getting pretty sick of looking at you."

"I'll bet you are at that. Say, why didn't you marry a good-looking fellow, Marg?"

"Because I'm always kind to dumb animals."

After they had eaten, they went out into the garden
for a few minutes before going to bed. The fog had
disappeared and the moon, big and white, was low in
the sky. The breeze blowing up from the Pacific was
damp but mild and it felt good on their faces.

"Look at the stars," said Marg. "Isn't this great?"

"You bet."

They stood in silence for a while with their arms
around each other, then Marg said:

"You just be careful with your money, Jim, and we
can stay out here a long time, and help the folks, too.
You didn't start betting tonight, did you?"

Jim hesitated.

"No."

"Stick to it. That's all foolishness. We'll never have
anything if you start gambling again."

"Listen. I'm going to be careful. This meet's going
to run for a hundred days or more, and then Mr. Bright
and Fallon and another man are going to open a track
up at 'Frisco. We're set for the winter and then some."

"Then what?"

"Don't worry. I've got a deal in now. When Mr.
Bright takes you up it means something. Say, I been
thinking. We've got to get a car. You can't get around
out here without a car."

"It would be nice. Do you think we can afford it?"

"Sure. I was talking to a fellow tonight. He said the
used-car market was shot. Said you could pick up a
Ford in good condition for a couple hundred dollars."

"Well."

"And then we could ride around and see things, and

you could take me to the track and come after me if you wanted to."

"That would be fun."

"All right. Tomorrow we get us a car. Whoopee! Ain't that swell, Marg?"

Chapter II

J<small>IM FELT VERY PROUD OF HIMSELF WHEN HE DROVE UP</small> to the racing-plant in his new car. Although he had driven a good many of them, he had never owned one before. Jumping about the country, he had never had any use for one; now it was different. A shiny, practically new sport roadster, with two extra tires in chromium covers at the sides, rumble seat and all; of course he'd had to pay more than he had intended, but Marg didn't know that. She thought it was a wonderful bargain.

He parked his car against the fence just outside the back gate, locked it, then got out and stood looking at it.

"Some job, you bet."

While he was looking, Bud Diegel drove up in a Cadillac 16, parked it beside Jim's Ford, then said:

"Hello, Turner! Been buying yourself a new bus, I see."

"Yeah. I like it, too. But I'll trade you if you'll throw in a couple of extra tires."

Diegel tried to laugh, but he didn't have much use for Jim. He thought he was a big, ignorant roughneck, and he was tired of hearing Valery talk about him; Valery said that Jim Turner was the nerviest man she'd ever known, and when he asked, "In what way?" she said, "Every way."

"Going in for the schooling?" asked Diegel.

"Yeah. Thought I might like to see it. I know horses pretty well. But I don't know anything about dogs."

"Valery's got some Australian pups she thinks are pretty hot. Personally, I don't like those big, lubberly dogs."

They went in, showed their cards to the gate-man, then crossed the inclosure and stood leaning on the rail at the side of the judges' stand. The big plant looked different in the daytime, cheaper and cruder. The center field under the dazzling California sun was a mere expanse of brown dirt; at night, with the floodlights turned away from it, it was mostly in the shadows and seemed to be covered with sod; this illusion puzzled Jim and he stood staring.

Eddy Clemens, the presiding judge, standing in the doorway of the glassed-in judges' stand, waved a hand at them and told them to come in. He gave them chairs and offered them cigars, which they accepted.

"We're going to school Willy Judas after we get through with this hand-schooling," said Eddy. "Thought you might like to get a close look at him. A lot of wise ones think he can take Dark Hazard."

"When's the match race?" asked Bud.

"Saturday night."

"Going to let Valery's dog in?"

"No; don't think so. He couldn't beat Dark Hazard in an eight-dog race with everything in his favor. That Wolf's Crag dog knocked Dark Hazard all over the track still Round Robin couldn't beat him. What do you think he'd look like in a three-dog race?"

"That was only one race. I think Valery's dog can beat both of them other dogs. Give him the outside; that's what he likes. Stick the black dog in the middle. It'll make the betting good."

"And give Willy Judas the rail, eh? That would be swell. This race is going to be five-sixteenths and Willy loves it. No, I don't think I can use that Australian dog."

"What does Billy say?"

Eddy colored and chewed on his cigar.

"I don't care what Billy says. I'm presiding judge till I hear different."

The timer called Eddy and he turned and waved to the rabbit man in the tower above the grandstand. The man nodded and signaled to the mechanic in the pit at the head of the first turn. The mechanic raised the rabbit out of the pit and set it, then waved "O.K."; the man in the tower gave the controls a turn and the rabbit started around the track, looking very lifelike.

"We'll see what them big Australians can do, " said Eddy.

Six men were standing just beyond the judges' stand, holding six big greyhound pups between their knees. When the rabbit came round they let them go, and they all made a break for the flying bait, jostling one another. At the first turn two of them lost the rabbit, and, stopping, stood looking about them in a dazed way. The rest flew round the turn. A little black dog was hugging the rail like a champion; the two Australian pups were running wide, but they were really running, and a woman in the grandstand began to yell.

"That's Valery," said Bud, with a laugh. But Jim was interested in the pups, and paid no attention.

When they hit the stretch the four remaining pups were spread clear across the track. The little black dog was still hugging the rail; a white dog was next to him, a nose ahead, but fading fast, and the big Australians were far on the outside, but close up to the leader. The white dog and one of the Australians fell back, the pace being too hot for them; but the other Australian finished with a great burst of speed and nosed out the black dog at the wire.

"That little Kashmir King pup is short," said Eddy, "but he'll make a great track dog. See him hug that rail?"

"What about Valery's pup?" asked Bud, smiling.

"I don't like them dogs that run all over the track." Eddy turned and called to the timer, "What do you make it, Tommy?"

Tommy told him and Eddy wrote it down.

"Now," he said, "you'll see a real dog."

"Here comes Valery," said Bud, getting up.

Jim saw her running across the inclosure. She had on a flannel shirt, a pair of linen riding-pants, and brown leather boots. She vaulted the fence and, putting her arms around the big Australian pup, kissed him; then patted the man leading him on the shoulder.

"Ain't that silly?" said Eddy, turning his back.

Bud winked at Jim. Everybody but Jim knew that Eddy had made a strong play for Valery and had merely been laughed at. Eddy was no beauty with his gold teeth, but he always had plenty of money and was used to having his way.

Valery came in the judges' stand, lit a cigarette, and sat down, panting. She was out of breath from her run.

Down the track a groom was leading out Willy Judas, the Florida champion; he was a big white-and-brindle dog, seventy-five pounds, with a shambling gait and the suggestion of latent power in his sloping back and his stout shoulders. He hadn't run at the Crescent City track yet and everybody was curious about him.

"There's a dog," said Eddy.

"Round Robin can beat him," said Valery. "I'm willing to bet he can."

Eddy merely snorted. Valery turned to Jim.

"Big boy, you're looking after Mr. Bright's interests. He wants everybody to get a square deal, don't he? Well, talk to that so-and-so there. I haven't got a chance as long as he runs things."

Eddy's face was red.

"You've got as much chance as anybody else. No more and no less."

"Nice boy, what? Eddy, you ought to be a real judge, instead of a race-track judge; you ought to be in the Supreme Court. You're funny enough. Don't you think he's funny, Bud?"

"Let him alone, Valery."

Eddy shifted, then went out to signal to the rabbit man in the tower. Valery caught Jim's eye and winked. She was sure looking good; she looked better dressed in a flannel shirt and riding-pants; if she didn't wear such loud dresses, and ear-rings and bangles like a snake-charmer she'd be a mighty swell woman. Thirty-five; she must be thirty-five, maybe older, and she could pass for twenty-five. It was funny when you considered the life she led.

"Jim," she called, "you're looking old and settled. Marriage don't agree with you."

"Never felt better."

"Don't lie to me. You're sinking fast. Don't you think he's got a married look, Bud?"

"Why don't you lay off of people, Valery? People don't like to be razzed all the time."

Valery flared up; her eyes flashed.

"Blah! Don't try to tell me what to do. I don't like it."

"There he goes," said Eddy. "God! Look at him break. Looks like he come out through the glass."

They all stood up to watch Willy Judas take the turn. He was flying after the rabbit, which hit the turn at a terrific rate of speed. Willy leaned at an impossible angle, but hugged the rail; he gathered speed in the stretch and whizzed past the judges' stand, throwing dirt with his big feet.

"Nineteen seconds flat," yelled Tommy.

"What do you think of that?" Eddy demanded. "And that big pooch don't begin to run in the three-sixteenths distance. He never hit his stride till he made that turn."

"I still think my dog can beat him," said Valery. "Going to let him in, Eddy?"

Eddy coughed, looked uncomfortable, then rubbed his hand over his face.

"Well, I ain't going to be tough about it. I'll talk to Fallon. If he says it's all right, why, I'll let him in."

"You know," said Valery, "you're all right, Eddy. You're a good guy and I could go for you if it wasn't for those gold teeth."

"Valery!" said Bud, wanting to laugh.

"She's the insultingest woman I ever saw," said Eddy, with dignity. What was wrong with his gold teeth? Other women liked them.

When the schooling was over Bud Diegel went up to the main office to see his brother, and Valery walked out to the car with Jim.

"How do you like my new buggy, Val?"

"Fine." Jerking her thumb at the Cadillac 16 she asked, "How do you like mine?"

"Going to marry Diegel?"

"Maybe. Listen, I haven't got a dime. If my dogs don't win some races pretty soon I'll have to feed them grass. I'm that low."

"What about Diegel?"

"I don't tell him nothing. I ride around in that Cad sometimes so hungry I could eat tripe. Is that a laugh?"

"How much do you want, Val?"

"I wouldn't take your money. Did you really think I was panhandling? I was just making conversation. Is your wife nice?"

Jim's face lit up and he began to smile. Valery held up a hand.

"Don't say it. I can see it in your eyes. It's too bad. I'm bored to death in this dump. We used to have fun going places, old boy."

"And how! But I'm through with the bright lights."

"Love in a cottage. Well, there's worse things. Good-by. Here comes my pash. Look at him hurrying, afraid he'll miss something. Isn't he a damned fool?"

Chapter III

A RECORD CROWD JAMMED THE GRANDSTAND AND OVER-
flowed into the betting-sheds and the inclosure; it was
the usual Saturday-night crowd increased by those who
had come to see the Florida champion, Willy Judas, in
the match-race. Eddy Clemens had decided to make a
four-dog race of it; that way the betting would be
heavier and more evenly distributed. He had added
Jim King, a good distance dog, to the three entries already announced—Willy Judas, Round Robin, and
Dark Hazard. With Jim King in the 1 box a lot of the
sharpshooters would bet on him, figuring that there
might be a jam at the first turn and that he might get
clear. Once in front, Jim King was hard to catch, as
he was a veteran track-dog and kept close to the rail;
any dog that passed him would have to go round him.

The betting was heavy on the ninth race. Timber
Wolf broke like a bullet out of the 8 box, cut across in
front of the field, took the rail and held it, winning
easily. The crowd had made him the favorite, and he
had closed at even money; hats were thrown into the
air, men hugged one another, then there was a break
for the cashiers' windows where the tickets were redeemed.

Jim hadn't bet on the race. He sat in Fallon's box,
leaning on the rail and staring down into the shouting,

laughing mob in the inclosure. Behind him Bud Diegel and Valery were pounding each other; they had won a good bet. Fallon sat next to Jim, with his hat tilted over his eyes, smoking a cigar imperturbably.

Finally he observed:

"Some crowd."

"Never seen a bigger one."

"Did Billy Diegel tell you we had a visit from the sheriff's office right after the third race?"

"No. Did you?"

"Yeah. It's the big crowds and the publicity we're getting. Some of us may have to stand trial. Test case."

"That's tough. Why don't they let you alone?"

"Oh, some of the long-hairs want to get their names in the paper, and, besides, the merchants don't want all this money coming our way. That's the way it always is. They may beat us, too. It's tough with a play like this."

"I'll say it's tough." Jim didn't care very much as far as he was concerned, but he knew that this would worry Marg. He sat staring out into the crowd, thinking what he would do if they did close the track. Maybe Bright would give him another job.

Fallon said:

"Not betting tonight, are you?"

"I haven't been. I can't bet much on my salary. I may get a few tickets on the match-race."

"Willy Judas ought to walk in. I told Eddy not to put him on the outside, because if he breaks fast and cuts over, it's all off. Dark Hazard don't like the distance; he's a sprint dog. And neither one of the others is in the same class."

Valery leaned forward and tapped Fallon on the arm.

"That remark will cost you just ten dollars."

"How so?" Fallon demanded, grinning.

"Ten even Round Robin finishes ahead of Willy Judas."

Bud laughed.

"Val's just won a bet and she's feeling cocky."

"That's highway robbery," said Fallon. "I'll give you two-to-one Willy Judas beats your dog."

"Done. Twenty-to-ten."

Valery pulled Jim's hair.

"Why so silent, boy? You haven't said a word all evening."

"What should I say?"

Valery snorted and turned to shake hands with a man who had just come into the box; the man had on corduroy pants and a brown suède windbreaker; his face was tanned and he looked strong and rugged.

"Hello, Lou," said Fallon. "I want you to meet a guy who thinks you've got the best dog in the world. Turner, this is the man who owns Dark Hazard, Lou Gorman. Turner, here, works for Bright."

Gorman shook hands with Jim, accepted a cigar, and sat down. Valery and Bud Diegel went out to cash their tickets. Jim sat looking at Gorman. It must be wonderful to own a dog like Dark Hazard. With a smile, he recalled how proud he used to feel when he was introduced as the "guy who raced Gold Leaf." There was nothing like it in the world.

"Think I'll have to get a few tickets on your dog in the next race, Mr. Gorman."

Gorman laughed.

"You've got more confidence in him than I have. He don't like the distance. Futurity is his speed. He may get out in front, but Willy Judas finishes like an express train and he can run all night. He's got the world's record for three-eighths and seven-sixteenths. If it was a futurity, I'd have a fistful of tickets on Pat. . . ."

Jim interrupted with:

"Who's *Pat*?"

"Who's what? Oh, Pat's Dark Hazard's kennel name." Fallon laughed.

"What are you trying to do, Lou, keep the odds up? Don't worry about Turner. He'll go light."

Gorman shrugged and, reaching into his pocket, took out a handful of tickets. Half of them were win tickets on Willy Judas, half of them were place tickets on Dark Hazard.

"I figure he ought to place. Personally, I think Willy Judas will walk in if he don't have bad luck. They schooled him futurity Thursday morning and he ran it right at the track record and he hadn't hit his stride. Don't pay no attention to me, though; I'm almost always wrong." Gorman laughed and put the tickets back in his pocket.

They sat smoking and watching the odd-board across the track; all four dogs were being played heavily; but Dark Hazard was by far the favorite and Round Robin next. Jim King was three-to-one; Willy Judas dropped from three to two-and-a-half-to-one and stayed there. Gorman laughed.

"The crowd's afraid of that Florida dog. They're

going to bet Pat off the boards. Looks like a chance to win a good bet." He got up and started out of the box. "I'm going to buy me some more Willy Judas tickets."

"The handicapper thinks Willy Judas will win," said Fallon.

Jim said nothing. He sat watching the board. He had come to the park with the intention of betting fifty dollars on Dark Hazard. But if the dog's owner wasn't betting him to win, why, he'd be a sucker to throw good money away just for sentimental reasons. He was sure taken with that black dog; the other evening at supper he had talked about him so much that Marg had finally told him to change the subject, he was driving her crazy. And the night before he had dreamed about him. He sat with a cigar burning up between his fingers, watching the odd-board and thinking how wonderful it would be to own that sleek, jet-black dog. That would be living.

"Two-to-five," said Fallon. "I'd hate to bet my money on him at that price. Look, Willy Judas has gone back to three-to-one. I'll have to bet him myself. All the boys think he's a cinch at five-sixteenths."

Turning, Jim saw that the grooms were leading the dogs out into the paddock. He got up. "Think I'll walk down and take a look at the hounds."

"Going to bet the Florida dog?"

"I think so."

Jim tried to avoid the pushing and jostling of the crowd by walking through the betting-shed instead of the inclosure; but the betting-shed was jammed; he saw long lines in front of each window and there was a staring, excited mob in front of the downstairs odd-board. It took him a long time to elbow his way to the paddock; the grooms were already leading the dogs up onto the glassed-in stage, where they stood in a line each on his proper number, while the crowds round the paddock stared at them. Jim King was wearing the No. 1 blanket, blue; Round Robin the 3, yellow; Dark Hazard the 5, green; and Willy Judas the 7, white.

"I don't like that Dark Hazard dog," said a woman, pointing. "Look how he stands there, like he was asleep. I like that big funny white dog."

"All right," said the man with her, "that's a hunch. Let's bet on him. What's his number? Seven?"

"His name is Willy something."

"Never mind his name. We'll just sock our dough on number seven."

Jim laughed to himself. Suckers; and picking the smart-money dog by accident. It was nearly post-time and the crowd around the paddock had begun to melt away. Jim managed to get up to the guard-rail directly in front of the stage. Willy Judas was as restless as a cat and kept switching his tail and twisting sideways, trying to get away from the groom. Round; Robin barked incessantly; Jim King tugged at his leash and the groom could not keep him in any position long. But Dark Hazard was calm and stood close to the groom, his tail down, his ears lowered, and a look of indifference in his pale amber eyes. From time to time Jim saw the other dogs looking out into the crowd, raising their ears with interest at a sudden movement. But Dark Hazard was remote and dignified, staring far over the heads of the people crowding the guard-rail, or else staring casually through them, never seeing them, like a lion in a zoo. Jim didn't know whether he liked that or not. He had been familiar with dogs all his life, particularly hunting-dogs, pointers and setters, and he was used to their calm, dark, friendly eyes. Dark Hazard hardly seemed like a dog at all; there was something wild and remote from man in his steady stare.

The five-minute bell rang; the grooms slipped on the muzzles and took the dogs down the incline which led to the track. Jim could feel the excitement of the crowd. The loud-speakers were announcing:

"Option windows close in five minutes. Last warning."

People started for the betting-shed, running from all directions.

Jim was still undecided. He saw the racing-secretary, Boyd Lambert, leaving the office behind the paddock inclosure. He waited.

"Well," he said when Lambert came out, "what do you say?"

"Willy Judas. He ought to win from the outside. I saw him beat better ones than this at Miami Beach."

"What about the black dog?"

"He's short. He's a sprinter."

These guys ought to know. Jim ran for the betting-shed and got his money up just in time; forty win tickets on Willy Judas. Then he made a dash for the box just as the warning bell rang. The box was full; Billy Diegel, Fallon, Lou Gorman, and his trainer Tex Willis, Valery and Bud Diegel were all standing up; they were shorter than Jim and he could see over their heads. The lights went out, and a deafening, grandstand-shaking roar burst from the crowd as the dogs broke from the starting-box.

Jim saw Dark Hazard's green blanket in front. Willy Judas was at his heels on the outside; Jim King and Round Robin were having a race of their own, trailing. Valery took one look, then fell into her chair with a groan. Bud said: "Never mind, Val," and patted her shoulder, but she pushed his hand away.

Dark Hazard hit the turn on top and gained two lengths on the Florida dog, who was running a little wide. Jim King was on the rail, three lengths back, Round Robin outside of him. Jim cursed himself for a sucker, and made up his mind that he'd never bet against that black dog again, no matter what anybody said. But, turning, he noticed that Lou Gorman's face was calm and in a moment the trainer, Tex Willis, said:

"Here he comes, Lou. He's catching him, he's catching him. Pat's shot his bolt."

They were swinging into the back turn. Dark Hazard was still on the rail, coming like a rocket, but the big Florida dog, running easily with a long, tireless, loping stride, was slowly overtaking him. Jim held his breath and waited; maybe the smart money was right, after all. The two dogs hit the stretch, running neck and neck, Willy Judas on the outside and going strong. Willis said:

"All right. He's got him. Go cash your tickets, Lou."

The crowd was in a frenzy now, screaming and bellowing. Dark Hazard was hugging the rail persistently; Willy Judas moved ahead of him half a length then seemed to hesitate. There was a long violent roar from the crowd and Willis said:

"Holy smoke! Look at this! Where did he come from?"

Valery jumped up and began to yell. Round Robin, running wide, was overtaking the leaders at each jump; Willy faded, but the black dog hugged the rail, put on a final dizzy spurt, and crossed the finish line, beating the fast-closing Australian dog by a scant neck. The stands shook with the tumult.

"Robin nipped that Florida dog. I'll be damned," said Willis.

Lou Gorman laughed.

"That shows how much I know about dog-racing. My cinch bet runs third and my own dog wins the race. How's that, Turner?"

Jim shrugged.

"That's the second time I bet against your dog, Mr. Gorman."

Valery was capering about the box, shouting:

"I guess that big boy can run, can't he? One more jump and he'd had him."

"Got any place tickets, Val?"

"I'll say I have. And, Fallon, you owe me, don't forget." She put her arms around Jim from the back and whispered in his ear. "Big boy, let's go places. Pat Desmond just opened a big joint on the drive. Anything you want. Hundred-dollar limit and all the champagne you can drink." Bud Diegel took her by the arm and shook her, his face scarlet.

"What do you mean, Val? What do you mean?"

"Oh, I forgot," said Valery.

Gorman turned to leave the box. Tex Willis was still standing with his mouth open, looking at the track.

"Well, I'll be!" he said, fervently, then turned and without another word followed Gorman out of the box.

Jim watched the dogs being led back to the kennels. Dark Hazard was walking along calmly, his head down and his mouth open, panting. Jim King, who had finish a bad fourth, was prancing about, waving his tail and jumping as if he had done something.

A sudden thought, coming from nowhere, struck Jim with surprising force. "Some day I'm going to own that black dog. Some day I'm going to race him. He'll be all mine."

He turned to Fallon.

"What do you suppose Gorman wants for that black dog?"

Fallon looked at him with surprise.

"He wouldn't sell him. The only way anybody could get him would be to claim him, and who's crazy enough to claim a dog for five thousand dollars?"

"That's a lot of dough, ain't it?"

The crowd was leaving the stands now. The floodlights over the track had been switched off. Valery turned to Jim.

"Did you hear what I said about Pat Desmond?"

"I heard you. I ain't interested, Val. Can't afford to gamble. I lost a hundred tonight on Willy Judas I never should have lost."

After checking up, Jim walked slowly out to his car. There was a thick fog coming up the boulevard from the ocean and the air was damp and heavy. He had a hard time starting his car; it missed and backfired. He sat cursing it, suddenly overcome by an irritation which had been growing on him all evening. Here he was a cheap piker; a hundred-a-week guy, afraid to bet; the bottom falling out of his stomach just because he had lost a hundred dollars. Hell!

But when he got home, Marg had an oyster-stew waiting for him and he sat down, smacking his lips, his irritation gone.

"I thought you'd like it on a cool night like this. See, I built a fire in the fireplace. Isn't it cozy?"

"Sure is. Say, that's good stew."

"Eastern oysters are kind of hard to get out here. You have to buy 'em by the dozen. Isn't that a scream? Imagine oysters by the dozen."

Jim laughed and finished the stew, then he sank back, lit a cigarette, and sighed with contentment.

"Well," said Marg, with a laugh, "did the wonder-dog win?"

"He sure did, and I . . ." Jim caught himself up. He had almost spilled the beans.

"You what?"

"I didn't think he would," said Jim, saying the first thing that came into his head.

"You didn't think he would! Why, you told me he couldn't be beat!"

"I know. But I got to talking to some of the wise guys and . . . Say, his owner even didn't think he'd win."

Marg looked at him for a long time, then she said:

"Jim, are you betting?"

"Me? No. Didn't I tell you I wasn't?"

"Well, I just wondered. Why don't you let me keep that money for you? We may need it."

"I'll take care of it."

That night, as soon as Marg was asleep, he got up

and counted his money. Why, good Lord! Where had it all gone? He started to figure, but got mixed up, shrugged, and went back to bed. It would be just too bad if the reformers managed to close the track!

This worried him and he turned over on his back and lay staring at a patch of light on the ceiling, and the longer he thought the more irritated he grew. But of a sudden he remembered Dark Hazard. That beautiful, miraculous black dog. Five thousand dollars was a lot of money, but after all he'd won more than that in Chicago in a few hours. What had Val been saying about Pat Desmond? A new place on the drive; hundred-dollar limit. Well, Pat was on the square, all right; no doubt about that. Maybe . . . but no. He turned. Marg was sleeping with her face toward him and he could hear her breathing. A wave of tenderness swept over him. Marg was so small and helpless, lying there asleep. She had her own worries, Ma and the rest! It would be awful to let her down.

He heard the clock strike three, then he began to drift into sleep. He saw a huge crowd; hats were flying into the air, and people were dancing around, hugging each other. "Dark Hazard wins! Dark Hazard wins!" He walked through the crowd, smiling proudly, and a man turned to point: "There goes the guy who owns Dark Hazard."

All night long the black dog in the green blanket ran through his dreams, and he woke up the next morning thinking about him, and all through the day the miraculous black dog was in his thoughts.

Chapter IV

WHEN JIM WOKE UP THE SUN WAS STREAMING INTO THE bedroom window; he rolled over on his back and lay with his hands under his head, staring out at the tall palm across the street which stood rigid in the dazzling light of midmorning. Pretty swell to wake up to a morning like this. Back home the folks were tramping through the slush and blowing their noses. Imagine; yesterday afternoon the thermometer read seventy-nine at three o'clock, and the sun was really hot, too hot, if anything. First of February, and weather like this. Of course the native Californians talked about the weather too much, bragged about it, in fact, till you could hardly stand it. All the same, he'd hate to go back to Chicago. He lay whistling, looking out into the sunlit street, and thinking with satisfaction of the nice spot he and Marg were in. No more sleet down your neck; no more wet feet and zero weather. Suddenly he smelled coffee boiling, and with an exclamation he jumped out of bed and began to dress.

Marg was already seated when he came out into the little corner of the kitchen, with benches and a table between, which they called "the breakfast room."

"Morning, Marg. That coffee sure smells good." He made this observation every morning and Marg usually laughed at him about it. Today she neither laughed nor replied, and Jim could see that there was something wrong. He sat down and began to eat. Finally he raised his eyes:

" 'Smatter, Marg?"

Without replying she showed him the morning paper. A headline read: DOG-MEN INDICTED: CONSPIRACY CHARGED. Jim glanced at it indifferently.

"Yeah. Billy Diegel told me he thought they could beat the indictment. I see they didn't. Well, maybe they can beat the case. They've got two court rulings on the option system already."

"Are you mixed up in this, Jim?"

"Me? No. I'm not an employee of the park. Don't get all excited, Marg. Everything's going to be all right, anyway. The reformers forced the sheriff to do something, that's all. The sheriff don't like it any better than we do. You know, Marg, it's funny about them reformers. I never did understand them. We're not hurting anybody. Why don't they just stay home and tend to their own business? They don't have to come out to the track if they don't want to."

"They think gambling's wrong, that's all. All my people do."

"All right, if they think it's wrong. All they've got to do is stay home."

"Don't talk that way, Jim. You know that some people feel that they ought to look after the people that can't look after themselves."

"Like prohibition. That's a laugh. Marg, tell you what I think. I think people ought to look after themselves."

"Some people can't. If they can find a place to gamble, they'll gamble. But I don't care about that. It's just being mixed up in a thing like this. I wish you could get into something that's . . . well, more re-spectable."

Jim did not know that there was a long line of May-hews speaking through Marg. She did not know it her-self. But she did know that if Ma found out about this indictment and all, she'd worry herself sick. Marg sat thinking, turning over and over in her mind the very thoughts, brought up-to-date merely, that her own mother and her grandmother and her great-grand-mother had turned over in theirs. She came from a long line of native Americans of the Scotch-Irish, Protestant, Puritan variety. Her female ancestors had been horri-fied and made combative by the male wildness of the frontier; they had wanted to smooth out this rough-ness. Why must men fight and drink and gamble? It wasn't at all necessary. No reason why they should not be models of industry, sobriety, and tractability. These women fought under cover, and as the years passed their influence grew. Civilization softened the men; they went into business, became clerks and middlemen and real-estate salesmen and bankers, and as a result of these insignificant pursuits gradually lost their foot-hold and became tame parlor cats, and with it, moralists and reformers, echoing, without knowing it, the opin-ions of their wives. These native American, Protestant Puritans were the Abolitionists of the Civil War, deadly fanatics, hating the South not only because of its slav-ery, or not even principally because of it, but because in the South life was on a larger scale, viewed more tolerantly, with a breadth of vision and comprehension which to the Abolitionist was *immoral*. The Abolitionists' grandsons were prohibitionists, continuing, without knowing it, their great-grandmothers' struggle against the dangerous living of the frontier. And so when Marg spoke a long line of Midwestern Puritans was speaking through her. Jim was born of different stock and had never come into contact with that timid feminine abstraction known as respectability; he could never quite grasp Marg's distinctions.

"No more night-clerk jobs," said Jim.

"I don't blame you much for that," said Marg. "But, Jim, couldn't you . . . I mean when the track closes . . . couldn't you get a job that would pay just as well without . . ."

"Maybe, maybe." Jim answered, placatingly; he had been worried at first about Marg, but now he was pretty sure that this mood of hers wouldn't last long and everything would be all right. Naturally she was a little upset by that indictment; she didn't know how things were done. "If that's all that's worrying you, Marg, why, forget it. Fallon thinks he can beat the case."

"But it's awful having those men tried like criminals and you being mixed up in it. And, anyway, that's not all. You've been gambling, haven't you?"

Jim hesitated, laid down his fork, and scratched his head.

"Yes."

"You know you promised me you wouldn't." Jim turned his head and began to look uncomfortably out the window. "I wouldn't spy on you and try to pry into your affairs; you know that, don't you, Jim? Well, your clothes looked so baggy that I was going to press them. Why you won't keep yourself looking more neat I don't know. But when I was taking things out of your pockets I found a lot of tickets, nearly a hundred dollars' worth. Jim, do you know how much you've got left out of all that money you won in Chicago? A little over three hundred dollars."

"I know, Marg. Things have broke tough and then I spent more for the car than I told you about. And, good Lord! it's hard to be around that track every night without betting a little."

"That's just what I was saying. If you couldn't gamble at all you'd be all right. But, Jim, couldn't you get one ticket on each race and let it go at that? You don't have to bet a lot to have a good time, do you?"

"No, I don't," said Jim, with decision, "and from now on that's what I'm going to do."

"Well, I hope you stick to it. I got a letter from Ma this morning and they had to let George have some of that money we sent to them. Isn't that awful? Oh, if I was home I'd certainly light into him."

"George is a drinker. You may have a lot of trouble with me, Marg, but I'm not a drinker, anyway."

"And that isn't all George is. He always did fool around with women. And what taste! Well, you saw the one he married."

"Yeah. I spotted her for a flusie right away."

"You see, Jim, you've got to be careful. If I could do anything about it, I would. But what can I do? I think it's mighty nice of you to be as good as you are about sending money to the folks. There's no law to make you. . . ."

"Oh, that's nothing. I like to do that. Say, Marg, while you was getting ready to press my clothes, did you see my pay check?"

"Yes. I did. For two weeks, you mean?"

"Yeah. I'll make you a present of that. I'll indorse it and you get it cashed and you can send as much as you want to Ma. Come on, give me a kiss and smile a little. I want to eat my breakfast."

Marg laughed.

"No matter what happens, pig has to have his breakfast."

"You tell 'em, baby. I stutter."

Marg came over and sat on his lap.

"You know, Jim, there must be something wrong with me. I'm not like my folks at all. Ma would think you were awful. I'd like to see Ma's face if you'd say to her: 'You tell 'em, baby. I stutter.'" They both burst out laughing and Jim began to choke. Marg pounded him on the back so hard that he tried to pull away from her.

"Ouch! I been married so long I can't take it any more."

"Getting to be a sissy, aren't you?"

"Well, that ought to please you. That's what you want me to be."

"You're crazy. I just want you to be grown up, that's all, and not go around lying like a little boy so you can have your own way."

"Do I get to eat my breakfast or don't I?"

Marg warmed up the coffee and poured him out another cup, then she sat down and said, casually:

"And another thing, while I'm on the subject, I think you're going to be a father."

Jim spilled coffee down the front of his shirt and sat with his mouth slightly open, staring at Marg.

"Don't look at me like that. I'm not sure yet. But I think so. You see what you got yourself into by coming to Barrowville? You will have to settle down now."

"Well, I'll be!"

After breakfast Jim sat staring out the window at the mountain range far to the northeast; it was sharply outlined against the vivid blue sky; great puffy white clouds hung low over it. Pretty nice with big mountains in sight! Fallon was telling him that there had been a heavy snowfall at Arrowhead and Big Bear. Winter sports, skiing and all that stuff, and right outside the door he saw birds sitting in a little bush and all around it was green and summery.

"What a day!" he said to Marg. "Say, let's take a ride over to the Kiowa Kennel and see Dark Hazard. Tex Willis told me he'd let me see him any time I wanted to."

"Is that the dog you're going to buy for only five thousand dollars?"

"Quit kidding, Marg. If I was rich I'd buy him; he's wonderful. If, see? But it don't cost nothing to look at him. Come on. It will be a nice ride. It's too nice a day to stay in."

"All right. Let's go. I'll drive."

"O Lord!" said Jim. "This will be a nice ride, all right."

"Well, I'm just learning."

"If you see any trucks, go around them; don't try to go under them."

Tex Willis seemed a little embarrassed by Marg's presence. He flushed when she spoke to him and tried for ten minutes to get rid of a cud of tobacco without her seeing him; finally he excused himself, disappeared into the kennel, spat out the chew, and came back smiling.

When they came up, he had been working on a big red dog, carefully polishing his coat with a cloth dampened with coal-oil, and while he talked to them he shifted the leash from one hand to the other, as though he didn't know what to do with the dog.

"What dog's that?" Jim asked.

"That dog there is Little Prince. By Kashmir King out of an Australian bitch; don't recollect her name. He's only twenty-two months old; hasn't run much. He's a world-beater; going to be a champion sure as shooting. He won his first four starts against aged track dogs, so they kept moving him up and moving him up, till they had him just under the tops. It was at St. Louis. Kind of a sharp turn and three dogs broke together and took an awful spill at the turn. Jinx, here, got hurt; got all scratched up and cut one of his pads bad. But we schooled him yesterday and he beat some pretty fair dogs ten lengths. They'll put him in tough on the strength of that schooling race, but he's a fast breaker and ought to win straight off. In a little while he'll be running against Willy Judas and dogs like that. Lou thinks he's the best dog we got."

"The best dog you got! What about Dark Hazard? And say, I'd like to have my wife see him."

"Lou's got Pat with him. But he'll be here in a minute. Wait till I put this dog in his crate and we'll have a talk. Excuse me, missus."

"That Little Prince dog is beautiful," said Marg. "I like that color. What do they call it?"

"Red fawn. Wait till you see a real dog."

Marg laughed.

"I think you've gone crazy over that Dark Hazard. I'm beginning to get jealous."

Tex Willis came back. Jim offered him a cigar and they lit up. Marg walked over and peeped into the kennel, then came back and said:

"Clean as a pin."

"Yessum," said Tex. "We aim to keep it that way. Keep your kennel clean and you'll have no sick dogs; that's what Lou says. Wasn't you asking me about Pat?"

"Yes," said Jim. "I thought he was your best dog."

"In a manner he is. But he's delicate. Gets hurt easy. Liable to get knocked out any time. He's more trouble to me than the rest of the kennel. Not that he's a uneasy dog. He ain't. He sleeps all time and you can't get him out of that crate, except by coaxing him, 'less it's time to go to the track. Then he's raring. He's a finicky dog. Won't eat sometimes, just because he takes a notion. He worries hell out of Lou. Excuse me, missus. He's the most expensive dog Lou's got, and he's liable to be no good like that. Light boned; delicate. Lou holds his breath when Pat goes round that first turn; lot of dogs get hurt there, like Jinx. No, sir. Lou likes a ruggeder dog, like that distance dog he's got—

Comedian. There's a dog can eat tacks, and if other dogs bump him on the track they fly in all directions. Course he ain't got Pat's speed, but he'll win more money week in and week out. No; Lou's figuring on Little Prince as his top. As I say, Pat's liable to go off like that. Anyway, he's a sprinter, even if he did beat that champion distance dog, Willy Judas. Willy ain't at himself yet; he ain't used to the climate and I understand he's having some trouble with his kidneys. He's tough when he's right."

Marg was a little bit bored by all this and turned away. But Jim listened intently. Tex Willis and Lou Gorman probably knew more about dogs than he'd ever know; all the same, he'd rather own Dark Hazard than all the Kiowa Kennels' other dogs put together, including Little Prince and Comedian.

"It's a wonder Lou don't sell Dark Hazard."

"Know anybody that would pay five thousand dollars for a dog? If you do, he's probably locked up. Lou won't take less."

"Why?"

"Well, right now he's running top. And he's been a pretty expensive investment. Lou paid a record price for him when he saw him school nineteen and one-fifth seconds as a pup, and damned if he didn't go off on Lou after about four races. Sore foot. It wouldn't bother most dogs, but it bothered Pat. Had to lay him up. And then, Lou carries trip insurance on him and he's spent a lot on him other ways. Lou beefs about him all the time, but I think he's Lou's pet at that. Here he comes."

Lou Gorman turned the corner, leading two dogs. When he saw Jim he began to laugh.

"Pat," he said to the dog, "here's your public."

The dog looked up at Lou, raising his ears. Lou laughed and gave the leash of a big brindle dog to Tex Willis, who said: "Here's that Comedian dog. Ain't he a dandy? Look at them shoulders." But Jim was looking at Dark Hazard.

Marg laughed and said to Lou:

"He's forgot I'm here."

"Well, I guess you're Mrs. Turner. Pleased to meet you." Then he turned to Jim. "Like him, don't you?"

"I sure do."

"In that case, I'll tell you what I'll do. If you'll promise to take good care of him and let him sleep with you and the missus at night, I'll sell him to you for four thousand nine hundred and ninety-nine dollars and fifty cents."

"He's got the fifty cents," said Marg.

Lou laughed and handed Jim the leash.

"Want to hold him?"

"You bet."

Jim took the leash gingerly, and stood looking down at Dark Hazard. The dog's coat shone with an almost metallic luster, jet black; high lights glinted on his long, round, smooth neck.

"Had him out sprinting him on the prairie. He's fit as a fiddle right now. Some of the newspaper boys showed up and took some pictures of him. The crowd likes him, comes out to see him. Nice race he ran against Willy Judas."

Jim said nothing. He ran his hand carefully down Dark Hazard's long, smooth, sloping back; all black and shining except for a thin, white scar.

"What's this?" he asked.

"Barb-wire scar. He got loose in a field after a rabbit."

"Look at his ribs," said Marg. "You don't feed him enough."

Lou laughed.

"That's the way a greyhound in condition looks, Mrs. Turner."

While they were talking, Dark Hazard raised his head and, with a graceful movement of his neck, slipped his muzzle into Jim's hand, then gently nibbled at his fingers. Dark Hazard's eyes did not seem so remote now. The dog and the man looked at each other for a long time. Jim was elated.

"Say," he cried, "he was chewing my fingers! Did you see him? Me and this dog are going to be friends. You're all right, black dog; you certainly are all right."

Lou winked at Tex over Marg's shoulder; his wink said, "Isn't that Turner a damn fool!"

On the way home, while Marg drove, Jim sat silent, staring at the dash. Marg was preoccupied with her driving and paid no attention. Finally Jim said:

"Did you see him, Marg? He looked up at me and sort of chewed my fingers."

"I tell you I'm getting jealous."

Chapter V

WHEN JIM WENT THROUGH THE BIG ENTRANCE GATE INTO the racing-plant, he barely acknowledged the friendly "hello" of the gateman. He was feeling low. For the first time in over a year he and Marg had had a real quarrel, and it had all come up over nothing, or so it seemed to him. That afternoon they had driven to Redondo Beach. It was a fine cool day; a good stiff breeze was blowing and there was a little fog. A pale gray light was diffused over the water which looked milky with a strange, wan, silvery cast. They had lunch in a little restaurant which overlooked the ocean; then they walked out onto the huge circular cement pier. At the farthest reach of the circle there was a crowd of men fishing. Jim and Marg stood watching them, and when one of them pulled in a sand-shark Marg squealed and shrank back and they had a good laugh. Gulls were everywhere; clouds of them were flying about over the fishermen; groups of them patrolled the pier, walking stiffly on their thin legs, tame as cats; some sat on the light-poles and fouled the sidewalk with their white droppings. Marg and Jim leaned on the railing beyond the fishermen, to watch some pelicans, great heavy birds with big pouched bills. Marg had never seen a pelican before and was very much interested. Jim had seen them at New Orleans and he got to talking about that strange town, about its funny houses with doorbells in the gates, its cemeteries where people were buried in dresser-drawers, and its niggers who spoke French. Marg said she'd like to see New Orleans and Jim thoughtlessly remarked that they might run down for the racing-season. Marg said nothing; she closed up like a clam and Jim couldn't figure out what was the matter with her.

On the way home she didn't have a word to say, so Jim started to talk about the greyhounds, just to make conversation. He told her about how hard it was to raise pups and how they were coursed, then hand-schooled, then box-schooled and made ready for track running. She listened merely. But his subject ran away with him and he began to talk about Dark Hazard and how he had won his last race from a field of champions and near champions by four lengths, how he was jostled at the break, jammed at the turn, but broke loose on the back stretch, got the rail and was never headed. Jim said that he was the greatest dog in the world and that he'd give five years of his life to own him.

Then Marg started to talk. Jim was astonished by her anger and sat staring at the road, driving mechanically. He did not know very much about women, but he did know that they were more subject to irrational moods than men; and after listening to Marg for a minute or so he decided that she was suffering from "nerves," merely, and would soon be all right again. What he did not know was that Marg had kept silent while things had been piling up on her, and his casual suggestion that they "run down for the racing-season" as if they were millionaires, and his wild enthusiasm for a dog worth five thousand dollars, had set her off.

On Thursday night there had been a special racing-program on and Jim had persuaded her to go. The atmosphere of horse tracks had always repelled her; she found the dog track much worse. The men Jim introduced to her were uncouth and ill-dressed, talked with their cigars in their mouths, swore, laughed loudly, and "kidded" her. A man named Bud Diegel was the best of the lot, but his grammar was worse than Jim's, if anything, and that woman he had brought with him was simply awful. Valery somebody. And worst of all she had announced that she was "one of your husband's old girl-friends" and she was very familiar with him all evening, called him Buck, a name Marg detested and never referred to, and pulled his hair. Why, the woman looked like she ought to be riding an elephant in a circus parade! Besides, Jim had lost fifty dollars on one race and she would never have known it if this woman hadn't spoken up. She and Jim had bet together on one of the woman's dogs.

Jim had been so embarrassed about the whole thing that she had said nothing, but she had made up her mind that she would go to the dog track no more. She would stay home and read or work on a bedspread she was making or go to a movie.

On top of all this she had got a letter from Ma telling her that George had come home broke and was now working in a poolroom. Ma wrote that, sick as Pa was, he had got himself into his clothes so he could give George a good talking to. Pa said that a man had no authority lying in bed, and after talking to George he had been so worn out that they had had to send for Dr. Moss. George working in a poolroom in Barrowville was too much. It was a terrible disgrace. Ma said that even Sonny, only seven years old, was ashamed of him. Ma said that George was living in a boarding-house on Railroad Avenue and that Pa would not speak to him or even have his name mentioned. George Mayhew living on Railroad Avenue, where all the roughs of Barrowville stayed!

This was bad enough, but it wasn't the worst. She was pretty sure now that she was going to have a baby, and what kind of a life would a baby of hers have? Jim was rapidly settling back into his old habits. He would never be anything but a gambler, a hanger-on at race-tracks, undependable, slack. And thinking about all this, she had suddenly realized that Jim was little better, after all, than her brother George. This thought startled her and she was surprised that it had never occurred to her before. Only Jim's extreme good nature, his apparent lack of selfishness, had blinded her.

Poor Ma and Pa! They had done their level best over a long period of years. They had wanted their children to be somebody, respected members of a respectable society, as they themselves had been. But Edward had died during his first year at the state university; and they had later learned that he was a heavy drinker and had been suspended for misconduct. George wasn't worth his salt; never had been; a weak, selfish little man, who married an awful woman and was deserted by her, even. And she herself was nothing to brag on; she had married Jim when she could have married Pres Barrow, the sort of man her people liked.

She poured out all these stored-up grievances at once and Jim was dumbfounded. She started out by complaining that she had no friends, that, due to their scheme of living, it was impossible to meet anybody she could associate with, as she wouldn't be seen with any of those race-track people.

Finally Jim said:

"Listen, Marg, if you feel that way, why did you marry me?"

And she replied:

"I don't know."

Then she went into the bedroom and shut the door. Jim had never seen her so wrought up before. He felt lost. He waited for a long time, but she didn't reappear. Depression settled on him. He wasn't himself unless he had Marg's approbation. He read the paper, smoked and waited, but there wasn't a sound. When the clock struck eight he got up and went to the bedroom door; it was locked. He called:

"Marg. Good-by. I got to go to the track."

She didn't reply.

So Jim did not smile and nod and make some facetious remark as he was in the habit of doing when the gateman greeted him; he merely inclined his head slightly and passed on into the inclosure, where there was the usual mob milling about, and went up into Fallon's office on the mezzanine. While he was crossing the mezzanine the lights were switched off in the grandstand, people began to yell, and the whole structure trembled; the first race was being run. There was a stranger in Fallon's office and Billy Diegel introduced him as "Jimmy Dakin, racing-secretary from up North."

Dakin was a big young man with rugged features and a cheerful grin. He told Jim that all the arrangements had been made for the opening of the new dog track south of San Francisco and that Bright had a third interest.

"I had a letter from him this morning. He said I was to talk to you; spoke highly of you, too, Turner. Very much pleased with your work. You're to move up North as soon as this meet's over. And take charge for Bright."

Jim turned to Fallon.

"How long you figuring on keeping this track open, Fallon?"

"Till the first of March or better."

"What about the trial?"

"Well, we're charged with conspiracy to violate the gambling laws, a felony. They've got to prove criminal intent. How they going to do that when we got the permission of the Crescent City Council to run?"

Dakin laughed.

"We ain't going to have a bit of trouble in San Fran. People up there go for racing in a big way. Not like the Iowa farmers down here."

"Say, we get the crowds."

"Sure. But racing will always be on the edge down here. Too many blue-noses and long-hairs."

"They're a funny lot," said Fallon. "My people were from Iowa. And my old man thought that a man who took a drink or bet on a horse-race was no better than a murderer. Consequently, I take my liquor straight and run a race-track."

Dakin laughed and said:

"Speaking about liquor, why don't we have a drink to celebrate the new track or something?"

"You don't care what you celebrate, do you? What about you, Turner? You've got a face a yard long. A good stiff one wouldn't hurt you any."

"I don't go for hard liquor much. But . . ."

"Oh, hell!" said Fallon. "Have one, have one."

Fallon took a big silver flask and four silver jiggers out of his desk drawer and they all had a drink.

"Ah," said Dakin, "that hits the spot. That's good stuff. Where do you get stuff like that in this God-for-saken spot?"

"What do you mean God-forsaken?" Billy Diegel interposed. "Ain't the movies here?"

Fallon laughed.

"What a crust, asking me where I get good stuff! It's right off the boat. They scraped it off. You haven't met many of these Frisco boys, have you, Turner? They think Southern Cal.'s the jumping-off place."

Jim smiled feebly and took another drink, which Fallon had poured for him. Dakin grinned.

"Well, ain't it? Aimee McPherson and the movies and the place lousy with hay-necks from the corn-belt. Boy, I'd hate to live here."

"We're doing all right. Let's have another drink."

They had two more and Jim felt somewhat better. He started to take an interest in what was being said and he roared with laughter at some of the stories Dakin told. Gradually he began to resent Marg's attitude. Why should she talk to him like that after all the money he had given her for her folks? Not many men would hand it out like that. When a man got married he didn't marry a whole family. Most guys would blow up, that's all.

After the second race Jud Stein came in with a sardonic smile on his long, thin face.

"What do you think? A new pup won the second race and paid five hundred and four dollars to win and sixty-four dollars and twenty cents to place. Is that something?"

"Good for the park," said Fallon. "We'll have a record crowd Saturday night on the strength of that. Let's have another drink. I've only got enough left for a round. No use saving it."

"Here's looking at you," said Jim.

Just before post time for the eighth race Jim left the office and went down to Fallon's box. He had been looking at figures till his head swam. Bright thought that the expenses at the park were much too high. Jim had told Fallon about it and Fallon had turned the matter over to Jud Stein, who had gone over all the accounts with Jim, trying to find out where they could cut down. This was a part of his job that Jim hated; he had nearly gone to sleep twice and Stein had laughed at him. That liquor certainly had a powerful wallop. Coming out into the fresh night air after a couple of hours in an ill-ventilated, smoke-filled room, Jim had to restrain a strong impulse to laugh and kick up his heels.

He sat down and counted his money. He had only seventy-five dollars in cash, but he had a pay check for two hundred in his pocket, and he felt pretty secure. Boy, but he had certainly got rid of that Chicago winning fast; he had no idea where it had gone. While he sat thinking about how money slipped through his fingers, somebody touched him on the shoulder. He turned. Tex Willis put his lips close to Jim's ear and whispered:

"The boss thinks Little Prince has got a good chance in this race. Course it's his first race at this meet and he may need it, but he's fine as frog's hair and his schooling's been good. He's only got one dog to beat, Timber Wolf, if it's a true race. Jim King can't run from the bottom."

"Thanks, Tex."

"It's O.K., Lou told me to tell you. Lou's took a liking to you. Don't let it go no further. He's five-to-one now and we may win a good bet."

Jim sat swearing to himself, wishing he had more money to bet. He had half a notion to cash his pay check; Marg didn't know yet that he had got it; but finally he decided not to, and counted out fifty dollars. If Little Prince came home at five-to-one, he'd have some money; if he didn't he'd still have twenty-five in cash and his pay check. He went down to the betting-shed and bought twenty-five preferred tickets on Little Prince. When he got back to the box, Fallon was there with Lou Gorman.

"Did Tex get you?" asked Lou.

"Yeah. Thanks."

"He's gone to three-to-one. Hell!" said Lou. "I didn't think they'd bet him like that."

"One of the tip-sheets picked him," said Fallon.

The dogs had been put in the starting-box and the grooms were trotting down the track. Jim paid no attention to them now; he was used to them; the ballyhoo

no longer offended him. Lou Gorman took out a cigar
and began to chew on it.

"If he only breaks," he said, fervently. Then he
leaned forward. "Look! He's got his head right against
the glass! He's going to do it, by God! He'll make a
shirt-tail shoot for that first turn and if he gets the
rail, it's all over."

The light went out, the rabbit came whizzing round,
and the dogs broke from their boxes as if fired from
the mouth of a cannon. Timber Wolf was two lengths
ahead when they passed the judges' stand and he beat
the pursuing Little Prince to the first turn by a length
and a half. Jim King was close up on the outside; the
rest of the dogs got into one of those deadly first-turn
tangles and were left behind. Timber Wolf held his
lead and at the eighth was going strong; Jim King
ran wide and lost ground; Little Prince, a rail-runner,
swung in behind Timber Wolf and hung at his heels.

"Damn!" said Lou. "If the Wolf don't move out a
little we're sunk. Jinx loves the rail."

The crowd was yelling wildly and urging Timber
Wolf on; he was the favorite and had closed at even
money. But he swung wide coming into the stretch
and Little Prince slipped in on the rail.

"He's in," said Lou, calmly, sinking back.

But Timber Wolf was game and Little Prince could
not gain an inch. They ran neck and neck down the
straightaway, and as they neared the wire Jim jumped
up in his excitement and tried to pull Little Prince
home with violent movements of his arms and shoulders.
Little Prince won by a nose. Jim sank back and, taking

off his hat, mopped his forehead. Somebody came up behind him and put a hand on his shoulder.

"Well, you pulled him home with your body-English,
damn you." It was Valery.

Lou sighed, threw away his cigar, and got up.

"Well," he said, "we won that one by a whisker. I
didn't know the Wolf had that much stuff. Looks like
the old Kiowa Kennel is going to win both feature
races."

"Why don't anybody ever tell me anything?" Valery
demanded.

"You didn't ask me," said Lou, pinching her nose.
She stamped on his foot and laughed loudly when he
winced. Lou Gorman thought he was such a he-man!
Jim turned.

"Think Pat's going to win?"

"I do," said Lou. "He's breaking better than he ever
did and he loves the futurity distance. Willy Judas
will be tough, and so will that mutt dog from Australia.
But I think Pat will win. If he does, that will be four
wins for us tonight, two of them features."

"Oh my! aren't we big-shots," said Valery. "And don't
call my dog a mutt or I'll break out and tell you what
I think of you."

"I was kidding, Val. I like that dog of yours. If I had
him I could make a champion out of him. Wait a minute! Don't fly off the handle. He's too heavy. Take
two pounds off of him and he'll beat the best, even
Pat."

"He's so thin now you can almost read a paper
through him. On your way, big-shot."

"Listen," said Lou. "if you want to make a little

money I'll tell you how to bet; Pat to win and the Australian mutt to place. It's a tip."

"Say, Lou," called Jim, "if I come down to the paddock after the race will you let me see Pat?"

"Why not? Val, this friend of yours has fell in love with my dog. I got a special policeman to watch him, afraid Jim, here, will steal him."

"Lou," said Jim, half serious, "would you sell him to me for five thousand dollars?"

"Would he!" Valery exclaimed. "He'd be crazy if he wouldn't. I'd sell you my whole kennel for five grand, and throw myself in to boot."

"What good are you? You can't run," said Lou.

"I can go too fast for any gent from Tulsa, Oklahoma."

"Listen, Lou," Jim insisted, "would you?"

Lou looked at Jim for a moment, running his eyes over Jim's face as if to figure out what was in his mind.

"Well," he said at last, "of course I wouldn't want to lose him. He's a champion. No, I don't think I'd sell him. But you could claim him."

When Lou had gone Valery sat down and lit a cigarette. Fallon propped up his feet and sat fanning himself; he had had a drink or two too many and was burning up. The loud-speaker announced:

"The Kiowa Kennel, a member of the Pacific Coast Greyhound Association, will repurchase the preferred options on their greyhound, Little Prince, for twelve dollars and twenty cents. . . ."

Jim turned to Valery.

"I got twenty-five tickets on that baby, Val. That's

. . . let's see, a little over three hundred dollars. Not so dusty."

"You're lucky. I'm going to bet with you the last two races."

After a while Fallon went back to his office. Jim and Valery sat watching the odd-board. Dark Hazard was being played heavily, but so were Willy Judas and Round Robin; the other dogs were long prices, except Tulsa Flier, a flashy blue hound, which had been moved up into the top class, due to a string of wins in the cheaper races. The racing-secretary had given him the 1 box and had placed Donegal, a slow starter, next to him in the 2 box. Tulsa Flier had everything in his favor, and if there was a jam of any kind at the first turn, he should hit the back stretch on top. He had the best outside chance in the race, and there were smart ones betting on him.

Valery watched the changing odds for a while, then she said:

"How's your wife, Buck?"

Jim turned to look at her.

"All right. Why?"

"I just wondered. Sort of stuck up, isn't she?"

"No. I wouldn't say that. She just don't like race-tracks, that's all."

"She certainly gave me the cold shoulder. How come you married her, Buck?"

"I liked her."

"Do you still like her?"

"I'll say I do."

"It's funny she'd marry a guy like you."

"Ain't it? I never could figure it out. Her folks thought I was poison."

"How come you never asked me to marry you, Buck? Or am I getting into politics now?"

Jim laughed.

"Don't be foolish. You always had 'em standing in line."

"I never kept you waiting much, did I?"

"No, not much."

"You were always such a big tramp. You never did give a damn whether school kept or not, did you?"

"I guess not."

"Well, you do now."

"You're right."

Valery sighed, then sat swinging her foot.

"Yep. You're getting as damn dull as everybody else. You used to be a whiz, boy."

"They slowed me down. Listen, the wife's going to have a kid. Can you feature old Buck walking the floor all night with a kid?"

"Yes, I can."

"Look! Round Robin's four to one. He ain't getting the play I thought he would. You know what Lou said. Pat to win and your dog to place. That's the way I'm going to bet."

"Tulsa Flier's a good place bet out of the one box."

"You better string along with me, Val. I think I'm lucky tonight."

Valery opened her purse and took out fifty dollars.

"Here. This is the works. Bet it any way you please for me. I'm getting so I couldn't pick the winner of the chariot-race in 'Ben-Hur.'"

"If you lose, don't squawk."

"What do you mean, dope? You must be thinking about somebody else. Did you ever hear me squawk?"

"No," said Jim, patting her on the shoulder, "I never did."

She pushed his hand away.

"Don't pat me that way. I'm not your sister or your maiden aunt. Boy, how you've changed!"

Jim went down into the betting-shed to cash his tickets, then he bet a hundred and twenty-five dollars to win on Dark Hazard and seventy-five dollars to place on Round Robin. On his way up the stairs to the mezzanine he bumped into a little man with a thin red face and a wry neck; the little man was not exactly a hunchback, but his head was set low and at a peculiar angle and his puny body gave an effect of deformity. He had on a dirty gray flannel shirt and his clothes were creased and stained as if he had slept in them for weeks.

"Buck!" the little man said in a high, piercing voice, seizing Jim's sleeve.

Jim looked at him for a moment, then his face lit up.

"Hunch Dolan!"

"Howdy, Buck! One of the boys told me you was working here. You're looking prosperous, Buck. How they coming?"

"So-so."

Jim was shocked at Dolan's appearance and couldn't take his eyes off him. The last time he had seen him Hunch was wearing a fine tailored suit, a diamond horse-shoe pin that was the real McCoy, and he was throwing money around with both hands. Hunch had always been a fool for luck. His horses used to stumble in some way, and if there were any breaks at all, Hunch got them. He had always had money to burn. Five years ago he had paid eighty-five hundred dollars for Tate Jamieson's filly Nelly Boyle, and everybody had laughed at him, but he had won her out in no time. Plain lucky.

"They been coming tough for me. For a fact, I haven't got but thirty cents. Can you feature that? Me, with only thirty cents. It all hit me at once, Buck. I got sick, had to go down to Arizona for my health, and everything sort of went to hell. I ain't had any luck since. Listen, Buck, can you stake me to fifty? I got a hot one in the next race. I hate to pass him up."

"I'll let you have twenty-five, Hunch. But save out some coffee money. What's hot?"

Jim held out the bills and Hunch took them quickly and stuffed them into his pocket.

"Tulsa Flier. I know the guy that owns him. It's a clean-up."

"Don't you believe it, Hunch. Stick your dough on Dark Hazard."

"I know what I'm doing, I know what I'm doing," Hunch insisted. "I tell you I know the guy that owns him. It's a clean-up. Buck, you never had a hotter one in your life. Tulsa Flier's in."

"Well, don't forget; save out some coffee money."

Jim knew there was no use trying to talk Hunch out of it; he himself had had hot ones like that. He knew the symptoms.

"Coffee money! If that baby stays at five to one, I'll

have some real money. He's in, Buck, I tell you, he's in."

Jim laughed. Hunch nodded several times, then hurried down the stairs into the betting-shed. Jim saw him at one of the windows, buying tickets. After the race he'd have the thirty cents he started with and would be around hunting another hot one, then, finding it, he'd be panhandling for a stake. There was no end to it.

When Jim got back to the box it was empty. He sat down, counted out Valery's tickets, and waited. Pretty soon she came back, switching herself among the crowded boxes, like a nervous filly at her first race. Val had a way of making every man within a radius of fifty feet look at her. And she wasn't bad, not half bad, Jim told himself; if only she didn't paint so and wear all them rings and bangles. She sat down, then took out her vanity-case and began to rearrange her hat.

"Just had a long-distance from Bud."

"I wondered where he was."

"He's up at Sacramento. His wife has got him in some kind of jam."

"His what?"

"Oh, he's divorced. Something about alimony payments. The wife's raring, going to sue him, I think."

Jim gave her the tickets. She glanced at them and said:

"I hope you're right."

"I feel lucky. Say, I saw Hunch Dolan. Boy, you wouldn't know him."

"That's the results of a misspent life. He gambles, you know, and drinks. How can people do such things?

I saw him after the third race. He tried to tout me and hit me for a loan, but I said: 'No ishfay today, umpchay.' I never did like that guy. When he's got dough, he makes a noise like a brass band and don't know us common folks. When he's broke, he whines. He used to high-hat me when he was racing First Out and Nelly Boyle. Buck, I feel like the devil tonight, like the bottom's dropped out of everything. Let's go some place after the races."

"What a chance!"

"Don't tell me you're virtuous. You just don't like me any more."

"I like you all right, Val."

The grooms were leading the dogs out. Valery leaned forward and put her hand on Jim's knee and tried to talk to him, but he was looking at Dark Hazard and paid no attention to her. The black dog was walking along, calm as usual, with his tail held close to his body; he walked so daintily that his feet seemed scarcely to touch the ground. He was wearing the pink six-blanket. Willy Judas was putting on an exhibition of violence, jumping as high as the groom's shoulder and shaking himself; then straining on his leash like a wire-haired fox-terrier. The groom had his hands full.

There were exclamations from the crowd. "Look at that white dog. He's sure raring to go. That guy can hardly hold him." Many rushed out to get up a last-minute bet. But they were just throwing their money away.

Tulsa Flier broke like a shot and beat Dark Hazard to the turn, with Willy Judas and Round Robin pursuing. But Dark Hazard took the rail from the flier

effortlessly in the middle of the back stretch and drew
away, running with such terrific speed that he nearly
caught the mechanical rabbit going into the far turn.
After that it was merely a question of which dog would
finish second. Dark Hazard was five lengths to the
good as he swung into the home stretch; Tulsa Flier,
Round Robin and Willy Judas were running neck and
neck.

Jim sat watching the black dog come in. But Valery
jumped up and began to yell:

"Come on, Bobby! Come on, Bobby! It's your mamma
calling, Bobby! Come on home, Bobby!"

Bobby came home, beating Willy Judas for second
by a nose. Tulsa Flier had tired badly during the final
drive and was outgamed for fourth place by Shanty
Irish.

Jim stood up to watch the groom lead Dark Hazard
back. There were tears in his eyes. What a dog! What
a dog! But Valery was wildly excited and, throwing her
arms around Jim, began to kiss him. "You picked 'em
one-two, honey. You picked 'em one-two." He got very
red in the face and pushed her roughly away. She stared
at him in surprise.

"What's the matter, Buck?"

"Nothing. Only get the hell away from me."

She sulked. She did not know that she had aroused
Jim by flinging her arms around his neck and kissing
him. Finally she shrugged and said:

"I think I'll go some place else."

"Go ahead."

"What's wrong with you, Buck? I was only fooling."

"All right. I'm going to run down and see Pat, anyway. You got your tickets, ain't you?"

"Yes. Want me to cash yours?"

"No, thanks."

He got up and left the box without looking at her.
He was a little worried and pushed his way heedlessly
through the crowd. He had enough trouble without
getting in a jam with Valery. But she did make him
want to go places and do things, throwing herself up
against him and kissing him that way. He knew that
Marg would never forgive him if he got mixed up
with another woman; she was that way. She jumped
on him for gambling and being irresponsible, but that
was because she was worried about the future; if he
had plenty of money she wouldn't care at all and everything would be lovely. But no foolishness with women!
That was out. And he didn't blame her. He knew how
he'd feel if Marg would happen to get mixed up with
some man. Why, the bottom would just drop out of
things, that's all.

The loud-speaker was announcing something. He
paused.

"Ladies and gentlemen, I know that you'll all be interested to hear that Lou Gorman's great dog, Dark
Hazard, has just equaled the world's record for the
futurity distance, covering it in the remarkable time of
twenty-eight seconds flat and defeating a field of the
fastest greyhounds in the United States. . . ."

There were cheers and applause and Jim smiled to
himself. Pat was the greatest dog in the world, and Lou
Gorman was a lucky stiff. Lord! how he'd like to own
that sleek black dog! That would be living.

The grooms were leading the dogs down the incline into the paddock when Jim came up. Willy Judas was still jumping about and acting wild, but Dark Hazard was as calm as ever. The dogs were led to an inclosure behind the stage and turned over to their handlers, who were waiting with leashes and blankets. Jim went in the paddock gate, nodded to the paddock judge, then went up the walk which led to the inclosure.

The inclosure was in semi-darkness and at first Jim could distinguish only vague shapes of men and dogs; then his eyes became more accustomed to the light, and he saw Willy Judas with his blanket on, being led up and down by his handler. A dog was standing in the heavy shadows cast by the back of the stage; a man was bending down behind the dog, examining one of his legs. Jim walked over quickly.

"Is that you, Pat?"

The dog looked up, and Jim began to scratch his head. Tex Willis got to his feet.

"I'll be dogged if he ain't a little lame in that off hind leg, but I can't see nothing wrong with it. He's a damn delicate dog. I reckon we better lay him up a week."

"What a race he ran!"

"Didn't he? He near caught that rabbit on this turn here. He'd sure busted up that race if he had. Come on, Pat. Get your blanket on."

The dog turned his head to look at Tex, then he stood stockstill while the blanket was being put on and buckled. When Tex was through with him he got up very close to Jim and nuzzled his hand. Jim was deeply pleased.

"That dog sure likes me, Tex. He sure does."

"He's a right affectionate animal. He's lived on the fat of the land all his life; never had no rough usage; so he's as kindly as a bitch. Nice animal, he is. Too nice, I tell Lou. Lou babies him."

"If I had the money, Lou wouldn't have this dog long."

Tex laughed.

"Well, you could have him, for all of me. I wouldn't give five hundred dollars for him as he stands. He'll go off on Lou some day and never come back. I'll be mighty surprised if he's got a year more of racing in him. Anyway, a man can't make no money with a dog like this. Give me five thousand dollars worth of hamburger hounds, any day. Come on, Pat. Let's take a walk."

Jim stood watching Pat being led away. Pat minced along, never straightening out his leash; accommodating his pace to Tex's. At the corner of the stage he lifted his leg like an ordinary dog, and this struck Jim as very strange.

Jim cashed his tickets, then he stood looking up at the odd-board. The tenth and last event was a hurdle race. There was a seven-year-old dog in it, Bonny Cutlet, and he was going begging at fifteen to one. Old Bonny had been a top dog in his day. Jim had seen him schooled for the hurdles, and while he didn't like the jumping much, he was fast as an arrow on the straightaway. Jim laughed to himself and bought four win tickets on him. He might come in.

There was nobody in the box, so Jim spraddled over

three of the chairs, lit a cigar, and settled back with a sigh of comfort. Pretty good world. He had quite a pocketful of money now; he had petted Pat and been nuzzled by him; maybe when he got home Marg would be different.

He smoked and looked at the track and watched the odd-board; then he noticed that somebody was standing in the aisle just outside the box. He turned. It was Val. She smiled coaxingly.

"Can I come in? I'll be good."

"Come on in, Val."

She came in and sat down beside him. She was very subdued and for a long time said nothing. Her presence troubled Jim, and her actions worried him. He knew her pretty well; all this niceness was put on for some reason. Finally she spoke.

"Betting on this race, Buck?"

"Yep. Bonny Cutlet. Fifteen to one. No, he's down. Twelve to one."

"This is your lucky night, boy. You'll make it three in a row sure. Did you bet many tickets?"

"Four."

"I'm stringing with you. I'm going down and get four tickets on him, too. I tell you this is your lucky night. I can feel it in my bones."

She went out to buy the tickets. When she came back the dogs were already in their boxes. The distance was futurity, five hundred yards, and there were three hurdles, low wooden frames topped by broom-straw hazards.

The dogs broke fast and the hurdle champion, Pacemaker, darted ahead and rounded the first turn, one length in front of Flying A, who was coming fast. Bonny Cutlet was a poor third, hugging the rail. Jim laughed.

"My lucky night, eh?"

But Valery cried out. Pacemaker and Flying A had fallen at the first hurdle. Bonny Cutlet took the lead, and although he lost ground on the two remaining hurdles, he made it up on the straightaway, and hung on gamely to outstay a fast-closing red dog which had come from far back. Valery jumped up and yelled. Jim was a little dazed by the outcome of the race, and said nothing; then he noticed that one of the track attendants was running in the direction of the first hurdle. Jim stood up. Flying A was lying flat in the middle of the track; he had broken his neck in the fall. The track attendant carried him to the paddock; his legs were sticking straight out, very stiff, but his head was dangling.

"It's a damn shame," said Jim. "A nice dog like that."

Suddenly he thought about Pat and a sharp pang went through him. Valery paid no attention to the dog; she cried:

"We won! We won! He closed at ten to one, Buck. Four tickets ought to be worth about a hundred dollars."

Bonny Cutlet paid more than they had expected. When the loudspeaker announced that preferred options would be redeemed for thirty-three dollars, Valery shouted, "Hurray!" and even Jim smiled. He forgot the dead dog in his pleasure over having picked a long-shot like Bonny Cutlet. Val was right. It was his lucky night.

People were filing out of the big grandstand. The judges had gone and the flood-lights over the track were switched off. Jim said:

"Well, got to check up."

"I'll wait for you, Buck."

"No, I'm going straight home."

"Straight home? With the streak of luck you're in?"

Jim considered. Marg hadn't even said good-by to him. Why should he break his neck to get home on schedule?

"Let's make Pat Desmond's, Buck. It won't take long to clean up with your luck. Remember the time at Tia Juana?"

"I got to check up."

"I'll wait for you."

Jim looked at her, then turned and went up into the mezzanine. Let her wait. Maybe he'd go and maybe he wouldn't. Anyway, it had nothing to do with Val. She wasn't going to get him in any jam.

Jud Stein was waiting for him, and Jim sat down.

"Got four tickets here on Bonny Cutlet, but I didn't want to hold you up. So I didn't cash 'em."

"I'll cash 'em when we get through."

Suddenly Jim remembered Flying A.

"Too bad about that dog, wasn't it?"

"Oh," said Stein, opening the ledger, "they will get knocked off occasionally."

Pat Desmond's new place was on the outskirts of Hollywood, more than fifteen miles from Crescent City. Jim and Valery went in Jim's car, as Bud Diegel had

driven to Sacramento in the Cadillac. Valery kept talking to Jim about the track, about the bad luck she was
having with her dogs, about her trouble with Diegel.
Jim said nothing. He had had an extremely lucky
evening and he knew that a man ought to ride his luck,
as it ran in streaks, but he felt now that his streak had
left him and he regretted having come with Valery.
Luck was a funny thing; nobody knew very much about
it. Most people didn't believe in it, even. But he did.
He had seen too many strange things happen and he
himself had felt many times that peculiar urge, that
overwhelming confidence, which came over you like
a flash. One minute you were piddling along, winning
a little, losing a little; then suddenly something hit
you; you were a different man; your "luck was in,"
you were "hot," and if the streak lasted you were due
for a clean-up. But the streak was unpredictable. It
might last for twenty minutes or twenty hours. But it
could not last forever, and gradually you cooled off.
At the end of the streak you were just like other men,
uncertain, middling, stringing along with the pack.

Finally he said:

"I should've gone home. My luck's out. I can feel it."

"Don't be that way. Picking a long-shot winner in a
hurdle-race! That's not brains, that's luck. And your
luck's never out till you start losing."

Jim said nothing. Valery pointed out the turns to
him and showed him a short cut over the hills; and
finally they drew up before a long, flat cluster of imitation Spanish ranch-buildings, which were joined by
porches. Lights blazed in front and many cars were

parked round a circular drive. They heard dance music and laughter. Jim parked the car and Valery led him through a long grillroom, where people were eating and a jazz band was playing, and through a stucco corridor, hung with "Spanish" tapestries and oil-paintings of desert scenes, to a big wooden door with a grill. She knocked. A man took a look at them, then swung the door open.

"Good evening, Mrs. Diegel," he said.

Valery nodded and they went in. When they were some distance from the lookout, she said:

"I been here with Bud so much he thinks I'm the missus."

Valery left her coat at a little cloakroom at the foot of the stairs. But Jim took off his cap, rolled it up, and stuck it into his coat pocket. Valery laughed.

"What's the matter, afraid of a raid?"

"No. It's just a habit. I wouldn't have no luck at all if I left my cap back there."

They came out into a big room blazing with light. It was crowded and there were a good many people in evening clothes.

"Some of the swells come here," said Valery. "Pat's getting a good play. He's got a strong in out here. I don't know how he got it, as this county is supposed to be strict."

All the gambling devices were going; all you had to do was to take your choice. There was a crap-table, blackjack, stud poker, draw poker, bridge, chuck-a-luck, and roulette. Jim bought two hundred dollars' worth of chips, then stood scatching his head. Valery said she

was going to try the blackjack, but Jim had no use
for that game. He walked over to one of the roulette
wheels and stood on the edge of the crowd, watching.
Some swells were playing. He caught scraps of conversation, and from time to time he stared at these people,
puzzled. They didn't seem real, the women especially;
sleek as seals, bejeweled, most of them thin and looking none too robust. The wheel stopped; the croupier
began to rake in the money.

"Del," cried one of the women, "you've won again."

Del had been talking. She laughed.

"Oh, did I? How marvelous!"

The croupier spun the wheel. Another woman was
saying:

"And I said to Carter: 'No, thank you. I wouldn't
live in New York for *anything*. It's too provincial. Quite
the most provincial place I was ever in.' But I do love
San Francisco. Carter's buying a house there."

Jim edged up and bet fifty dollars on the red. He was
afraid of bumping these women and held himself rigid.
The red won. He left the hundred on. The red won
again. He left the two hundred on, but the croupier
shaved it half.

"Hundred limit," he said, without looking up.

People drifted away; others came up; but Jim continued to play, keeping his eyes on the wheel. But it
was no use, and he cursed himself for having come.
He kept seesawing, getting no place. Finally he cashed
his checks and, turning away, counted them; he had
won a little over a hundred dollars in half an hour.
This wouldn't do; he was cold, his luck was gone. He

walked across the big room, looking for Valery. He found her sitting on a lounge with a glass in her hand, talking to a big man in evening clothes. The man had slick black hair and a fine whisky face, red as a sunrise, with little purplish veins in his cheeks. He turned.

"Hello, Buck!"

"Hello, Pat! Nice place you've got here."

"Like it? How you doing?"

"Terrible. Up and down. Can't win, can't lose."

Valery drank from her glass, then said:

"I can lose. I'm flat already."

"Shall I charge some dough to Bud's account?" asked Pat, grinning.

"Not on your life. Let me have fifty, Buck?"

Jim gave it to her. Pat laughed.

"Seems like old times. You and Valery. What a pair you used to be! I hope you don't get lucky, Buck, like you used to. My overhead's high here."

"What a chance!" Jim sat down beside Valery. The thing for him to do was to go home. Marg would be worried as it was, though it was still early. When Pat Desmond had gone he turned and said: "Val, let's get going. I can't do a lick of good here."

"Wait till I lose this fifty. It won't take long."

She got up and went back to the blackjack table. Jim sat staring across the big gambling-room for a while, then he began to nod. But he was roused by a woman at a nearby roulette-table shouting: "It wins again. Thirty-three wins again." Of a sudden it all came back to him; Chicago, Johnny Mueller, that wild streak at the fifty-dollar limit place, and the three numbers which had leaped into his mind out of nowhere: 33, 24, 3. He rubbed his hands together and got up.

At a little after dawn Pat stopped the wheel.

"Buck," he said, "you're through, done, and finished."

A few of the swells had remained to watch this man who had such a tremendous streak of luck. They looked at him with a sort of awe. The croupier, pale with fatigue, cashed Jim in. Valery's eyes were bright and she stood leaning on the table, watching Jim count the bills and slip them into his pockets. He looked as bedraggled as if he had fallen into a pond. His collar had wilted, his hair was matted with sweat, and his face was streaked where he had rubbed his hands over it.

"Well," she said, "you're luck was in. I told you your luck was in, didn't I?"

Jim grinned wearily.

"It was a hunch. I just happened to remember one time in Chicago." He turned and looked about for a clock; then he noticed that a man was raising one of the curtains. The window was gray. "Marg!" he said, getting up. "My God! What time is it?"

"It's nearly six o'clock," said the croupier.

Jim pulled his cap out and put it on, then he started for the door.

"So long, Pat. My luck was sure in tonight."

"It sure was," said Pat, trying to smile. "Well, it's a good advertisement for my place, anyway. It shows my wheels are straight."

Valery ran after Jim and caught him at the door.

"Say, what about me?"

"What do you mean what about you? Come on. I got to hurry."

They drove along in silence for a long time. The sun was just coming up over the hills. The atmosphere was heavy. A thick mist was rising from the land and the upper rim of the sun shone through it with a misty, vague, silvery radiance. Jim was still a little dazed and his eyes were heavy, but suddenly it all burst on him at once. *He could buy Dark Hazard now!*

"Hurray!" he cried. "This sure was my lucky night. You hear me, Val? I'm going to buy myself that black dog. Boy, what a break for old Buck. It's the first one in years."

"Don't forget I got you to come."

"You're right. If it hadn't been for you, I . . . Say, Val, how much do you want? I ought to give you a split on this dough."

"Don't be silly. I played on your money all night. Don't feel sorry for me. I tucked away over a thousand dollars, just in case you might need it."

"You keep it."

"I intend to."

The sun was clear of the hills now. The air smelt damp. They saw dew sparkling all over the country-side.

"How much did you win, Buck?"

"A little over twenty thousand dollars."

"Hold me up; I'm falling. No wonder Pat had a face like a cigar-store Indian."

When they had driven through Hollywood, where the first street cars and the milk-wagons were beginning to appear, Val settled down and put her head on Jim's shoulder. Finally she patted his cheek and said:

"This is the most fun I've had in five years."

It did not sound like Val. She was all soft and cooing. Jim drew away slightly.

"Behave."

"Listen, Jim, you know I don't give a damn for Bud Diegel."

"It's all one to me whether you do or not."

"You're a liar."

"Don't call me names. Say, Val, can you feature me owning that black dog? I can hardly wait."

She closed her eyes and pretended to be asleep. She kept getting closer and closer to him until he could feel her breath on his face. He drove with his eyes on the road, trying to avoid Val's cheek, but a feeling of contentment began to creep over him. Val was his kind, no mistake about that. She liked what he liked; they had a good time together; and she was a good sport with no ties, no family, ready to go any place at any time. Val never beefed; she took what came and made the best of it. But she had one great fault—she was too possessive. He remembered Tia Juana. What a nice mess?

It was broad day when he drew up in front of her apartment on the outskirts of Crescent City. The mist had risen and the sunlight was warm in the streets. He saw the tall palms standing rigid in the morning.

"You're home, Val."

She pretended to start up in her sleep; then, with a sudden movement, she pulled Jim's face down and kissed him. She was all warm and soft, and there was that sleepy, sensual look in her eyes he remembered so well.

"Get out, Val. I'm in a hurry."

"Buck, come on in. I want to talk to you. Only for a minute. I swear I won't try to make you stay."

"Get out, Val."

She sat up. The sleepy, sensual look had disappeared. "You mean it?"

"I mean it. Hell! the wife won't know what happened to me."

Valery laughed and got out. She looked at Jim with contempt.

"Well," she said, "they certainly slowed you down, all right."

Jim let himself in quietly. He had sure had a close one with Val; a little more pressure and he would have gone in with her. That would have been a damn silly move. What did she care about him? She wanted to have her own way, that was all. He had played it right. But the contempt in her voice still rankled.

He tiptoed through the living-room and peeped into the kitchen. No one there. Marg was probably asleep. It would be better not to wake her. He could tell her about his good luck after he had had a little rest. He took off his cap, threw it on a chair, and sat down on the lounge. Things began to swim in front of him. He was dead tired and his eyes hurt from staring for hours at the wheel. He lay down and began to drift into sleep. He saw the race-track; he heard the roaring crowd; a black dog in a green blanket was flying down the stretch, far ahead of the field—Dark Hazard. Jim sat up in confusion. Was it all a dream? He shoved his hands into his pockets, then he grinned and sank back. No it wasn't a dream; the money was there and the next time the black dog ran he was going to claim him. No use arguing with Lou Gorman; he'd just claim him for five thousand dollars and that would be all.

The bedroom door opened and Marg came out, fully dressed. Her face was very pale, Jim thought.

"Oh, you finally got home!"

"Listen, Marg, I'm sorry but . . ." He was so tired and his eyes ached so that Marg seemed to sway and recede.

"You picked out a nice time to stay away. Why didn't you say something when you came in?"

"I didn't want to wake you, Marg."

She sat down across the room from him.

"Wake me! I haven't been asleep. I got a special-delivery from Ma about ten o'clock and I wanted to talk to you about it, so I waited and waited until I couldn't get to sleep when I tried." Marg put her hand over her face and began to cry.

Jim got up hastily and started toward her, but she waved him away. Then she took out a handkerchief and wiped her eyes.

"I'm nervous, that's all. I heard all kinds of noises around here tonight."

Jim fell into a chair, very much ashamed of himself.

"Gosh! Marg, I . . ."

"Don't explain. It doesn't matter much. You're just like you always were." She paused and sat looking at the floor for a long time. "Jim, things are going pretty bad back home. Ma says that Pa can't get well. He's all cut up about George and wastes his strength talking about him. What would Ma do if Pa died? I think I ought to be there, Jim."

"But, Marg . . . !"

"Anyway, I'm going to have a baby and I'd rather have it at home. I don't know a soul out here. I feel lost."

"But, Marg, I couldn't leave here. I got my job and in the spring they're going to open a track at San Francisco, and anyway" . . . he hesitated, then he went on . . . "anyway, I'm going to get me that black dog and I got to be where I can race him. Either here or Florida."

Marg stared at him.

"You what?"

Without a word Jim got up and began to take money from his pockets, stack after stack of wrapped greenbacks. Marg held her breath. He put it all in her lap, then he said:

"There it is. Twenty thousand dollars. I guess I can afford that dog now, Marg, and we'll have plenty to run us, and besides I got my job. I had a streak of luck at Pat Desmond's place. Made him stop the wheel. See, Marg?"

Marg sat looking at the money in a dazed way, absently running her fingers over the stiff, new banknotes. Gradually her face cleared. Jim was somewhat puzzled by her expression. She did not look like *his Marg* now. She seemed remote. And he remembered with a queer sensation that that was the way she used to look before she had ever shown any interest in him.

Marg coughed, then in a rather unnatural voice she said:

"You've had streaks like this before, haven't you, Jim?"

"Sure. I had one bigger than this."

"What did you do with all that money?"

Jim shrugged.

"Well, it got away. I don't know. That was before I knew you, Marg. I was mighty careless then."

"Don't you think it's foolish to pay five thousand dollars for that dog?"

"Foolish! I should say not! Why, I can afford it now! I may never get another chance!"

Marg got up and handed Jim the money.

"You better put that in the dresser drawer, Jim. I'll get you some breakfast, then we'll both get some sleep. You must be worn out."

"I'm pretty tired. Say, Marg, you don't care if I get that dog, do you?"

"Why should I? It wouldn't do any good if I did, would it?"

"Well, I wish it was all right with you. We'll have all kind of fun with him. I'll bet you'll be as proud of him as I am. Want five hundred to send to your Ma?"

"Let's worry about that later."

"All right. But, you see, we can send Ma plenty now and you won't have to worry. You can have your baby out here, Marg, just the same as any place else."

"I'll think it over."

Jim went in the bedroom and put the money in the

top drawer of the dresser. When he came back Marg was starting to get breakfast.

They ate in silence for a long time. Jim was very hungry and swallowed the food with enthusiasm. Marg was preoccupied, but Jim didn't notice it. He sat laying away long strips of bacon and thinking about the sensation there would be at the track when he claimed Dark Hazard. Lou would rave; he was pretty sure of that. Any other dog-man would pocket the five thousand with a smile; it was a lot of money for a dog, even a world champion. But Lou was prosperous, had the top money-winning kennel at the track, and, besides, Pat was a sort of pet of his. Lou would probably protest the claim and try to get it annulled, but Jim knew that the track officials couldn't afford to annul a claim the way things were. Their whole system of operation depended on the legitimacy of claims; otherwise they would be liable to prosecution under the gambling laws of the State of California. Claims were the backbone of the option system of betting.

When he had finished the last strip of bacon, he looked up and found Marg, with her chin cupped in her hands, staring at him. She quickly glanced away, then took a sip from her coffee-cup.

"What was you looking at me like that for?" Jim demanded. "Do I look funnier than usual?"

"You never did look funny. I was just thinking what a big overgrown kid you are."

"Me? Say, I'm no kid after what I been through."

"Just the same, you'll never grow up."

"How come?"

"You never will, that's all. I like you, Jim. You've got a lot of faults, but you're all right. Want some more coffee?"

"Yes. I'll take another cup."

Marg poured the coffee, then she said:

"I think you'd have a lot more fun if you didn't have me tagging after you."

Jim had the coffee-cup halfway to his lips. He stopped, stared at her for a moment, then set the cup down.

"Say, you need some sleep. You've got the funniest ideas this morning."

She lowered her eyes and sat playing with a spoon, turning it over and over in her fingers. Jim finished his coffee, then he sighed, patted his stomach, and said:

"Ah! That breakfast hit the spot. Marg, wait till you hear the rumpus when I claim Dark Hazard. Boy, them dog-men will be running in all directions."

Marg looked up at him and smiled; then she came over and, with a suddenness that surprised Jim, put her arms around him and kissed him.

"Well," said Jim. "You do like me a little, don't you, kid?"

"Yes. Not much. But a little. You better get some sleep now. I'll clean up the dishes, then I'm going to lie down, too."

"Hey! I usually help with the dishes in the morning. I don't feel so sleepy now. Give me that dish-towel."

"No. Go to bed. Your eyes are hanging down on your cheeks."

Jim laughed and stood yawning and stretching, looking out the kitchen window. The sunlight was hot and

dazzling; the house next door cast a long, sharp, purplish shadow out into the street.

"You know," said Jim. "I like this place. But I can't
get used to it. The other day I was out in the yard, kind
of walking around, and I saw a lizard that long. Jees!
I jumped straight up. Back home the only lizards you
see are them little ones they sell at the county fairs.
You know, the fellow has them on a board with little
chains around their necks."

"Chameleons."

"Yeah. I saw this lizard and I give a jump. But he
just sat there and looked at me. Nervy little cuss. He
was sunning himself on that cement out there."

Marg paused in her work and stood looking out the
window.

"It is nice here," she said.

"Yeah. But some people like Frisco better. We'll go
up and see what we think of it this spring."

Marg made a queer sound in her throat and he
turned to look at her. She quickly took out her handkerchief and blew her nose. He was reassured.

"Well, if you don't mind, I'll hit the hay. I am
pretty tired, at that. It makes your eyes smart, looking
at that wheel. I see green and red spots when I look
out where the sun is."

"Go ahead. I'll be with you as soon as I get through
here."

Jim went in the bedroom, pulled down all the blinds,
put on his pajamas, and got into bed. Boy, it sure felt
good! He hadn't had a wink of sleep in twenty-four
hours. Slowly the world began to drift away from him.
A breeze blowing up the street from the ocean rattled

one of the blinds; he heard a truck pass the house with a jarring rumble. In the room it was dark and cool; outside, the sun blazed white in a pale sky, the palms cast thin, sharp shadows; far to the northeast the mountain range was smoke-blue, rising high above the Hollywood hills with their flat, red-tiled Spanish houses. He was falling, falling. He woke with a start. Marg was standing in the middle of the room. He thought that she had a queer expression on her face. But he must have imagined it, because the room was dark.

"You were snoring, Jim, and then you jerked all over and woke up."

"I dreamed I was falling. I'm so damn tired, that's it. Coming to bed?"

"In a few minutes."

He turned on his side and began to drift into sleep again. Marg kissed him on the cheek; or else he dreamed it. Suddenly he didn't know anything at all. He slept while the hands of the clock went round and round, and the shadows of the trees and buildings decreased and disappeared, then reappeared and lengthened. Night came down fast and the street lights, pale in the early evening, were lit all along the Ocean Boulevard. At the dog track the ticket-sellers opened their windows; the crowd poured in. A new pup won the first race and paid a long price. Fog drifted up from the ocean and misted the flood-lights. Valery sat in Fallon's box, wondering what had happened to Jim.

When Jim woke up the room was pitch black. He yawned loudly and stretched his arms high above the covers, then he reached for Marg; she wasn't there. Getting supper already, he'd bet. Marg was sure prompt about things like that. He lay on his back, listening for the pleasant kitchen sounds, but all he heard was the ticking of a little clock on the dresser. Strange! Getting up on one elbow, he looked at the crack under the bedroom door; dark. A little worried, he jumped up and switched on the lights.

"Marg!" he called, then waited.

Not a sound. He opened the living-room door and turned on the lights. Nothing. Then with a growing sense of dread he walked all through the little house, turning on lights and calling "Marg!" Where could she have gone? He stopped in the kitchen. All the dishes were washed and neatly stacked away in the cupboard. Suddenly he noticed how dark it was out-side; there was no sound of traffic on the boulevard; it felt late, very late. Swearing, he went into the living-room and looked at the clock. Twelve-thirty.

Panicky now, he ran into the bedroom, threw on his bathrobe, and, turning on the light at the back of the house, he went out to the garage. But the car was there. Then he thought about the money; twenty thousand dollars cash in an unlocked dresser drawer. There were always mugs hanging around those gambling-joints. Maybe they followed him home. Good Lord! maybe they had grabbed the dough and kidnapped Marg! Maybe she had woke up and . . . !

"If anybody touched her I'll kill the sons-of-bitches," he said aloud as he ran back to the house.

In the bedroom, the drawer stuck and he pulled at it frantically. Finally it came open and fell on the floor with a crash. He bent down. Most of the money was gone; he could tell that at a glance. But there was a sealed letter and he saw his name on it, written in Marg's small, neat handwriting.

Dazed, he picked up the money and counted it hurriedly; five hundred dollars. Then he hunted around for a cigarette, lit it with a shaking hand, and went into the living-room to read the letter. Sitting there in the empty room with all the lights going, he read:

DARLING JIM:

I have taken most of your money and probably by the time you read this I will be on my way home. I know that it is a pretty awful thing to do, but I think it is for the best. You were going to pay five thousand dollars for a dog and in a little while all this money would have been gone and we would have been just like we were before I got you to go to Chicago and look for work. Please think all this over. I am going to take some of the money and buy my business back. Pa will not live long and I'll be able to look after Ma and George. And when the baby is born I won't be pushed for money, as I am going to put most of this in the bank.

If you want to write to me, address your letter to the old address. I love you, Jim, but I can't stand that kind of life any longer. If you want to come here and live I will have a place ready by the time you get here. I know that you will be very much surprised at what I have done, but just think it over and try to see my viewpoint. I am very sorry about the dog, but it was just one of your wild ideas. I have left you enough money to get along on. If I were you, I'd get a small apartment or even a room. As you know, I did not take a lease on the house, so that is all right. I am crying as I write this and I can't see the paper very well, so that is the reason the lines go every which way. Good-by.

                                                MARGARET.

Chapter VI

THE SATURDAY NIGHT CROWD MILLED THROUGH THE
betting-sheds, jammed the grandstand, and overflowed
into the inclosure, where they stood six deep at the
guard-rails, waiting for the start of the feature race.
Sam King, owner and trainer of the Dallas Kennel,
which had just arrived from Florida, had entered his
great young dog, Trackmaster, for a match-race with
Dark Hazard. The Florida dog had broken all records
in the short distances, setting a new mark for the one-
turn quarter mile, and he was touted to beat the black
dog. Eddy Clemens had added Little Prince and Round
Robin to the race and had given Trackmaster the 1 box.
The betting was heavy and the figures on the illuminated odd-board at the side of the timer's stand
changed rapidly. Little Prince had been racing well
and was given the best outside chance; Round Robin,
as usual, was the unknown quantity, the dark horse.

The dogs had been slipped into the starting-boxes
and now the grooms, in their red huntsmen coats and
their black-visored caps, were trotting up the track toward the gate. Waves of excitement ran through the
grandstand; in the betting-sheds the floormen were
pushing their way through the crowd, shouting: "Get
your money up, folks. Last chance. Don't get shut out."

Jim leaned on the rail of Fallon's box and stared

out at the track. He had been drinking and his face
was red. Valery and Bud Diegel were just behind him,
arguing and laughing. Lou Gorman and Fallon were
sitting in a corner, talking in low tones. Fallon had
won his case in the courts and was explaining the moves
and countermoves of his attorneys.

The warning buzzer sounded and the loud-speaker
announced, "There goes the rabbit." There was a rush
for the rail. A great rumbling sound like the booming
of distant surf rose from the grandstand. Behind Jim
a woman yelled hysterically. Lou Gorman calmly lit
a cigar and went on talking with Fallon.

The rabbit whizzed into the stretch turn; a bell rang
sharply; the starter dropped his flag; and the dogs broke
from the starting-box, flying. Dark Hazard's green
blanket flashed first round the turn, with Trackmaster
and the other two dogs bunched behind him. Jim sat
with a cold cigar between his fingers, staring. They
couldn't catch him. It was no race at all. The farther
they went the larger the gap of track between Dark
Hazard and the three dogs grew. There was a lump
in Jim's throat at the sight of that sleek, handsome,
jet-black dog hitting the back turn, leaning at an impossible angle and hugging the rail. There was just
one dog in the world—Dark Hazard.

As the dogs came down the stretch the grandstand
shook with the tumult. People were yelling themselves
hoarse, urging the black dog on, though he needed no
urging. Running at a terrific rate of speed, he burst
across the finish line six lengths in front of Little Prince,
who had outnosed the Florida dog. Men capered in the
aisles, hugging one another and throwing their hats in

the air. The loud speaker announced that Lou Gorman's champion had again equaled the world's record
for the futurity distance.

In the next box, Sam King pulled his hat down over
his eyes and sat glumly staring at the track and trying
to roll a cigarette, spilling tobacco down the front of
his shirt.

"Some dog you got, Lou," said Fallon.

"Yep. Pat's all right. That's the last crack they'll get
at him for a while. I'm going to lay him up. See; he's
touchy in that off hind leg."

Valery leaned forward and tapped Jim on the
shoulder.

"Well, Buck, here comes your dog."

Jim said nothing. He sat leaning on the rail, staring
down at the judges' stand. Three of the dogs, held by
the grooms, were standing in a line behind Dark
Hazard. A woman with red hair, smiling self-con-
sciously, was presenting Dark Hazard's groom with a
huge silver trophy. Eddy Clemens, with a cigar aslant
in his mouth, was looking on with his hands in his
pockets. A roar of approval burst from the crowd,
drowning the presentation. The groom acknowledged
the trophy with a slight bow, then the march was played
and the dogs were led down the track to the kennels,
single file. Dark Hazard was in front, with his head
down, panting; he was stepping daintily to the music,
with his tail held close to his body and his back sloping.

Jim watched him out of sight, then he got up. Sam
King and Lou Gorman were shaking hands. Sam tried
to smile, but didn't manage it very well. Lou turned
and put his hand on Jim's arm.

"Turner, we're going to have a little celebration over at the kennel. Like to have you."

"No, thanks," said Jim. "Got to go check up."

Valery said something to him in a low voice, something insulting, he could tell by the tone; but he paid no attention. The crowd was leaving the stands now, talking and laughing. The flood-lights were switched off over the track.

In the office Stein, smoking imperturbably, was waiting with the ledger.

PART THREE

BARROWVILLE : 1932

SPRING

Chapter I

IT WAS A COLD NIGHT FOR MARCH, AND A CHILL, SHIFTING wind was blowing across the railroad yards, carrying with it dust and scraps of paper. Two men were sitting in a switch-house, smoking and staring at a pot-bellied, sheet-iron stove which was red hot in places. Outside, the semaphores rose into the sky, huge engines panted on the sidings, sending up steam, and bells rang, the iron clangor sharp and clear in the cold night.

One of the men was wearing a badge in plain sight on his vest and a holster strap could be seen under his coat. The other was a railroad employee, an old man with a grizzled mustache and a leathery, blackened face.

"Weather ain't what it was," the yard dick was saying. "When I was a boy we had winter, then we had spring and summer. They wasn't all mixed up every which way like it is now. We never had no real snowfall this year at all. When I was a boy we had snow on

the ground months at a time, good sledding, good skat-
ing."

"You're right. And I remember back a sight further
than you do, Charley. I recollect when we had a sure-
enough winter in this part of Ohio. I was born up
north of the state capital and we had drifts so high we
used to have to dig out. None of that now. We have
piddling snows and it either melts right away or gets
as dirty as hell."

"You're right."

The employee pulled on his pipe thoughtfully and
stared out the window.

"Blowing up for sure," he said. "As windy a day as
I ever saw. Well, when March comes in like a lion it
goes out like a lamb. I'm about ready for some good
weather. A man my age feels better when there's a little
sun to thaw him out."

"Yep. You're right. I got a touch of sciatica myself."

Down the yards there was a prolonged blast of a
whistle, the clanking of big wheels running over a
switch, and the labored chug-chugging of a heavy freight
making the grade at South Siding.

"That's her," said the employee, nodding. "Pretty
close to schedule, too. Understand they're having
mighty nasty weather down around Cincy. That's good
running."

"Dave Morrissey, ain't it?"

"Yep. As good a freight engineer as there is on the
Big Four."

The yard dick got up leisurely and stretched; then
he buttoned his coat.

"Got to look her over, Lafe. See you later. I'll come in to get a feel of this stove off and on."

"Many hoboes coming in?"

"Many! We got the jail full. Judge Savage gives 'em all thirty days and puts 'em to work on the parks. Plenty for 'em to do now. And if they don't want to work, let 'em stay out of this town, that's all. Summer's coming and they all follow the sun. Good-for-nothing, lazy bastards. Ought to deport the lot of 'em, even if they are mostly Americans. We got enough deserving men out of work in this town without a lot of lousy bums."

The yard dick waved and went out. The employee got up to stir the fire, talking to himself; he'd done a little bumming off and on, and resented what the yard dick had said. But he was old enough and wise enough to keep his mouth shut. It would never do to let anybody in this straightlaced town know that you had ever hit the rods.

The big freight from Cincinnati was just pulling into the yards when the dick came down along the tracks. He saw small, sparse snowflakes falling past the yard lights and swore briefly. Wouldn't the weather ever get decent? The engine stopped with a slow grinding of wheels and a sudden hiss of air-brakes. The engineer waved to the dick, leaning out from his cab. An oiler was coming up alongside the train. The dick saw a lantern moving toward him and called:

"Jerry! What say?"

"All clear, Charley."

The dick took out a cigar and lit it, then turned back to the engineer.

"Bad run?"

"Sleet on the tracks between Cincy and Hamilton. It slowed me down some, but I made up time between Dayton and here. How's tricks?"

"Nothing to brag on." The dick stood pulling on his cigar, the red ash lighting up his face on the inhale. The engineer did not seem very talkative, so with a shrug he turned, and was just going to start back for the switch-house when a dark figure slid down from a gondola. "Hey, you!" yelled the dick and made a grab, catching the man by the sleeve.

The brakeman came up on the run.

"Hold your lantern up here," said the dick.

"He's all right," said Jerry. "I'll vouch for this guy."

"Must of paid his fare," said the dick, with a laugh. "I warned you about that, Jerry."

"You warned me! Don't be a damn fool. Who are you to warn me?"

"Well, you burn these guys for the price of a ride and tell 'em everything's lovely, then I got to throw 'em in the can."

The hobo pulled away, jerking violently, but the dick, who was big and strong, caught him again and held him helpless with an armlock. The hobo was big enough, taller than the dick, but he didn't seem to have much strength.

"Hold your lantern up, Jerry. I want to take a look at this bird you say is all right."

Jerry swore, then started to raise the lantern, but the hobo, with a sudden rush of energy, kicked the dick on the shins, broke from him, and ran into the shadows beyond the siding. Cursing, the dick jerked out his electric torch and started after him, shouting: "Stop or I'll shoot! Stop or I'll shoot!"

Jerry made a loud, derisive noise with his lips, then he shrugged and glanced up at the engineer, who was laughing.

"I hope he falls down and breaks his goddam neck. He warned me! That guy was all right, Dave. And I never took a cent from him."

"That's what you say. When you going to cut me in on this petty larceny?"

Jerry shrugged and walked back toward the end of the train. The engineer sat leaning from his cab, watching the snow falling down through the powerful beam of the locomotive searchlight.

Half an hour later the yard dick came into the switch-house. The employee was staring at the stove.

"Well, any luck?"

There was a sardonic ring in this question which annoyed the dick, who didn't reply, but merely sank into a chair beside the stove.

"Snowing," said the employee.

"Yeah. A fine night to chase a bum across the yards."

"He got away, eh?"

"Yep. Lost him over on Fourth Street some place. I didn't get much of a look at him. Oh, well."

Chapter II

THERE IT WAS, JUST AS HE HAD REMEMBERED IT. THE OLD brick house standing well back from the street, with its iron fence, its brick walk, and the colored fanlights above the door; must have been built in the '80s. The hall light was on; he could see it glowing behind the pale-blue and amber glass; but all the windows were dark except those in the sitting-room, where a dim light was burning. But things were changed somehow. For a moment he couldn't figure it out, then he noticed, at the far end of the big lot, a small brick building with a show-window. Then he knew. Marg must have moved her millinery shop; must have built one on the old Mayhew grounds. He walked to the end of the lot and looked into the darkened show-window. In the back of the shop a night-light was burning, casting a pale, bluish glow over everything. He saw the silhouettes of row after row of hats.

He walked slowly back to the iron gate, opened it, and crossed the brick walk; then he hesitated. What would Marg say? He couldn't make up his mind to ring, and stood for a long time staring at the fanlight. But the wind was cold and blustering, whirling the sparse snowflakes and sweeping dust and scraps of paper up the street; he had exactly twenty-six cents and he was cold and hungry. That chase through the yards and across the dark quarter of the town had worn him out.

While he hesitated, a little man came up the street, walking briskly, the skirts of his long overcoat switching from side to side. He opened the gate, crossed the walk, and came quickly up the front steps; then he started back. Jim loomed tall against the dim light from above.

"Well?" said the little man. "Looking for some one?"

"Yes," Jim stammered, "I'm looking for Mrs. Turner."

"What do you want with her?"

"I want to see her."

"What about?"

Jim took a step forward.

"What do you care, pardner? What business of yours is it?"

"I happen to know Mrs. Turner pretty well."

"Well, I'm her husband."

There was a prolonged silence and the little man came closer, trying to see Jim's face. Finally he cleared his throat several times and in an unnaturally calm voice said:

"Oh, you're James Turner! Well, I'm Preston Barrow, very old friend of the Mayhews'. I'll ring."

Jim heard the old bell buzzing in the back of the house. He remembered one time, long before Marg had ever so much as looked at him, when he was rooming here and forgot his key. Marg came in her kimono to let him in, after having carefully put out all the lights. She said:

"Come in quickly. I don't want to take cold."

And he had stammered:

"I'm mighty sorry to put you to all this trouble, Miss Mayhew."

And then he had waited in the dark hallway until he had heard her door close upstairs, as he didn't want her to think that he was fresh or anything like that.

"Cold night, isn't it?" said Barrow.

"You're damn right it's cold. I'm froze."

Barrow coughed and they stood waiting in silence. Presently they heard footsteps; then the door was opened. Marg! She stood peering out into the darkness.

"That you, Pres?"

Barrow cleared his throat.

"Margaret, I . . ."

But Jim burst out:

"Marg, it's me."

He saw her hand drop from the door-knob. He saw her standing very still with her hands at her sides. Turning suddenly, she switched on the porch light.

"Why, Jim!"

Nobody moved. Barrow and Marg stood staring at a big gaunt man with a three-day beard. The man's eyes were sunken, his face streaked with soot, his clothes ragged. There was a short, painful silence, then Barrow said:

"I'll run along, Margaret. Maybe I'll see you tomorrow." He turned and held out his hand. "I'm glad to know you, Turner. I've heard a lot about you."

They shook hands in silence, then Barrow went down the steps. Marg called:

"Good-by, Pres. Come in, Jim. I don't know what to say to you. Why, I . . ."

She shut the door and he followed her down the

dim hallway and into the sitting-room. She sat down.
He took off his hat and stood turning it in his hands;
then he sank into a chair across from her. The room
was just the same as it had always been; there were
the same old pictures on the walls and the same musty
smell.

Jim coughed and said:

"I wouldn't bother you this way, Marg, but I'm flat
and I got sick down in Memphis. I lost thirty pounds.
Ordinarily I weigh around one-ninety. Take a slant at
me."

Marg looked at him for a long time.

"Jim, I might as well tell you I was just getting ready
to start . . . I mean, I'm going to get a divorce."

"Divorce? Going to marry that little guy, what's-his-
name?"

"I was thinking about it. He's certainly been fine to
me. Pa and Ma are both dead, you know."

"Yeah?"

"Yes. I don't know what I'd've done without Pres.
I had an awful time in the hospital. You don't even
know you've got a son, do you?"

"A son? What's his name?"

"I named him Edward, after Pa. Why didn't you
write to me, Jim?"

"Why should I? You sure did the run-out act on
me."

"I know, and took your money."

"Oh, the hell with the money. I would just have piddled it away. But it was the way you run out that got
me."

"Did you ever get that dog?"

"No. I never had any luck at all after you left. Marg, where's the kid? Does he look like me?"

"He's asleep. He's got hair like yours. I think he's going to look like the Mayhews."

Jim suddenly put his head down and began to cry. Marg sat for a moment staring at him, horrified, then she got up and came toward him, but hesitated.

"Jim, it's awful to see you like this. You look . . . Oh, your clothes and everything. Are you hungry?"

"I'm starved. I ain't had nothing today but a dough-nut. Excuse me for crying, Marg, but I'm all shot. I came in on a freight and a yard bull chased me. It damn near finished me."

Marg moved back from him.

"Jim," she said, hurriedly, "I'll get you some of Pa's clothes and you come back and shave. George and Sonny are out to a picture-show and I don't want them to see you like this. While you get ready, I'll cook you some supper."

Marg sat leaning on the kitchen table, watching him eat. He looked different now in a clean shirt and with his hair combed and the wiry bristles off his face. He was gaunt and thin, but his color was good and she could see that before long he'd be as big and robust as ever. All he needed was a little rest and some good food.

"Ah," said Jim, "that spaghetti sure hit the spot. Can I have another cup of coffee, Marg? Wait. I'll get it. I forgot how things was."

Marg ignored this and said nothing. Jim poured him-self another cup of coffee and sat down to drink it.

"So you got George behaving?"

"I have. He's doing fine. Been working at the Hurst Manufacturing Company for over a year. Shop clerk. He lives right here where I can keep an eye on him. Pres Barrow got him the job."

"This Barrow guy seems to be head man around here."

"Well, I knew him long before I knew you. I went to school with him. I should have married him years ago." Their eyes met, then Marg looked away quickly. "You can stay here tonight, Jim. We'll get things straightened out tomorrow. What are you going to do?"

"Don't ask me. First, I want a little money. Then I may look around for a job. I'm off race-tracks and gambling for life. Look what they done to me. I'd like to settle down to a nice easy job. I don't care about the pay, just so I don't have to work too hard."

Marg looked at him, then she burst out laughing, struggling to control her face.

"I'm trying hard to feel sorry for you, but I can't. I don't see how anybody could. You haven't changed a bit."

"Say, I sure feel better now. Marg, you don't happen to have a cigarette around the house, do you?"

"No, I don't think so. But there may be some cigars in the living-room. Sometimes Pres leaves cigars here."

"Oh, goddam him and his cigars. He looks like a sister to me."

"Jim, you must never talk like that about Pres Barrow. He's good as gold. Look what he's done for me. Anyway, you're jealous."

"Sure I'm jealous. Why shouldn't I be when some

guy comes along and grabs my wife? Who the hell wouldn't be?"

"And don't swear all the time."

The door opened and a small man, slightly bald, with a thin, delicate face, came in, followed by a boy. The man looked like a badly-drawn caricature of Marg. The boy was thin and had not yet grown up to his second set of teeth, but his color was good, his hair blond and of fine texture.

"Well . . ." said George, staring.

"Jim," Marg interposed, "this is Sonny Mayhew. You've met George."

Jim stood up, towering over George and his son, and shook hands with them.

Light was streaming into the room when Jim woke up. A lukewarm wind was stirring the curtains and there was a damp, fresh, earthy smell all about. Jim yawned and stretched his legs under the covers. These old-fashioned feather beds were certainly swell; soft as they could be; you sank away down into them and slept like the dead. He got up on one elbow and looked out the window. Spring. It was hard to realize that last night it had been snowing. Dew was shining on the bushes in the yard. He saw a robin jumping stiffly on its little legs, looking for worms.

He remembered the jolting freight, the long siege of the flu in a cheap rooming-house in Memphis. This was something like it. He was damn tired of jumping about the country, with a pocketful of money one day and broke the next. He was no youngster any more; his hair was beginning to get gray. Maybe it would be a good idea to get a job in Barrowville and try to settle down. Maybe Marg would take him back. It would be wonderful if she would.

There was a knock at the door. He sat up.

"That you, Marg?"

Some one coughed, then a piping feminine voice said:

"Missus says you're to get up and get your breakfast. It's past eight o'clock."

"Be right with you, sister."

"I'm the hired girl."

"I don't care who you are. I'll be right with you."

"Missus says to hurry."

Jim got up and dressed hastily. He felt like a new man already; all he needed was a little rest and he'd be as good as ever. He looked in the glass at himself. There wasn't an ounce of flesh on him, hardly. His Adam's apple stuck out like he'd swallowed an olive. But he wasn't soft; he still had some muscle. Combing his hair, he noticed how the left side was streaked with gray. "But you can't hardly tell it," he muttered, "on account of my hair's so light." Bending forward, he looked more closely at himself. Before, he had never thought about getting old. In fact, he had never thought about himself at all till he had had that long sickness. Hell! it was pretty terrible when a big strong guy like him couldn't hold his head up. After all, you couldn't live forever. No matter how rugged you were you eventually took the count. Gray hair was only the beginning; pretty soon you had to get glasses, then your teeth began to decay and come out, you got rheumatism and your legs creaked when you walked. After a while you couldn't walk; you just sat in a chair and thought about how strong you used to be and everybody cussed you under their breath for being in the way. He had thought this all out during the nights when he was unable to sleep and was so weak he could hardly move his hands.

One night when he was at his worst a couple of flusies, who lived above him, threw a party. Lying there sweating with weakness, he had heard them laughing and shouting and shuffling about to the music of a gramophone. There were drunken screams and the crash of falling chairs; later there was silence; then a woman began to sob hysterically, the sound rising and falling in the stillness. It was awful and he had lain thinking: "Wait till you get sick, you bums. Wait till you can't get out of bed without getting dizzy. Wait till you can't hold your hand up a minute at a time. Then you won't be throwing chairs around and drinking booze and acting like a lot of alley cats."

Being sick was just practice for being old.

He tied his tie hastily and got into one of Pa's coats. The old boy must have been a pretty big man in his day. The coat was too big for him. He left his room and went down the hall, thinking about those long nights in Memphis; but the sight of Marg sitting at the breakfast table, looking neat and fresh, drove all such thoughts from his mind.

"Morning, Jim," she said, with a smile. "I thought I'd better get you up before I left. Sonny's gone to school and George's gone to work. I've got to go pretty quick."

Jim sat down and began to eat. Good toast, good bacon, good everything.

"I'm going to lay my ears back and go to this food, Marg. Say, you're certainly looking fine. Better than ever."

"Oh, I'm getting old." Marg was pleased and sat looking at Jim, smiling in a friendly way.

"Old, nothing. I'm a spring chicken myself and you're six years younger than I am."

"Jim, you're getting gray."

"Hell! I thought I combed my hair so you wouldn't notice it."

She put her fingers to her lips.

"Watch your language, Jim. Lottie teaches a Bible class and you'd shock her to death. Anyway, Eddie's in the next room and boys pick things up soon enough."

"What's he doing in there? Why don't you bring him in?"

"He's had his breakfast. He's playing. I leave him there so Lottie can keep an eye on him."

Lottie came in with a new pot of coffee. She was tall and very thin, with a long neck, lank brown hair, and small, near-sighted eyes. She spoke in a high treble voice. Her hands were long, red, and big-knuckled.

"This is Mr. Turner, Lottie," said Marg.

"How do you do, Mr. Turner?" piped Lottie, putting down the coffee-pot, her face red with embarrassment.

"You called me, didn't you?" Jim asked.

Lottie misunderstood him.

"Yes, sir, I did. But the missus told me to."

Jim laughed.

"He just wondered, Lottie," said Marg, placatingly. "It was perfectly all right."

"Yessum."

Lottie went out.

"Good Lord!" said Jim. "Is that the kind they grow around here?"

"You mustn't make fun of Lottie. She's a very fine girl."

Jim ate in silence for a while. Finally he said:

"How's our old friend, Barrow? Has he been around yet this morning?"

"Jim!"

"Well, I just asked."

"I know what you mean. You'll like him when you know him. He's certainly done wonders. His father died and left things in a terrible mess. They used to be one of the richest families in Barrowville. But the foundry was a total loss and Pres was over his ears in debt. But he's got a small machine-shop running and he owns part of an office-building up town. He's surely a worker. He's got ten per cent of the debts paid already. . . ."

"What part of the office-building does he own?" asked Jim.

"If you're going to try to be smart I won't talk to you."

"Listen, Marg, I'm just feeling good. Seeing you again and all that. Say, this cooking is swell. Will you let me stay on as a star boarder? I won't make any trouble."

She didn't say anything, but sat with her chin in her hand, looking out the window.

"Marg," said Jim, putting down his coffee-cup and taking hold of her arm, "are you sure enough going to get a divorce?"

She got up quickly.

"I've got to run down to the shop. I don't know what I'm going to do yet, Jim. So don't be bothering me about it. Here." She handed him some money which she had taken from the front of her dress. "Get yourself some decent clothes. You know what I mean. No race-track clothes. A nice dark suit and some dark ties and white shirts. I'll see you this evening. I generally run down to the Ladies' Aid for my lunch."

Jim took the money.

"But, listen, Marg . . ."

"You can get your lunch up town or else come here and eat with Sonny. Quarter till twelve sharp. I'll see you tonight. If they have to alter the clothes, you wait till it's done. I want you to look nice."

Marg went out. Jim sat looking at the table for a long time; then he counted the money—one hundred dollars. Finally he shouted:

"Hey, out there!"

Lottie opened the door and peeped in. She looked scared.

"Got any more toast, Lottie?"

"No, sir. But I could make you some, Mr. Turner."

"How about an egg? Could you fry me one?"

"I could, sir. But . . ."

"But, what?"

"The missus might not like it. We only cook three eggs of a morning. One for each of them. Four this morning, counting yours. . . ."

"Well, make it five."

"Yes, sir."

Lottie went back into the kitchen, shaking her head. The side door opened slowly and Jim sat watching it. Seeing no one, he thought it was the wind and got up to close it. But it was Eddie, who was peeking at him.

"Hello, kid!" said Jim. "How's tricks?"

He stood looking down at the serious-faced, tow-headed little boy, trying to realize that the boy was his own. It was hard to do. Eddie seemed just like any-body's, some stranger's kid that you looked at, smiled at, patted on the head, and forgot.

" 'Lo."

"Come on in and sit down."

But Lottie called, "Eddie! Eddie!" in her shrill voice, and the little boy disappeared, shutting the door softly.

Jim sat down to wait for the egg and the fresh toast. He would have liked to hold Eddie on his knee and talk to him, but it never occurred to him to tell Lottie to let the kid stay. Lottie was managing him and that was that.

Pretty soon Lottie came in with the food.

"Lottie," he said, "I'm a big eater. I'm not like the Mayhew tribe. If I stay here you'll have to cook more than you do."

"If you stay here . . ." stammered Lottie. "I thought . . ."

"You thought what?"

"I thought you was married to the missus."

Jim looked at her shocked face and laughed.

"Don't get all excited. I am married to her. But I may not stay, all the same."

"Oh," said Lottie, relieved, "you might go away on business again."

"Yes," said Jim. "On business."

It was after six o'clock when Jim got home. Sonny let him in and said:

"Hurry, Uncle Jim. We're eating. We always eat on time. Aunt Margaret makes us."

"I see, I see," said Jim. It made him feel very queer to be called "uncle" by this strange boy and to be accepted into the family as if he had been away not three years, but three days.

He followed Sonny down the long hallway. When he stepped into the brightly-lighted dining-room George and Marg stared at him and Sonny cried:

"Oh, you got a new suit!"

Marg said:

"Sit down, Jim."

He sat down, and Lottie brought him his dinner. Eddie was sitting in his high-chair at the end of the table, alternately eating and playing with his food. From time to time Marg spoke to him, admonishing him. George ate in silence, looking at Jim out of the corner of his eye. Sonny stared frankly.

Finally Marg said:

"That's a nice suit, Jim. Did you get it big enough?"

"Yeah. It's way too big now. But I told the guy at the store that I'd probably gain twenty pounds or so before long so he allowed for it."

Sonny leaned over and whispered to his father.

"Dad, he said 'guy.'"

George bent over his plate to laugh.

After dinner Jim asked Marg if she'd like to take a walk, it was so nice out. But she shook her head and said that she was going to a movie with Pres Barrow. Jim didn't say anything; he just stood looking at her for a moment, then he turned on his heel and went back to his bedroom, beyond the dining-room.

It was warm inside and Jim took off his coat and opened the windows. Night was falling; the street lights came on as he watched, shining palely in the smoke-blue dusk. He heard the faint rumble of uptown traffic. Well, here he was back in Barrowville, Ohio, with no prospects and his wife going out with another guy. That was pretty good.

He looked around for something to read. All he could find was an old copy of the *American* and a small pamphlet. He sat down and picked up the pamphlet. It was something got up by the Barrowville Chamber of Commerce, and he saw Preston Barrow's name prominently displayed. Jackass! Swearing to himself, he read: . . . "Barrowville offers unusual facilities to the manufacturer . . . a railroad terminus . . . coal and water . . . population 67,098 at the 1930 census; estimated population over 70,000 . . . only fifty miles from the state capital . . . a central shipping point for the entire mid-West. . . ."

"Nuts!" Jim threw the pamphlet on the floor. The thing for him to do was to get a little money from Marg, not much, say a thousand dollars, and blow. Maybe he could pick up something in Chicago. Too bad about Bright dying like that, but maybe he could find Joe

Constantinesco or Johnny Mueller. Johnny was broke, though, or so he had heard. All the same, he could take a chance. No use being buried in this one-horse town, home of the Methodist Episcopal College and the Edgeworth Theological Seminary, as the pamphlet said. No, he'd be better off some place else. He couldn't stand having Marg a stranger, going around with some other man. A little of that went a long ways.

He picked up the magazine and tried to read it, but there was nothing in it but a bunch of "success" stories. How Joe Ipswitch of Oshkosh had built up his little chicken-raising business until now it was a national affair, shipping eggs, probably bad ones, and fryers, to all parts of the mid-West. Joe admitted that hard work had done it; nothing else; just hard work and a little vision, perhaps. Jim threw the magazine on the floor and sat looking straight ahead of him. A mild spring wind was stirring the curtains; the same damp, fresh, earthy smell he had noticed that morning was coming in the windows; the traffic sounds grew muffled. Presently he dozed.

Marg woke him. He stared at her.

"I thought you was going to a movie," he said, bewildered.

"I've been. It's nearly ten o'clock."

"Good Lord! No wonder I'm stiff."

Marg sat down across from him. He was not quite awake yet and her expression puzzled him. He couldn't tell whether she had been crying, or whether she was going to cry, or what. But he did notice that she looked different, somehow.

"Have you been here since dinner?"

"Yes. I dropped off to sleep. I was tired, I guess."

"I thought maybe you'd go out some place."

"Where could I go in a joint like this? You know I don't care much about movies."

After a long silence Marg said:

"Jim, I've talked things over with Pres. We didn't go to a movie at all. We just talked things over."

"Well?"

"Would you like to stay here?"

"That depends."

"Jim, I'm not going to get any divorce. I told Pres I thought you and me . . . that we ought to . . ."

Jim's face had begun to light up and he was half out of his chair, but Marg waved him back.

"Wait, Jim, before you say anything. I want to tell you something."

"Well?" Jim stared at her a little uneasily; there was something about the tone of her voice that worried him.

"You see, I didn't hear from you for nearly three years. I didn't know where you were. You remember I wrote in my letter that I'd have a place for you if you wanted to come. Well, you didn't come. Pres and I, we . . ."

"I get it," said Jim, in a loud voice. "You fell for that guy, Marg. Just because I wasn't here and you wasn't getting any."

"Jim! I won't stand for you talking to me like that. I've known Pres Barrow for years. I . . ." She began to cry.

Jim jumped up and started to pace up and down.

"All the same, what I said was right, wasn't it? Marg, tell me, wasn't it?"

"Partly . . . yes."

There was a prolonged silence. Jim stood still in the middle of the room as if he had just been hit with a sledge and was getting ready to fall. He couldn't believe it, and yet he knew it was true. He had always thought of Marg as absolutely untouchable except for himself. It was very still in the room; the curtains moved in the mild wind; he heard a car passing the house, going very slowly. He burst out:

"I'll wring that little mug's neck, that's what I'll do. I'll fix him so you won't know him the next time you see him. Making a lay out of you. That's what he done."

"He'd marry me in a minute. It was my fault. Don't be a fool, Jim. . . ."

He began to laugh; finally he sat down.

"Well, I'll be damned! No matter what happens, I'm never surprised. But this beats me. It was a hundred-to-one shot, sure enough."

Neither of them spoke. Marg wiped her eyes and sat staring at the carpet. The clock on the dresser ticked on and on; the wind died down and the curtains hung motionless; car after car passed the house, springs squeaking over the rough street. Gradually Jim's face cleared. He sighed, hesitated, then motioned for Marg.

"Come on over, kid. I haven't been in no convent myself."

Marg tried to smile, but Jim could see that she was thinking and that her thoughts weren't pleasant. All the same, she came over and kissed him. He pulled her down on his lap. She lay there for a moment with her arms around him; then she started to cry again.

"What's the matter, honey?" he asked.

"I wish I'd never left you, Jim. Now everything seems sort of spoiled."

"We'll get over it."

Chapter III

JIM LEANED ON THE CIGAR-COUNTER AND STARED OUT INTO Limestone Street, which was noisy and filled with late afternoon traffic. The sun was just going down behind the buildings on the other side of the street. The little town was pretty busy. Jim had not yet got over his surprise at the number of automobiles and people that paraded up Limestone Street all day long. You'd think you were in a city. But at night it was different. Barrowville, in spite of its Chamber of Commerce, its great number of automatic traffic-lights, its banks, theaters, restaurants, was a nine-o'clock town. At a little after eleven the streets were deserted; lights were out, except for an occasional all-night Greek dairy lunch; the city slept. The footsteps of the policeman sounded loud in the empty streets.

Jim laughed.

It was funny for him to be buried in a place like this. At least a little while ago he would have considered himself buried. Now he was happy. Things ran smoothly at home, due to Marg's top-notch management, and he had even got used to the routine of the cigar store. He opened up at eight o'clock sharp; he went off duty at six, the owner taking his place. It was strange the way it had happened. He had looked for work vainly for nearly three weeks, feeling mighty embarrassed at being the only one at the Mayhew house not doing anything. He had almost given up. But one day a job "snuck up on him." A man yelled at him on the street—Barney Sidler, who used to run a cigar-store in Cincinnati and was always betting on the horses at Latonia. Barney gave him the job. At nine o'clock in the morning he had been walking about, wondering what to do; at ten he was working. That was a break.

The cigar store was in the entryway of the largest office-building in Barrowville—the Marcus Block, twelve stories tall, with a great Gothic doorway. The store was nearly all glass on the entryway side and there was a sliding glass panel for bad weather. In fine weather it was wide open. Jim disliked being cooped up, and this place suited him. All day long, while the hands went round the clock, he leaned on the counter and stared out into Limestone Street. The store carried not only tobacco of all kinds, but cheap candy, chewing-gum, and mints, and it was patronized by most of the stenographers in the Marcus Building. They liked Jim. He was always smiling and never fresh. Sidler was delighted with him and at the end of two weeks gave him a small raise in salary.

Sunday the store was closed and Jim had the whole day to himself. He and Marg usually took a long walk out to the edge of town. Barrowville was built on a big river, which was muddy most of the time, and surrounded by interminable, flat farm country. The farms were the richest in the state; the soil was heavy black loam and grew wheat, barley, corn, and oats in profusion. The farmhouses were well cared for and set far back from the smooth macadam roads; the barns were enormous and clean, and huge silos towered above the other buildings. Marg and Jim would walk out along the old Madison Turnpike, now a national highway, with signs reading: New York, 564, or Kansas City, 538. Birds sang on the fences; ground squirrels scampered across the road, and buzzards circled. In all directions the rich, flat land stretched away to the horizon without a dip or rise.

Sunday evening they had a cold supper. Barrowville was very still on Sundays. The picture-shows were closed; no one shouted or laughed out loud. Sunday evenings depressed Jim a little, although he never said so. Marg sewed or wrote letters. He and George went back to George's bedroom and played seven-up. Marg said that while she thought card-playing was all right, there wasn't any use in playing before Sonny, who usually sat on the floor with picture books or worked at his mechano with an intent face. Eddie was put to bed in a little alcove just off Marg's and Jim's bedroom at seven o'clock. Sometimes they found him wandering about the halls in his fuzzy sleeping-suit. He wanted to be with the grown-ups. He was never punished for it. Marg merely talked to him.

Jim liked George, who certainly belied his looks. At a glance he resembled a temperance-lecturer or the superintendent of a Sunday school or the cashier of a country bank or a rich man's secretary, self-effacing, a nobody in his own right but dependable; an unobtrusive little man, with delicate features and thin, sandy hair. But George had more life in him than anybody in Barrowville as far as Jim could see. He had been places. Once he had bummed from Chicago to Seattle. Jim couldn't imagine this delicate little man bumming, and often sat looking at him. When they were alone George sometimes spoke of the "goddam Methodists," putting an enormous amount of venom in his words. But he was afraid of Marg and was much more amenable to her discipline than his own son.

The quiet, easy life at the old Mayhew house made Jim very happy. He took on weight and did not pay any more attention to the streaks of gray in his hair. The days passed, identical but without monotony. One day it suddenly occurred to him that he was heading for middle-age, that he was slowing down generally; that this was the reason the life suited him. But one look in the glass reassured him. He was the same as he had always been except for the gray hairs and a slight paunch.

He and Marg never spoke to each other except pleasantly. Marg had a girl in the store now and could do pretty much as she pleased during working-hours. She spent a lot of time refurnishing the house and cleaning things up. Jim always exclaimed at the sight of anything new and praised it; not because he ever paid much attention to his surroundings, but because he knew that it pleased Marg.

They never mentioned Pres Barrow, and he did not come to the house any more. Every day or so Jim saw him going into the Marcus Building, where his lawyers had an office. Barrow always smiled conscientiously, but hurried on. Pretty nice-looking fellow he was with his dark, handsome face and his well-pressed clothes. Not so small as Jim had thought. Jim was six feet two, himself, and considered all men under six feet insignificant.

Barrow was above medium height, if anything. Sometimes the thought of him rankled, and Jim's face got red with suppressed rage. But these moods didn't last long. In a minute or so he was smiling and radiating good-humor.

At six o'clock the *Daily Sun* truck drove up and the boy ran in with the late editions for the cigar store.

"Howdy!" said Jim.

"Hi, big boy! How's tricks?"

"So-so. What's new?"

"Is anything ever new around here? So long."

Jim took the papers and put them on the counter, then he changed his coat and stood waiting for Sidler, who was usually on time. It was nearly dark now and the street lights were flashing on all along Limestone Street. Most of the people had left the office-building, but a few stragglers were coming out. The scrubwoman came up to buy a paper and stayed to complain about her rheumatism. She was a woman of fifty, with a shape like a full sack and a dark, battered face. Jim could tell that she had gone some in her youth and once or twice she had got confidential, amusing Jim by her slant on things. Every night she stopped to buy a paper, every night she complained about her rheumatism. You could set the clock by her.

At ten after six Sidler came hurrying up. He was a small, fat man with a congested red face and a hooked nose. He talked with his hands and was very excitable.

"Am I late, Buck? Sorry. Didn't mean to keep you waiting."

"It's all right, Barney. Well, I've got to toddle. We eat on schedule."

"I wish I was you, with meals waiting and a nice wife. Ever since I lost Mom I ain't been no good. I get so damn sick of restaurants. Oh, well. Say, did you hear the latest?"

"What?"

"They're going to try to reopen Bellport."

"Yeah? They'll never do it."

"I ain't so sure. I was talking to a man today who thinks they will. Bellport ain't Barrowville, you know. First place, it's across the county line. Second place, it's full of Roman Catholics and Germans. Not like this Ku-Klux town. You wait."

"Well, it's all one to me. I'm done with that kind of stuff. I'm tired of being a bum."

"A bum? It's sport, Buck, sport. Ain't you a sporting man?"

"I used to be."

"You sure settled down, didn't you, Buck? Well, that's all right, too, if you don't overdo it. Don't let this town get you; it's deadly. But you've got a nice wife, all right. Old man Mayhew used to be pretty well known here. Kind of went to seed, didn't he? It's funny how all the old families around here have went to seed. All the business is run by new people. It's funny."

"It's the breaks."

"Yep. This depression has sure busted things up. Look at young Barrow. His old man was pretty rich for this burg. Now the boy's around begging everybody for more time, more time. Trying to save something. Oh,

well. That's the way it goes. Up and down. I'm doing
pretty well myself, right now."

Jim wanted to break away. Sometimes when Barney
got started he didn't know when to stop.

"Got to run, Barney."

"Go ahead, go ahead."

After dinner Marg sat down to write some letters, so
George and Jim went back to George's bedroom to
play seven-up. George got out the cards and sat shuffling them, but making no move to start the game. Jim
lit a cigar and said:

"Well, what's the delay? Afraid your luck ain't right?"

"Listen, Jim," said George. "Heard anything about
Bellport?"

Jim nodded.

"Barney told me something about it. It won't do. I
don't think they'll ever let them open."

"I think they will. I was talking to Roy Hartman
today. He's going to put money in it. He used to be a
good friend of mine before I went decent." George
laughed and began to deal. "Roy's all right. Calls me
up sometimes at the factory just to say hello. Thinks it's
funny because I'm a shop clerk. I used to work for him,
you know, till Marg came back from California. He's
got a big poolroom. Well, he thinks they'll open sure
and he offered me a job—cashier. Ten dollars a night.
It's easy. I told him about you and he says he'll fix you
up, too. Maybe if we both talk to Marg she'll . . ."

Jim sat shaking his head.

"Maybe you don't understand what I mean, Jim. I
mean we'll keep the jobs we've got. It's just like finding

the money. Ten dollars a night; one hundred nights; one thousand dollars. We'll be home in bed by one o'clock. Get a good night's sleep and be ready for our regular jobs. I could use a thousand dollars. So could you."

"No," said Jim, "I'm through with that kind of stuff. A guy always starts out all right. But he don't finish up that way. In a couple of weeks we'd be throwing up our regular jobs, and when the meet was over, where would we be? I'll tell you. We'd be following the ponies. No, I'm done with that stuff. Marg won't stand for it and I don't blame her. George, Marg and me never had a harsh word over anything else. It caused all our trouble."

George grimaced, then he looked at his hand and inquired:

"Stand or beg?"

"I beg."

"I'll give you one."

They played the hand out in silence, then Jim said:

"Well, high, low, jack, and the game for you, boy. You sure hold the hands."

"Four for me, one for you. Your deal. You think it over, Jim. If we both talked to Marg and told her we were each going to make a thousand dollars, why . . ."

"Not a chance, George. Play cards."

"Well, if you feel that way about it, why, I'm sunk. Marg would raise hell. Plenty. I guess I'd better forget it, but I do get sick of never having any money in my pocket. I beg."

"I'll pass the deal."

A little later Marg came in and stood watching the

game. From time to time she patted Jim on the shoulder. Finally he said:

"Why don't you take a hand, Marg?"

"All right."

She sat down, and George dealt the cards.

"Quiet, isn't it?" said Marg. "Eddie's been in bed hours and Sonny's asleep on the davenport. The house is certainly quiet when they're asleep."

"I beg," said Jim.

Marg leaned over and kissed him. He laid down his hand to hug her.

"Hey!" said George, "play cards."

When they were getting ready for bed Marg said:

"Jim, I want to talk to you a minute."

"All right, Marg; shoot." He struggled into his pajamas and sat down on the edge of the bed.

Marg was sitting at the dressing-table, combing out her hair, and she hesitated for a long time. Finally she said:

"I know you won't like me to bring this up, but it's about Pres Barrow."

Jim's eyes narrowed.

"Yeah?"

"It hasn't anything to do with me, Jim. So don't worry about that. It's this. I used to go to school with a girl named Betty Hamilton. She was my best friend. I left the state university in my second year, but she graduated. Then she got married to Ward Powell and came here to live. Pres and I used to go to her house all the time. He's a great friend of her husband's. Well, just about the time we got married and went away, they left

Barrowville. Now they're coming back for a visit and I've simply got to have them here, Jim."

"All right. Why not?"

"Well, Jim, we've got to have Pres here, too. They'll think it's mighty funny if we don't."

Jim didn't say anything, but sat looking at the floor. He didn't want that Barrow bird in the house, that's all, after what had happened. It was a little too much to ask. Funny Marg was so casual about it. He couldn't figure it out.

"Jim," said Marg, "I don't like to talk about it, but, listen, I know you've got things twisted. Pres doesn't know . . ." She stopped and went on combing her hair.

"He don't know what?" Jim muttered.

"He doesn't know I told you anything, if that's what's worrying you."

Jim turned and got into bed. That did make things a little different and to some extent explained Marg's attitude. All the same, it was hard to take.

"It will only have to be once," said Marg. "I'll explain it to Pres."

"Don't explain nothing. If you've got to have them people, have them, and invite him over. If he's got any sense at all you won't have to do any explaining. The less you talk to that bird the better I like it."

"All right, then. It's settled."

After a while Marg turned out the light and got into bed.

"Mad, Jim?"

"No."

"Well, why are you away over there then?"

Chapter IV

JIM WAS DISTINCTLY UNCOMFORTABLE. HE SAT ON THE edge of his chair, listening attentively to everything that was being said, and tried not to show his embarrassment. Marg had got him into a stiff collar and it was sawing his neck; his hair was plastered down so tight that it felt like he had a hat on. From time to time he glanced at George, who was sitting back swinging his foot and looking at the others with unconcealed boredom. Jim was mighty glad that George was there; it helped a good deal.

Marg had warned him to watch his grammar, as Betty was very well educated and her husband had at one time taught English in the Junior College. That was before he took that job with his uncle. Now he was successfully running a big business, so Marg said. Jim liked Ward Powell as little as he liked Pres Barrow, who seemed perfectly at ease, smoking a cigar and keeping the conversation going. But Jim noticed that Marg was having a good time; her face was flushed, her eyes shining, so he tried to be as amiable as possible. The four of them, Ward and his wife, Barrow and Marg, talked about people Jim had never heard of. There were long discussions about what had happened to this one and who had married whom till Jim's head began to swim. Who cared? From time to time George put in a sardonic comment and Marg looked at him sharply. Once Jim turned away to laugh.

Ward Powell, a red-faced young man with very sleek brown hair, a loud voice and glasses, was talking about a friend of his who had been very brilliant at school but had gone to the dogs, was "a washout." He had started out with the greatest prospects, but was now a mere insurance clerk at forty a week.

George coughed and said:

"I wish my boss would raise me to forty a week."

There was a short silence, then Barrow changed the subject. Jim could see that Barrow was no fool. He sensed the tension in the room, felt the impending clash of inimical points of view, and tried very hard to smooth things over. Powell belonged to the boom period of American life, and luckily had been practically untouched by the crash. His thinking was the thinking of the Coolidge era; he was a figure of the past, but didn't know it. He judged every man by the number of dollars he had in the bank, by the sort of car he drove, by his scale of living. He had a fixed standard. All above it were the decadent rich; all below it had gone to the dogs, were washouts. This sort of thing ruffled George's back, annoyed Barrow, but left Jim unmoved. It didn't matter a damn to him what a comic like Powell thought.

Mrs. Powell was a different matter. She was good-looking and Jim felt pretty sure that with a little encouragement she would be very nice and friendly. But she was afraid of her husband and listened with an air of approval to everything he said, echoing him when she spoke, and nodding agreement so often that it was funny. She had dark-red hair and dimples and looked like the sort of woman who giggled. Jim expected a giggle every minute or so, but it never came.

With surprise he noticed that Marg seemed to take a great interest in what Powell was saying and also nodded approval, though not so often as Mrs. Powell.

Time passed. The clock ticked on. Once George groaned audibly, but at a glance from Marg bent down and rubbed his leg and muttered something about neuritis.

Finally Barrow said:

"Why don't we play cards? Shall we play cards, Margaret?"

"It would be nice."

Mrs. Powell turned to Jim.

"Do you play?"

Jim cleared his throat and looked uncomfortable; he felt Marg's eyes on him.

"Yes, I do. I like draw poker best, but I'm not particular."

Mrs. Powell laughed.

"Oh, I meant bridge."

"I suppose we could play poker," said Barrow, hastily. "Why not? How about it, Ward? Shall we play some penny-ante?"

"Well, I don't like to be a wet blanket," said Powell, considering. "But, personally, I don't care much about poker. It's not scientific enough. All luck. No mental effort. I like a game that makes me think. Like contract. That's the game."

"Ever try cribbage or pinochle?" asked Jim. "Them's real games."

The Powells looked at each other quickly, then glanced away. Marg flushed. But George said:

"Any chump can play contract. But it takes a man with card sense to play cribbage or pinochle. You're right, Jim."

"Oh, I don't know," said Powell. "But I can't speak from experience. I've never played *those* games. My grandfather used to play cribbage, I believe."

Barrow laughed.

"We don't seem to be coming to any sort of agreement. What do you say, Margaret?"

"Why, we'll play contract, of course. George and Jim can play what they like."

"Good," said George, getting up. "That suits me to a T." He started out of the room, calling over his shoulder, "Come on, Jim."

Jim got up and stood looking about him with embarrassment. He wanted to make a break for the door, to get out without being noticed, but they were all looking at him.

"Do you play contract, Jim?" asked Barrow, bringing the "Jim" out smoothly.

"I never learned."

"I was going to say that you could take my place and I'd play some cribbage with George."

"Well, thanks. Excuse me, people."

He found George in the hall, waiting.

"Get your hat, Jim, and we'll sit out on the porch. It's a fine night. I want to cool off a little, anyway. Ward Powell raises my temperature."

Jim got his hat and they went out and sat on the front steps. It was a beautiful spring night, with a damp, lukewarm wind. The sky was clear and above the elms of Tecumseh Street the stars were sparkling. Children were playing hide-and-go-seek, using the corner light-post for the base. Jim saw them running in and out among the shadows, arguing and shouting. Cars passed from time to time. It was almost summer; you could feel it in the air and sense it in the attitude of the people, who were discarding overcoats, taking the curtains off their cars, opening their windows, and getting ready to let in as much of the good weather as possible.

"This is nice," said George. "It's a relief to get out here where it's quiet and dark and not contaminated by a so-and-so like that Ward Powell. He is the most odious bird I ever knew. He's just my age. We went to school together. He was one of those little sweeties who always tell the teacher everything, you know. A bookworm; always had his lessons. Damn! but he gets under my hide. He was teaching school over at Junior College when his cousin died and his uncle took him into the business. Then the uncle dies and he inherits the works. All accident. If it hadn't been for his uncle he'd still be teaching school. To hear him you'd think he was a Captain of Industry or something."

Jim cleared his throat.

"George," he said, "there's something I want to ask you. I'm always wondering about it. But I never wanted to say anything because I was afraid you wouldn't like it."

"What is it?"

"How come you're so different from your people? I mean, Marg and the people you was raised with. You're not like Powell or Barrow. You're more like me."

"I resisted, that's the answer. I had Methodism crammed down my throat from the time I was that high. It's the old story of the preacher's son. Pa wasn't a preacher, but he was superintendent of the schools and that's just as bad. I resisted, Jim. Pa made a bum out of me with the best intentions. See?"

"It's funny."

"This town is deadly. Narrow and bigoted. Look what it's done to Marg. Not that she isn't all right. She's one in a million. But she'd be a different girl if she lived some place else. I was mighty glad when she married you. And it helped her some. But she's right back where she started now."

"She certainly keeps things going."

"She does that. And I give her credit for it. I'll admit that I caused everybody a lot of trouble, but there was a certain amount of hell that I had to get out of my system. My brother Ed started at it early. He'd've been a bearcat if he hadn't died. He had more nerve than all the rest of the Mayhews put together."

They sat in silence, looking out into the shadowy street. The front door was open and they could hear the others laughing and arguing mildly over the bridge game. Once Jim heard Marg say, "Oh, Pres!" in such an intimate voice that he cleared his throat uncomfortably and shifted his feet.

"Pres, now," said George, "is a different matter. He was always regular, from grammar-school on. His old man's money didn't make a bit of difference. He was just one of the kids. And when his old man died and left him broke, he didn't fold up. He went to work. And there isn't anything he wouldn't do for Marg, or for any of us, for that matter. They don't make them any better than Pres Barrow."

"No," said Jim, hesitating, "I guess he's all right."

George laughed.

"He's been hanging around after Marg ever since I can remember. They had an awful case in high school. We used to make his life miserable. Marg always could twist him around her finger. Marg's pretty good at twisting, don't you think?"

"Yep, I do. George, maybe she'd be better off if she was married to Barrow. I kind of feel out of place around here sometimes."

"So do I. Thank God there's not many of the Powell breed around any more. Most of them are broke. The Hoover prosperity took care of them. They're mighty quiet when they're broke. Don't worry about them."

"I'm not worrying about them. I'm worrying about Marg. She's not like she was in Chicago or out in California. I don't know how to say it, but she's . . ."

"She's going Barrowville. We'll all go as we get older. You're going it, too, Jim, even if you don't realize it. You're getting fat and satisfied."

"Yep. I am. I like this place here, and I like the kids. Sonny's a dandy and so is Eddie. And then everything runs along so smooth."

"Oh, well," said George, "we're slowing down. We're getting along toward that certain age. All we can do is make the best of it."

They heard Mrs. Powell laughing loudly and they heard her husband's oracular voice explaining a play some one had overlooked.

"They don't know we're here," George observed.

"Let's take a walk. I know where we can get some good beer, Jim. Shall we?"

"I don't care. Only we can't stay long."

After the second beer George began to warm up. His home manner had entirely disappeared. He smiled at Jim, narrowing his shrewd little eyes, and he told stories about his adventures that were very funny.

They were sitting in the back room of a little German grocery beyond the railroad tracks. It was musty and smelled of vinegar and tar soap. Above their heads burned a bluish, old-fashioned gas-light, which flickered and cast elongated shadows on the wall.

George ordered another beer for each of them, then he began to tell Jim about a man named Huston he had met in the West.

"Everybody called him Useless," George said, "but he wasn't. He was the shrewdest bird I ever met. He had the biggest poolroom west of Kansas City and he owned some runners. His son used to say: 'Here comes the old man's belly around the corner. He'll be here in half an hour.' Huston weighed about three hundred pounds. His son said he hadn't seen his navel for twenty years. They were always kidding him about being fat, but he said all his fat was around his waist and none of it in his head. And he was right. He'd bet on anything, on the weather if there wasn't anything else handy, and he was always hanging around the race-tracks. One time at St. Louis he caught a dip putting his hand in his pocket. He grabbed the dip and held on to him. The dip says: 'Mister, you got me all wrong. You thought I was going to take something out of your pocket, didn't you?' And Useless says: 'Well, I knew you wasn't going to put nothing in!' "

Beer-warmed, George talked on and on, reliving his life around the theaters and tracks, and telling Jim about the queer people he had met. Jim hardly knew him. He wasn't George Mayhew, Marg's brother, now; he belonged to that great army of drifters, that fraternity of hop-scotchers, Jim had known all his life—Johnny Mueller, Tom Lift and a hundred others. All of them as irresponsible as children and as likable; throwing their money out the window, never worrying about the next meal, always optimistic. And gradually the present faded away. The horses were running, gamblers were grumbling about the odds, crowds shouted and the grandstand shook. He saw rain slanting across a center field; he smelled wet turf and horse sweat and liniment.

"George," he said. "It's after ten o'clock. We better be getting back."

On the way out they met Harry O'Brien, who owned the barber shop and poolroom just around the corner. He shook hands with Jim and George, and they stood talking.

"Did you hear about Bellport?" he asked. "It's all set. Everything's O.K. The mayor and the city council give them a permit. A hundred-day meet. Horses in the afternoon and dogs in the evening."

"What!" said Jim. "Dogs? They haven't got no dog-track at Bellport."

"They have now. They built one. They got two tracks, two grandstands, everything. I was talking to Roy Hartman just before I come in here. You ought to hook up out there, George. You'll make something while it lasts. I understand they're going to give the cashiers and option-sellers fifteen bucks for day and night. If I didn't have my business I'd ask Roy for a job."

Jim and George walked home in silence. Jim was struggling with himself, trying to put a memory far back in his mind so it wouldn't bother him during the meet. When they reached the gate George said:

"I hate to pass that up. I could make fifteen hundred dollars. Fifteen a day and me working for thirty-two fifty a week."

"Yes," said Jim, "but it won't last. Anyway, Marg wouldn't let you."

George didn't reply.

The Powells had gone. Barrow and Marg were sitting in the living-room, looking very solemn. Jim and George, although they had chewed gum and eaten mints, diffused a rich, beery odor through the hall. Marg began to sniff; then she laughed.

"You ran away to drink beer, didn't you? The Powells wondered where you'd gone."

Barrow got up quickly and smiled.

"Why didn't you invite me?" Barrow shook hands with George and Jim, then he started for the hall. "I've had a very pleasant time," he said. "You know, it's nice here. I envy all of you living like this. I batch it. It's been nice seeing you, Turner. I wish"—he hesitated, looking from one to the other—"I wish I could see more of you people."

"Drop around then," said George. "Seems to me you've been avoiding us lately. You used to be here enough."

Both Barrow and Marg flushed. Jim noticed it and

he also noticed the glance which passed between them. It worried him, made him feel insecure.

That night Marg kissed Jim lightly, then turned away and settled herself for sleep. Jim put his arm around her and got very close to her, kissing the nape of her neck, but she said:

"Good night, Jim. I'm awfully tired."

Chapter V

BARNEY SHOWED UP NEARLY HALF AN HOUR AHEAD OF time. He lived a rather lonesome life and liked to talk to Jim. Although he had been in Barrowville for nearly four years, he was still considered a newcomer and had made few friends. He did not come into the store, but stood on the customer's side in the entryway, leaning on the counter. He was very much excited about the Bellport track, had a Racing Form in his pocket, and could talk of nothing else.

While they were talking Pres Barrow got out of one of the elevators and stepped up to the counter to buy a cigar. Barney was very friendly and recommended a new brand he was carrying. Barrow bought a handful, lit one, then said:

"How are you this evening, Turner?"

"Fine."

"I haven't been in lately."

"I thought I hadn't saw you."

"No. I've been up to Cleveland on business. I really believe things are beginning to pick up."

"I hope so, I hope so," Barney put in. "Not for myself, because my business has been pretty good. But on account of everybody. Things were sure nice in 'twenty-seven."

"They certainly were. I don't think we'll ever have

times like that again. Well, good-by. Remember me to Margaret, Turner."

"Nice young man," said Barney. "Not like most of these stuck-up bastards around here. Ain't this a funny place, Buck?"

"I don't know. I like it, all right."

"Yeah, but you've got a family. You ought to be like me. Nobody gives a damn what happens to me. I haven't got no friends, hardly. Two afternoons a week I go down to a pinochle club on Anthony Wayne Street; you know, Pete Schmidt's. Used to be an old-time saloon. Nice place it was, too, before they voted dry. Best German beer I ever tasted except in Cincy. Good local beer, too. Remember that dark Frederick Barbarossa beer? Ah! that was beer! Yep, I play pinochle two days a week; the rest of the time I look down my nose. Not now, though," he went on, his eyes shining; "now I got a place to go every afternoon. There ain't nothing in the world like horse-racing, Buck. Sport of kings is right. Boy, don't I get a thrill when them babies hit the stretch. Wow!"

Jim shrugged.

"You can afford it."

"I can afford it!" Barney snorted. "I ain't rich. I got a little money. I got some Liberty Bonds. I got a business. But I ain't rich. But why should I worry? I'm over fifty. I got nobody. I can't take my money with me when I kick off. No, sir. But I do wish Mom was here to see them horses run. She loved it." Barney turned away. Jim saw tears in his eyes and coughed uncomfortably.

"Well," said Jim, finally, "I don't blame you a bit, Barney. That's what you like and you ain't hurting anybody. Go to it. Me, I'm done with all that stuff. I don't even read the entries."

Barney laughed.

"You're afraid to read the entries, ain't you, Buck?"

"No. It's not that. I just want to forget about all that stuff. You never was a no-good tramp like me, Barney. A millionaire one day and a bum the next. You always had more sense."

"I'll admit I don't plunge. You was always a plunger. That's the trouble with you. I remember the first time I ever heard of you, Buck. It was at New Orleans. You'd just made a strike at Charley Futrelle's. I remember Mom and I was anxious to see you. When we did see you, you had on a dirty old sweater and you looked like you'd just got off a freight. Billy Considine told me that you was buying shoes for every busted swipe and exercise boy at the track. A little while later I saw you borrowing money from Billy."

Jim's face clouded, then he laughed.

"Yeah. I used to be pretty crazy in them days." He stood leaning on the counter, thinking. Pretty soon the clock over his head struck six sharply and he saw the scrubwoman coming in. She came up to buy a paper and Barney inquired about her rheumatism, winking at Jim.

"You don't need to wink," she said. "My back's killing me tonight. And my right knee's swelled up like a washtub."

"You should've saved your back a little, about forty years ago," said Barney.

The scrubwoman said nothing. A wide grin spread

over her battered dark face, then she winked, and started
for the elevator.

When Jim got home Marg met him in the hall and
kissed him, then she said:

"Don't say anything about George at the table. I'll
tell you about him later."

Sonny was already seated at the table with a bowl
of steaming soup in front of him. Eddie was in his high-
chair, banging on a plate with a spoon.

"Eddie! Mustn't!" said Marg.

Jim grinned and kissed Eddie on the head. Sonny
said:

"Hurry and sit down, Uncle Jim. I can hardly wait
to eat this soup. I saw Lottie making it, but she wouldn't
give me any."

Jim sat down quickly.

"All right, Sonny. On your mark; get set; go."

"Jim!" admonished Marg, laughing.

Sonny ate as fast as he could, scarcely taking a breath.
Then he stopped and laughed. Eddie was laughing, too.
Jim looked at them with a sigh of contentment. It was
pretty swell to come home to a nice family like this.

Lottie came in with Jim's soup.

"Good evening, Mr. Turner."

"Good evening, Lottie."

"Dad won't be home to dinner," said Sonny. "Had
to work."

"I see," said Jim; then he looked at Marg, who shook
her head slightly.

They ate in silence for a while. Finally Eddie upset
his mush and milk and said: "Oh, hell!" with a serious

He ought to be home here with Sonny, even if he is working at Bellport. He can go out every day on the bus, and come home at night when he's through; then I'll at least know what he's doing."

Jim sat staring uncomfortably at the carpet. Marg had sure had her share of trouble with him and George. It was too bad.

"Jim," she said, after some thought, "I want you to go out to Bellport tonight and bring him home. You tell him he can work out there if he wants to, but I want him home nights on account of Sonny. If you can get him to come home tonight, why, Sonny will never know the difference. We'll tell him the factory is busy and that George has to work every night."

"I'll try, Marg. But you know George. He'd listen to you a lot quicker. You better come along."

"No," said Marg, sharply. "I wouldn't go out there for anything. People in Barrowville hate that place."

"Not all of them," laughed Jim.

"The ones that count do."

Jim cleared his throat and got up to get his hat. No wonder George blew up, if that's the way Marg talked to him. He was momentarily irritated himself. Marg was so positive about things. If people did not think like her, they were wrong. She never considered the possibility that there might be two sides to things.

"And, Jim," she called, "I'm trusting you. No betting."

"You don't need to worry about me. I'm through with that stuff for good. I don't even read the entries in the paper, dogs or horses." He put on his hat, but hesitated; then he took all the money out of his pockets and gave it to Marg, saving out a five-dollar bill. "There you are, kid. How's that? I'll just take this five along for fare and things like that."

"Oh," said Marg, smiling happily, "you don't need to do that, Jim. I trust you."

"You keep the dough. Then you'll know I won't be gambling. I'll do the best I can with George, Marg, and that's as good as a preacher can do."

Marg kissed him.

When Jim entered the racing-plant the second race had just been run. The grooms, dressed as bell-boys, with short red jackets, white trousers, and red pill-box caps with gold straps under their chins, were leading the dogs back to the kennels. Jim saw the familiar blankets blue, red, yellow, purple, green. . . . He stopped on the stairs. There was a black dog wearing a green No. 5 blanket. Jim began to tremble slightly, then he laughed. Hell! that was a rough-headed big dog, with high hind quarters, big-boned and clumsy.

Jim looked about him with surprise. He hadn't expected to see such a nice dog-plant at Bellport. The old horse-plant hadn't been much—a big, roughly-built stand, a mediocre track which was awful when it rained, cheap pine stables, everything crude and hastily thrown up. But the dog track was A-number-one. The huge grandstand was built on a framework of steel and painted white; the boxes along the front were white and green, with fine chairs and decorations; the timer's stand was the last word in up-to-date equipment, with electrical boards for the odds and results. The center field was well sodded and the flood-lights were on tall white-

and-green poles, making the track as light as day. The
girl ushers were dressed in comic-opera military uni-
forms, reminiscent of Crescent City, and Jim paused at
the top of the stairway to stare down at the crowd milling about the inclosure and the paddock.

The third-race dogs were being led up onto the
glassed-in stage at the far end of the plant. A wave
passed over the crowd, which began to move in that
direction. Jim saw the dogs standing close to the grooms
on the brilliantly-lighted stage, staring out at the people
jammed at the guard-rail. It was a warm, early-summer
night; there had been a shower in the afternoon; there
was the good smell of damp turf in the air. Jim breathed
it in with a smile. Above the vague rumbling which
rose from the crowd he heard the dogs barking in the
jinny-pit. Some one touched his arm; a voice said:

"Program, mister? You can't tell one dog from another without a program."

"No," said Jim, and hurried up the stairs, crossed
the stand, and went into the mezzanine.

He didn't know where George was working, but he
thought he'd try the mezzanine first. The mezzanine
was jammed; there were long lines in front of all the
option-windows and the floor-men were walking about
in the crowd, calling: "Get your money up folks and
avoid the rush. Dogs go to post in ten minutes."

Jim wandered through the crowd, looking at all the
men behind the grills. Finally he saw George at one of
the windows where tickets were cashed. He was staring
out idly and indifferently into the mezzanine; he had on
a green eye-shade and was smoking a cigarette. Jim went
up to the window.

"Hello, George!"

George blinked.

"Well! Don't mean to tell me you're breaking over, too. Marg *will* have a spasm."

"No. I come out to see you."

"That's different. Say, did you ever see such a crowd? Boy, what a plant! And dogs! They've got the best dogs from California and Florida; all the top-notchers. They've got the dog that won the five-thousand-dollar sweepstakes at Baden, Top Sergeant. And they've got that ten-thousand-dollar Australian dog, Maori. Both of 'em running tonight. I'd like to get out and get a look at 'em."

"George," Jim interposed, "Marg wants you to come home . . ."

"No. Not a chance."

"Listen, you don't get me. Marg's sorry she blew up that way. She said it was just because it happened so sudden. . . ."

"Don't bother me, Jim."

"Wait a minute. She says she don't care if you work out here. It's all right. But she wants you to come home on account of Sonny. She says you can live at home and take the bus out here every day. She . . ."

"Why didn't you say so?"

"I was trying to."

Suddenly George began to laugh. He laughed so hard that he had to lean against the partition for support. Jim just stood looking at him. Had George gone off his nut?

"Hey!" he said, a little bit irritated. "What the hell are you laughing at, George? What's the idea?"

George gasped and wiped his eyes.

"It's you, Jim. You ought to see yourself. You look like the little girl in 'Ten Nights in a Barroom.' 'Father, dear father, come home with me now.' Honest to God, Jim, I never saw anything funnier in my life. Did you ever think you'd come to this?"

Jim grinned and lowered his eyes.

"It's on account of Marg. You know I don't care what you do, George."

"You're all right. If Marg will let me be and not give me that virtuous talk all the time, I'll come home. I'd rather live at home, anyway. She's right about Sonny. I intended all along to stay at home. But Marg rubbed me the wrong way with all that talk."

"Well, that's settled," said Jim, delighted. "I'll wait for you. We'll go home together."

"Good. I'll be able to leave right after the last race. You know, Jim, I'm mighty glad things turned out this way. I found out this afternoon that I wasn't as wild as I thought I was. I'll tell you it made me sick to think I wasn't going to be with the family any more. If Marg hadn't jumped all over me the way she did, I'd've gone back and apologized."

"Swell," said Jim, grinning. "Well, I'll walk around and look things over."

"Don't lose your shirt."

"Don't worry. I left all my money with Marg. I haven't got but five dollars."

George started to laugh again. It made Jim feel pretty foolish, but he didn't say anything. Overhead, the off-bell rang and the grandstand shook with the tumult. The mezzanine was deserted except for the ticket-sellers and the cashiers. Jim waved at George and ran out to watch the race. He got to the rail behind the boxes just as the dogs hit the stretch, three of them running neck and neck. Near the wire a new dog slid through on the rail and won by a nose; there wasn't a length's difference between the first four dogs.

Jim felt the excitement of the huge crowd. He began to get hot all over.

"That's sure real handicapping," he said to a man standing next to him. "When you see four noses on the post the racing-secretary knows his business."

The man laughed.

"You're talking over my head, brother. This is the first time I ever saw the dogs run."

"Like it?"

"I'll say I like it. They sure got a steady customer. I'll be here every night. I can't afford to bet very much; a couple of tickets a night. But it's all the same to me. I get a wallop out of it whether I bet or not."

"So do I. I was out in California when they started dog-racing out there. I didn't think I'd like it, but I did. As a matter of fact, I worked at the Crescent City Track."

"Yeah? That's my idea of a job. I'd work for nothing at this track."

Jim stood at the rail, talking to the man till post time for the fourth race. Crowds moved behind them, packed from rail to rail. At all the stairways there were uniformed track policemen, keeping a path open; the inclosure was full.

"Well," said the man, "I'm going to bet one ticket on the number four dog in this race. I like white dogs."

Jim laughed and turned to watch the man push and

elbow his way to the mezzanine. Imagine a guy picking winners by color! That was a good one. He was just turning back when he saw a familiar face in the crowd. His heart missed a beat.

"Tex!" he shouted.

Lou Gorman's trainer looked about him, trying to locate the voice; then he caught sight of Jim, and hesitated for a moment.

"Turner! Good Lord. A sight for sore eyes! I ain't seen you since the first 'Frisco meet."

They pumped arms.

"How's things, Tex?"

"Middling. Come on down to the box. Say, I'm glad to see you. I don't know many of these Eastern guys. Only a few of the old bunch here."

They went down to a box in the A section and Tex gave Jim a cigar. They lit up, but before Jim could speak, the off-bell rang, the mechanical rabbit came whizzing round and the dogs broke from the starting-box. It was a runaway race. The white dog shot from the 4 box like a bullet, took the turn at a terrific rate of speed, and came home alone, with the 1, 6 and 8 dogs two lengths behind him, fighting for second money.

Jim laughed.

"That's good. I was talking to a guy just before you come up, and he picked that four dog because he liked his color."

Tex shrugged.

"It ain't such a bad way to pick 'em, after all. I know every dog by heart at this track and yet I set here all last night and never won a bet."

Jim turned to watch the dogs being led back to the

kennels by the grooms. He was trembling with sup-pressed excitement. He wanted to ask Tex all about Dark Hazard, but for some reason he couldn't frame a question. Finally he asked, indifferently:

"Where's Lou? Is he around?"

"Lou! Didn't you hear about Lou? He went like that." Tex snapped his fingers. "A big strong guy like Lou and it hit him all of a sudden. He just dropped over, and when I come in, there he was lying on the kennel floor and them dogs were raising holy hell, jump-ing against their crates and howling. Doc said it was a athletic heart. Lou used to box and play baseball and he never took no care of himself; wouldn't train proper. He went just like that."

Jim was stunned and sat staring at the track. He re-membered Lou's rugged, dark face, his big shoulders. Why, he'd've bet that guy would live to be eighty.

"It sure was a surprise to me," said Tex. "I couldn't believe my eyes when I seen him. I rolled him over and I tried to bring him to, but he was stony dead. He sure was. And them dogs didn't really settle down for two days." Tex tossed away his cigar and took out some scrap tobacco. "Chew, Turner? No? I'm trying to break my-self of the habit. But damned if I can take any liking to smoking-tobacco. When a man's around the grandstand, though, and meeting a lot of high-class people, he can't be chewing all the time." Tex crammed a big chew into his mouth, then he went on: "I own the Kiowa Kennel now. I ain't just a trainer any more."

He glanced out of the corner of his eye at Jim to see if he was properly impressed. He seemed to be, so Tex smiled affably.

"Yep. I got the best dog in the world right now. That is, I'm running him. He belongs to a rich guy out in 'Frisco. Top Sergeant. We won the Baden Sweepstakes in a walk with him. He's as fast as greased lightning, strong as a bull, and he weighs seventy-five pounds. Wait till you see him tonight. He'll take some of the run out of that Australian dog. You watch."

Jim hesitated for a long time, then he blurted out:

"You got Dark Hazard?"

"Yes. Why?" Tex looked at Jim with surprise, then his face lit up and he laughed condescendingly. "I remember. You was dead stuck on him out in California, wasn't you?"

"I sure was."

"If I ain't mistaken you was talking about buying him for five thousand dollars." Tex threw back his head and laughed. "Well, you're sure a lucky guy you didn't. Course I knew it was just talk. But I remember you coming over to the kennels with the missus and I remember Lou saying that maybe you was crazy enough to claim Pat for a long price like that. Hell! He's no good. I'm running him over the hurdles."

"You're what?" Jim demanded, dazed.

"I'm running him over the hurdles. He's got to pay his feed bill, some way. He's no good on the flats any more. Practically a three-legged dog; his left hind leg ain't worth a damn. And he don't like the hurdles any too well, either. He props. But he's so damn fast between hurdles he beats them hamburgers once in a while. Hurdle races pay good money. I been trying to get me a good hurdle dog for some time, but they ain't for sale—that is, at a price a man would pay. . . ."

Jim interrupted with:

"Can I see him?"

"Why, sure! Come over to the kennel some time."

"No. I mean, tonight."

"Well, if you'll just set still you'll see him. He's running in the tenth. I'd take you down right now, if you're that anxious, but he's in the jinny-pit, waiting for the race."

"Excuse me," said Jim, jumping up. Tex looked at him with surprise, then shook his head. Lou always had said that this Turner guy was a nut. Jim came back with a program and, sitting down, leafed through hurriedly to the tenth race. Dark Hazard, running in a hurdle race! He couldn't believe his eyes. The beautiful, miraculous black dog running with the hamburgers usually reserved for the hurdles: old broken-down dogs, wild young pups, fighters, bad actors, short-bred dogs of all kinds, the riffraff of dog-racing. Jim stared at the program in unbelief. And that record! Dark Hazard hadn't won a race in five starts. Twice he had fallen. Once only had he been in the money, third by six lengths. Jim sat clearing his throat and staring, stunned, at the program.

Dark Hazard was the bright spot of his past, as beautiful as a dream. When he thought of him at all it was as an easy victor, a sort of supernatural dog, unbeatable, running effortlessly against the best flesh-and-blood dogs. But what chance did they have? The box flew open, the bell rang, people raved, and the miraculous black dog tore round the stretch turn and finished at dizzy speed, the other dogs merely racing for second money. Hadn't won a race in five starts against hamburgers? Jim pushed back his hat and ran a shaking hand across his forehead.

". . . Lou babied him too much," Tex was saying. "He's a finicky eater and he likes to have his own way. I put the iron into him, tried to learn him proper dog ways, but he was too far gone. He had one good season after Lou died, then he went to pieces. Wasn't worth his food and freight. I tried to sell him, but everybody was wise. He's got good breeding and he used to be pretty fast, so we bred him, but he didn't throw no pups. Four in one litter and three in another, and not one of them worth a good goddam. He's a sure enough bad-luck black dog. Some black dogs are good luck, like that Top Sergeant dog; other black dogs are poison. Pat always was hell for hard luck."

Jim just sat there as Tex talked on.

"It was funny about me. Lou popped off just like that, like I said. His people didn't know nothing about dogs. His old man's a preacher down in Oklahoma, and he never had no wife. So I bought 'em from the estate for practically nothing, Little Prince and all. One day I was a trainer, the next day I had about the best kennel ever trained. Funny now, ain't it? Yes, sir. I had top kennel at Baden, where they pay real money. I been going like who-shot-the-cat."

"I see you got him in for five hundred dollars," said Jim, at last.

"Yeah. If he keeps on his feet, he may make me a little money in the hurdles. He ain't got nothing to run against here. No good hurdle dogs."

Jim cleared his throat and sat staring at the track. Tex paused, hesitated for a long time, then observed:

"It's funny how things go. Ain't many of the old bunch here. Tommy Mason, remember him? he's got his dogs here. Most of them old plugs, no good. Remember he had the best kennel next to Lou that year at Crescent City? Well, he's got all he can do to pay his feed bill now. And remember Val Wilson?"

"Yes, I remember her."

"Well, that big dog of hers, Round Robin, got away from her trainer and they never did find him. Tough, ain't it? She sold all her dogs after that. Didn't get nothing for 'em, either. She married that slick-haired guy with the big car. Billy what's-his-name's brother. Recollect? And they got in some kind of a scrape up in 'Frisco. A woman fell out of a window, or jumped out, or something, at a party. And Val and her husband and some other people was held for investigation. But they let 'em go. I understand she and her husband busted up. He probably lost his dough."

Jim sat silent, staring, while Tex talked on.

Waves of excitement ran over the crowd as the star dogs were led out for the feature race. Top Sergeant and Maori were the favorites and both had been backed down to even money. The rest of the dogs were long prices.

Tex leaned on the rail, staring down the track at the futurity box. He was chewing his tobacco like a cow chews a cud. Jim looked at him with distaste. So he put the "iron into Pat," did he? Jim had half a notion to take him behind the grandstand and give him a hell of a good licking.

"Watch him break," said Tex. "He breaks faster than

Pat ever did and he hugs the rail just as good. He run the five-sixteenths at Baden in 31 3/5 and beat the best they had five lengths. He ought to eat 'em up here in the futurity."

When the dogs broke, Maori flew out on top, but Tex's dog caught him before he had reached the turn and ran neck and neck with him round into the back stretch, but couldn't seem to pass him. It was a runaway race; the other six dogs were far back, jostling and maneuvering for third. Tex sat with an expression of acute anxiety on his long, sunburnt face. "Git him, Bill. Take him, Bill. Now you got him." Jim had nothing against the dog, but he hoped that he'd be beaten. Here was Tex sweating with suspense, all eyes for this big young dog, and over in the jinny-pit, forgotten, was Dark Hazard, waiting to run against the hamburgers in a hurdle race.

But Top Sergeant won, running a fine race from the outside and putting on a spectacular finish.

"There's a dog," said Tex; then he jumped up. "See you later, Turner. Got to go down and look after Bill. Ain't he a prime specimen? Class wrote all over him."

Jim sat watching the dogs being led back. In front of the judges' stand a woman was waiting with a big silver trophy. Top Sergeant was acting up, jumping and writhing, and the groom had all he could do to handle him and at the same time take the cup from the rather nervous woman, who moved back apprehensively from the plunging dog and offered the trophy at arms'-length. There were cheers and laughter from the crowd, which swelled into a roar as the dog broke loose and tore down the track toward the gate. The paddock judge jumped out and caught him. The crowd was delighted at the informal antics of Top Sergeant, and Jim sat silent, listening to him being praised. Greatest dog racing, the champion of champions, the Man-o'-War of dog tracks.

Jim shrugged and muttered to himself.: "Big clown of a dog. You never seen Pat acting up like that. He's a gentleman."

Standing up in the box, Jim saw the hurdle dogs being led up onto the stage. At that distance it was hard for him to see them, but he made up his mind that he wouldn't go down to the paddock. He was too wrought up. Sweat was standing out in little beads all over his forehead and his hands were clammy. He might get excited down there and make a fool of himself. He could look at Pat on the track; that would be close enough.

The minutes dragged. He sat watching the fluctuations of the odd-board. Dark Hazard: eight to one. Jim laughed to himself. What in hell was the matter with this bunch of dummies? Finally he jumped up and started for the betting-shed. He'd have to get one ticket on the black dog just for old time's sake.

George saw him crossing the mezzanine and waved to him, smiling sardonically. Jim bought one two-fifty ticket, feeling like the cheapest of pikers, then he went over to George's grille.

"Just bought one ticket for luck on a dog that used to run out West."

"You plunger," said George, laughing.

When Jim got back to the box the dogs were being led down past the judges' stand. Jim looked for the green No. 5 blanket, but a big, raw-boned white dog was wearing it. Then he remembered that Dark Hazard was in the 2 box. He stood up and leaned on the rail. There he was, walking daintily along, as quiet as ever, with his tail held close to his body and his back sloping in exaggerated fashion. He seemed a little unfamiliar, though, in the red No. 2 blanket. But his coat was as jet-black and as glossy as ever and he looked like what he was, a prince of dogs, among this awkward, battered lot.

Jim was so excited that he wanted to talk to somebody. He turned to a man in the next box.

"See that black dog? He used to be top dog on the Pacific coast. He's a whiz."

"Yeah?" said the man indifferently. "Well, he don't look like much to me. What's he doing in a hurdle race?"

"He's old."

The dogs were slipped into the starting-box and Jim stood breathing with difficulty, staring at the starter, who had his flag poised. The rabbit came whizzing round, the lights went out, and the starter dropped his flag. Dark Hazard broke on top, flew past the judges' stand two lengths in front, and hugged the rail at the turn, leaning at an exaggerated angle. At the first hurdle he was three lengths in front, but he hesitated before taking the jump, and the big white dog caught up with him.

"Yeah," said the man in the next box, sarcastically, "he's pretty good. Lost three lengths on that hurdle."

"He's no hurdle dog," shouted Jim.

"I'll say he ain't."

Dark Hazard and the white dog ran neck and neck for a few yards, then Dark Hazard pulled away, a gap of track appeared between them, and the black dog, flung by his own momentum, took the second hurdle without hesitating. The crowd began to urge on the white dog, which was the favorite. He hung on gamely and pulled away from the other dogs, hugging the rail a short distance behind Dark Hazard.

Jim began to yell:

"Come on, black dog. You got 'em beat a mile, black dog. Show 'em what you got, old boy."

But at the third hurdle he fell. Jim saw him strike the wooden support head on, miscalculating his jump; he saw the white dog flash past him, heard the violent, deafening roar which arose from the stands, then, hardly knowing what he was doing, he ran from the box and pushed heedlessly through the crowd. As he ran down the stairway he caught a momentary glimpse of Dark Hazard lying stretched out in the middle of the track.

When he got to the far gate a track attendant was carrying Dark Hazard to the paddock. His legs were stiff and he was lolling his head. Jim began to sob. The track attendant looked at him with amazement, then said:

"He your dog, mister? He sure knocked himself cold on that hurdle."

"Is he dead?"

"Don't know. I got to take him in for the vet to see."

The vet was waiting inside the office. Jim saw Tex running toward them and gritted his teeth. That big heel, putting a dog like this in a hurdle race. Somebody took hold of his arm and pushed him. The gateman said:

"You can't go in there."

Jim said nothing. He merely hit the man with the

back of his hand, brushing him aside. Tex, coming up out of breath, panted:

"He's all right, Charley. Let him in."

The gateman stood with his hand to his face, staring. The track attendant put Dark Hazard on a table and Jim, Tex, and the vet stood looking at him. He seemed very crumpled and thin, lying there.

"Well," said Tex, "that's the end of that son-of-a-bitch. He's never been nothing but trouble."

The vet bent down.

"His neck ain't broke. He just got knocked cold. He'll be all right."

"All right or not," said Tex, "that's the end of him. He always did prop for the hurdles. Think what he'd do now. He wouldn't jump a hurdle now for a beef-steak. He's done. If he comes round, give him the gas, Doc. He's a bad-luck dog."

Jim took Tex by the arm and Tex winced.

"Wait a minute, Tex. If you don't want that dog, give him to me."

"I never give a dog away in my life."

"Well, you ain't going to give him no gas."

Tex tried to pull away, but couldn't. Then he laughed foolishly. There was something shining out of Jim's pale eyes that disturbed him.

"You heard what I said. I never give away a dog in my life. If you want him, he'll cost you twenty-five dollars."

Jim let go of Tex quickly and reached into his pocket. He had one dollar and seventy-three cents. He stood staring at the dog a moment, then he turned and said:

"I'll be right back. I'll give you your twenty-five, Tex. But I'll kill you if you touch that dog."

Tex laughed again foolishly. The vet said:

"He's coming round. We won't touch him, big boy."

The crowd was leaving the park now. The flood-lights had been switched off. Jim ran across the inclosure and up into the mezzanine. George was leaning against the wall with his hat on. He had a cigar between his fingers and he looked very well pleased with himself. Jim grabbed him.

"George, give me twenty-five dollars."

"Hey!" said George, pulling away. "What is this?"

"Don't argue. Give me the twenty-five."

"All right. All right. But don't scare me to death. What's the idea, Jim?"

"I'm going to buy a dog."

"You what?" With the money in his hand, George leaned back against the wall to laugh. "He's going to buy a dog. This is the best ever. I want to see Marg's face when we come home with a dog. Have you lost your mind, Jim?"

Jim pulled the money out of George's hand.

"No. Far from it. Meet me down at the side gate, George, and get a taxi."

"Say, a taxi to Barrowville will cost us six dollars."

"We can't walk, can we?"

When Marg heard the taxi stop outside she got up and opened the door. It was late and she had begun to worry. She heard the taxi-driver say:

"Good night, fellows. Thanks." Then she heard him say something that sounded like, " 'Night, old boy, good old boy," but she didn't pay much attention.

She saw Jim and George come up the walk. Was there a dark shadow between them, or did she imagine it?

They came up onto the porch. The shadow was a tall greyhound. She started.

"Well . . . what . . . ?"

"It's Dark Hazard, Marg," cried Jim. "He got hurt in a hurdle race and I bought him for twenty-five dollars."

They came into the hallway and George stood grinning. The dog looked about him timidly, his pale amber eyes remote. Marg stared for a long time, then she sat down on the hall seat and began to laugh.

"You should have come after me yourself," said George, still grinning.

The dog looked from one to the other, standing with his body pressed tightly against Jim's leg.

BARROWVILLE : 1932

EARLY FALL

Chapter I

"THIS SURE KEEPS US FIT, GEORGE," JIM WAS SAYING. "Why, I've took off twelve pounds since the middle of August. I ain't got no belly to speak of at all, any more."

"I feel better myself. Not that I need to take any weight off; I've always been trying to put it on since I can remember, but I certainly feel a hundred per cent better. A man don't get enough exercise pushing a pen."

"No, nor selling cigars. Though I do stand on my feet practically all day. You, Pat! You're the cause of it, old boy. If it wasn't for you George and me would be pointing for the old folks' home."

Pat looked up, raising his ears; then he rubbed against Jim's leg.

"You're a great old dog, Pat, a great old dog," said George.

They were walking up the Madison Turnpike. There

was the smell of fall in the wind and the fields were bare. Smoke rose slowly from the farmhouse chimneys, hanging in spirals in the heavy air. Leaves were falling, littering the road in places; big russet oak leaves streaked with red, pale-gold maple leaves. The men walked slowly, smoking and looking off over the flat gray and brown landscape; the dog walked sedately between them, never tugging at his leash, letting them set the pace. He looked in fine shape, his coat shone like jet; his limp had almost entirely disappeared.

As they were crossing a field into a grove, a big fox-squirrel jumped up, ran swiftly across a bare space, and climbed a tree. Pat was off like a shot, but the leash caught him short and whirled him around. He lit flatly on all fours, facing Jim, who laughed and said:

"That won't do, Pat, that won't do at all. You'll pull my arm out of the socket. You know you're not supposed to do that, Pat." The dog lowered his eyes and turned his head away timidly. "By God!" Jim said to George. "That dog's got more strength than a runaway horse. If we ever jump up a rabbit, grab ahold and lay down or we'll be minus a dog."

When they reached the grove, Jim sat down on a stump and Pat stood very close to him, with his body pressed against Jim's legs. George caught up a stick and made a few half-hearted attempts to knock down some green walnuts, then he sighed, sat down, and took out a pipe. From where they sat they could see a white farmhouse; cows were standing about the stable-yard near the haystack; beyond, the turnpike curved off gray and flat toward Cincinnati. There was the good smell of burning leaves in the air.

It was Sunday, about noon. Farmers were passing in their Fords on their way home from the crossroads church or from the churches in Barrowville. Some of them leaned out to stare at the greyhound.

George said:

"Does Sunday ever bother you, Jim?"

"Yep. It used to before I had Pat. Sunday around here gives me the willies. It's something in the air."

"I can still feel it, and Sunday's been the same as any other day to me since I was fourteen. When I was a kid it was awful. We had Bible-reading after breakfast; then we went to Sunday school; then we stayed for church and learned all about what happened to sinners, how they were burned to a cinder but never consumed, and other juvenile trash like that. Then we went home and sat on a chair till papa told us we could get down. Sometimes mamma read us stories from the New Testament. We were just barely allowed to breathe. After supper we had family prayers. God! it was awful! And I can't shake it off; never could. I still lower my voice on Sundays."

Jim laughed.

"Well, I'm different. I never went to Sunday school much; once or twice to please my mother. My old man thought it was all rot."

"This place is deadly," said George, puffing on his pipe. "I resist. But Marg is sinking fast. Ever notice?"

"She seems different sometimes."

"She is different. She's been going backward ever since she came home from California. She even looks different."

"She looks a little older."

"Not only that. She's beginning to look like Barrow-ville. And lately she's been worse than ever." George knocked out his pipe and refilled it, tamping the to-bacco down with a pencil. "You know, Jim, sometimes I think it's all due to Pres Barrow."

Jim was a little startled and looked sideways at George.

"You what?"

"Well, he sort of stands for this place. In a way, you know. He's better than most, but still he belongs here. A pretty nice fellow, regular, but a little too respect-able, little too narrow. You know what I mean. And Marg has more respect for him than anybody living."

"I guess she has."

"When you first came back he stayed away. But now he's getting to be a member of the family and sometimes he bores me till I think I'll have to insult him. He's smug. As I remember it, he didn't used to be. But maybe I'm changing, too. Maybe I'm going the other way. Hell! If I was ten years younger I'd light out. But I'm sunk. If I had had any sense I'd have gone West with the dogs. I had a chance to. But on account of Sonny and Marg I stayed. And then Marg went to all the trouble of getting me my job back and . . ."

They sat silent, looking off over the fall landscape. The sun was shining palely now, casting a faint glow over the woods. A dense cloud of migratory birds flew above them, making a shadow. Pat stirred and barked, but did not tug at his leash. Jim sat stroking his head.

What George had said worried him. Principally be-cause George had merely put into words his own vague thoughts. George was keen and saw things with his little observant eyes and he could talk about what he saw. Jim recognized his superiority in this respect. He felt pretty dumb, compared with George. Marg was changing, turning into a housewife. She did not seem happy any more, was always worried about some slight thing in spite of the fact that things ran more smoothly than ever before. George had his old job back and was getting steadier every day; never touched a thing but beer, and never gambled. Sonny was healthy, well behaved, doing well at school. Eddie was getting bigger and stronger. And he, himself, worked day in and day out, saving his money, contributing his share to the upkeep of the big old house and never complaining. What more could Marg ask?

She had everything that she wanted . . . except one thing. Jim flushed, thinking about it. Barrowville had forgotten the Mayhews; they had sunk. Pres Barrow, direct descendant of the pioneer who had founded the town, was the only one of the old families who ever came near. Barrowville objected to both George and Jim. They were sports; that settled it. There was no sporting blood left in the great-great-grandsons of the pioneers; they had degenerated into petty business men, Sunday-school superintendents, prohibitionists, managers of anti-tobacco campaigns, reactionary politicians, and the like. They said "No" to every manifestation that seemed at all dangerous to them and they hated and feared all men who said "Yes." Vitality had entirely disappeared from the ruling class. Only the people across the railroad tracks were alive; the immigrant

Italians, the second-generation Germans, and the swarm-
ing Irish. Marg felt this pressure very strongly and Jim
knew it, although he only came to the realization
gradually.

But what could be done about it? Nothing that he
could think of. He turned to George.

"You know, sometimes I wonder why Marg ever married me. It's funny."

"Well, after all, she's my sister, and Ed's sister, too.
She had some kick left in her in spite of the way she was
raised. But that kick's about all gone."

Jim nodded in silence and stared at the road where
the Fords were still passing. Marg was very kind-hearted,
no doubt about that, but she objected very strongly to
Pat. She did not want people to think that Jim was one
of those dog-track persons; and she said that if he went
around Barrowville leading that dog all the time nobody would ever have anything to do with him. At first
Jim was very much surprised by Marg's attitude and he
had argued with her. Now he kept silent, but did as he
pleased in regard to Pat.

He got up every morning at five-thirty to walk him, as
a greyhound man told him that that was the only way
to get the dog back on his feet. He walked him from one
and a half to three miles, then he took him back to the
little shed at the end of the lot where he kept him,
rubbed his bad leg down with a special liniment, then
fed him, giving him a balanced dog food which he
bought at a pet store. He took him out for a short walk
after dinner every evening; then he put him to bed. The
dog loved to sleep and never barked or howled or caused

any trouble. Eddie would go out and peer in at him, calling, "'Lo, dog. 'Lo, Pat," but Sonny, a rather timid boy, was afraid of him, intimidated by his pale, remote eyes. But he was impressed by him, too, and sat of an evening drawing pictures of him. George loved the dog and encouraged Sonny in his attempts at portraiture. Marg said they had all gone crazy.

At Sunday supper everybody was intensely uncomfortable. It was Lottie's night off and Marg carried the food into the dining-room, assisted by Sonny, who succeeded in breaking two cups. There was a short silence, then Jim laughed, but Marg said:

"It's not funny, Jim. Sonny, can't you be more careful? Everything goes wrong around here."

George shrugged and stared at his plate. Jim flushed and glanced at Barrow, who looked away uncomfortably, clearing his throat. Finally the broken pieces were picked up and Marg sat down. After a while she tried to be very affable, patted Sonny on the head and called him "her good boy," and spoke very kindly to Jim. But somehow things never got straightened around. The tension in the room was slightly relaxed but never entirely removed.

After dinner, Marg put Eddie to bed. Sonny got out his paint-box and began to color a picture he had drawn of Dark Hazard. When Marg came back Jim was down on the floor, showing Sonny how to paint the blanket.

"Make it green," he was saying, "and put a white number five on it. When Pat was running, that's about the only blanket he ever wore."

"But why?" Sonny demanded.

"Because he was so great they had to put him in the middle, see, so maybe the others would bump him when he broke out and slow him down a little. If they didn't he was a cinch."

Marg looked at Barrow and shrugged. Barrow smiled politely.

"What's a cinch?" asked Sonny.

"Why, a cinch is . . . it means he would win easy. When a dog is very hard to beat you call him a cinch."

Sonny took a pencil and printed under the drawing: "Dark Hazard, the cinch."

George laughed.

"Sonny," he said, "you're just like your Aunt Marg. He still don't understand you, Jim."

"Well, what's the diff?"

Later, after Sonny had been put to bed, they played cards. Jim had learned to play bridge because Marg liked the game, but he played indifferently and often exasperated all of them by his mistakes. Barrow was icily polite, Marg shrugged and looked at the ceiling, but George sometimes lost his temper and often he seemed so comical that Jim burst out laughing. Jim was unable to understand how they could get so wrought up over a game of cards. He had played stud poker with men who would bet a thousand dollars on the turn of a card and his pulse had never quickened. Cards as a form of gambling had never appealed to him. To play bridge for nothing was merely a bore. But he stuck it out Sunday after Sunday, sometimes barely able to keep his eyes open.

At ten o'clock they stopped playing and Jim went out to the shed at the end of the lot to see if Dark Hazard was fixed for the night. He flashed his electric torch into the crate and the dog opened his eyes. Jim gave him fresh water, then he reached in and patted his head. The dog turned over on his back and stretched out his front legs. He loved to be rubbed, so Jim rubbed him for a while, talking to him. Then he covered the crate with a blanket, said, "Good night, Pat. Sweet dreams," and went back to the house, muttering to himself:

"Pretty damn cold out there for that dog tonight. I don't want him to catch pneumonia, now that I got him doing so well."

He let himself in at the side door; this door opened into a short hall which ran at right angles to the long front hall and formed an L around the base of the front stairway. The big hall was in darkness. At the far end the porch light cast a pale glow a few feet inside. The front door was open. Jim saw Barrow and Marg. Barrow had his overcoat on and his hat in his hand. Jim could not see their faces, but they seemed to be tense, staring at each other. This worried him and he halted for a moment, scarcely breathing. Marg put out her hand suddenly and spoke in an entirely strange voice, low-pitched and intense:

"Pres! You mustn't come here any more!"

Barrow shook hands with her briefly, then turned and went out. She shut the door. Jim heard her sigh. Then she turned and started up the stairway. He coughed and came noisily down the hall.

"That you, Jim? I'm tired. I'm going to bed."

"Good night, Marg. Think I'll sit up awhile and talk to George."

"Good night."

It was one o'clock before Jim felt at all sleepy. George had gone to bed about twelve and the house was very still. Jim had just finished a story in an adventure magazine. It was about a rum-runner who started out as a tough river-front kid, worked himself up till he was skipper of a rum-schooner, and concluded his career by being reformed by a school-teacher. The ending disgusted Jim and he threw the magazine on the floor. He couldn't picture this husky and profane man settling down to the humdrum of shore living. That was the trouble with all the stories he had ever read; they weren't true. The writers didn't know what they were talking about. Guys like this rum-runner didn't settle down; they got shot or drowned or sent to federal prison. Marg was always telling him that he should read more. But why read a lot of junk that wasn't even true? He never could see Marg's point. Of course Marg thought that the adventure magazines and the detective magazines he bought were pretty terrible, but the stuff she read was just as bad; worse, if anything, because it wasn't even exciting. Stories about dressed-up people and the trouble they had staying married; or else a story about a girl who had two suitors and couldn't make up her mind which to take; or a story about one of them modern girls who told her father where to get off and was always doing "daring" things. Jim sometimes gritted his teeth over a story like that in what Marg called one of the "better" magazines. He'd like to have a daughter

like that; he'd warm her pants for her and put her in
her proper place.

He got up and yawned, then he noticed that the room
was cold. It had been fairly warm that afternoon and
they had let the furnace go out. A small gas-heater was
burning in the living-room, but it didn't give off much
heat. Jim listened. The wind was banging a shutter at
the back of the house. Cold out, and windy. He thought
suddenly of Dark Hazard out there in that flimsy shed.
He didn't want him to take cold. He was doing so well.
He looked as lithe and sleek as he had ever looked; his
bad leg was sound, though he still walked a little gingerly on it, due to habit. A cold would knock him all to
pieces. Taking up his electric torch, he went out.

The next morning Marg found Jim fully dressed,
lying on the living-room lounge, asleep. The dog was
stretched out on the floor beside him. When she came in
the dog looked up and stared at her intently with his
pale eyes. She began to laugh. Jim was always so brisk
in the morning now, getting up at five-thirty to walk
the dog. But the walk had evidently been too much for
him this morning. She took a step toward him, intend-
ing to shake him. But the dog raised his long sloping
head and growled softly. The dog had always seemed to
her just a toy. But now she realized how formidable he
was; nearly seventy pounds of hard flesh and muscle,
swift as the wind and strong as a mastiff; with gleaming
white fangs. She remembered Jim telling about how
these dogs were used to course coyotes on the plains; a
coyote or even a wolf was no match for them. She
stepped back and called:

"Jim!"

Jim rubbed his eyes and sat up. He saw a look of fear on Marg's face, then he heard Dark Hazard growling.

"Pat!" he said, sharply.

The dog raised his ears and looked up at him, then he lowered his head in shame.

"You mustn't growl at Marg, Pat. She's your mamma." Marg was very much annoyed.

"I'm no mamma to a dog," she said. "If you paid half as much attention to Eddie as you do to that . . . that animal, you'd . . ." She hesitated.

"Now, now, Marg. I've got to look after him, don't I? It was cold out in the shed, so I brought him in here."

"You brought him in here to sleep?"

"He's as clean as I am."

"Cleaner, probably."

Jim flushed. Marg was always complaining that he didn't take enough baths, didn't wash his hair often enough, never thought of his personal appearance.

"You're just sore 'cause he growled at you, Marg. That's all. If you'd make friends with him he'd like you as well as he does me."

"I've got other things to do. Come get your breakfast. It's nearly seven-thirty."

"Seven-thirty! I won't have time to walk him today."

Marg turned and left the room.

A BOY FROM THE DRUG STORE ACROSS THE ENTRY WAY brought Jim his lunch each day—a cup of coffee, a sandwich and a piece of pie. Jim took it into a little alcove at the back of the store and ate it when he had time.

It was Saturday noon and he stood leaning on the counter, waiting for the boy with the lunch. The day was cloudless and pleasant and the September sun was warm in the streets. People came out of the big elevators in the foyer and hurried past on their way to lunch— smart little stenographers, snappy-looking, running out to shop, their high heels tapping lightly on the floor; young clerks lighting cigarettes and grinning, glad to be out in the air for an hour; dignified older men, salesmen and executives, puffed up with their own importance. Some of them stopped to buy tobacco or candy. The older men bored Jim, the young men puzzled him, and the slim little stenographers with their rouged lips and their pert faces made him feel like an old man, fat, gray, and out of the running. But he smiled at all alike and was very popular because of his unvarying good humor.

The boy brought his lunch and Jim took it back to the alcove. He drank the coffee quickly, then took a bite out of the sandwich before he was interrupted. He waited on a customer, then hurried to the alcove. He kept this up till the sandwich and the pie had disappeared, then he sighed with satisfaction, took a few puffs from a cigarette, and went back to lean torpidly on the counter.

The outgoing rush was over. The elevator boys were standing in the foyer, talking. Occasionally a few people drifted in or out, some stopping at the cigar counter. Presently Jim noticed two men standing across the entryway by the mail-chute, looking at him. They seemed out of place. They were big, chunky men with weathered, red faces, tow-colored hair, and coarse features. But they didn't look tough; they looked good-natured, and rustic. They were dressed in city clothes, but Jim was pretty sure they were farmers. Their actions puzzled him. They stood eyeing him, but as soon as he glanced in their direction, they looked away. He noticed that they were nudging each other and finally he heard one of them say, "No, you."

A man came up to buy some cigars, then one of the farmers walked over, hesitatingly, and said:

"Are you Mr. Turner?"

"Yep."

"Have you got a greyhound?"

"Yes, I have."

"Well . . . Pete, come over here. This is the guy."

Pete came slowly, grinning and averting his eyes. The first man said:

"My name's Herman Reuterdahl. This is my brother Pete. Mr. Sidler was telling us you had a greyhound. He says it's a very good greyhound. Been run on the tracks some."

Jim laughed.

"I'll say he's been run some. He was a top dog in California."

The brothers glanced at each other, grinning. Herman said:

"My father plays pinochle with Mr. Sidler and he is always talking about that greyhound. We thought we'd just come in and see you about him."

"That's right," said Pete.

"See me about him! You mean you want to buy him?"

Herman laughed.

"No, not buy him. We got more greyhounds now than we know what to do with. We thought we'd just come in, being's it's Saturday, and see if you'd like to bring him out and race him. We got a farm about three miles north of town. We got twenty greyhounds."

"He's been hurt. I been nursing him along. I just got him for a pet."

The brothers looked at each other, grinning.

"Well," said Herman, "we been thinking if he's so almighty good maybe you'd like to run him a little. We got some pretty fast ones. I got a pair of them in a trade and we raised a couple of litters just for fun. We been coursing some jacks with them. It's fun. We like it."

"Ever race them on tracks?"

"We never did. But the pair we got in the trade has been raced. In the East at Kensington, Pennsylvania. They was pretty good dogs there, too. The bitch can run the five-sixteenths around thirty-three seconds, they tell me. We got a couple of big male pups that are as fast as lightning."

Jim began to get interested. Pat was in pretty good shape; the walking had kept his weight down; he wasn't but two or three pounds over his usual running weight. Lord! it would be wonderful to see him sailing along, with his nose close to the ground. He was the fastest thing alive when he was right.

"Well," said Jim, "I don't know. I might come out some Sunday."

Herman scratched his head.

"We don't have much time on Sundays. We go to church over in Bellport and we stay most of the day over there with our relatives. We're Catholics, you see. There ain't but one Catholic church in Barrowville, and we like the cathedral in Bellport better."

Pete spoke up.

"We thought, this being Saturday, you'd be off work in the afternoon."

"No. I've got to work. Sunday's the only day I can get off."

The Reuterdahl brothers held a conference, then Herman said:

"We'd like awful well to see that dog of yours run. Couldn't you call up Mr. Sidler and ask him to let you off for the afternoon? He's the one that started this. He told my father your dog could beat anything on four legs, and to tell you the truth, we don't believe it. We got some mighty fast pups. The old dog's got a bad leg, but he can run some, too. The bitch is in whelp."

Jim understood them now. They wanted to give his dog a beating so they could crow about it to Barney. A thrill went through him. Beat Dark Hazard with some old pick-up dogs! Culls, the dog-men called them. What a chance!

"All right," he said. "I'll call the boss."

The Reuterdahl brothers took him home in their old Ford. He ran into the house, shouting: "Marg, Marg!" but Lottie opened the kitchen door and said:

"There isn't nobody here but me and Eddie, Mr. Turner. Sonny's down at the Y.M.C.A. playing indoor baseball. George had his lunch and went uptown. I don't know where the missus is."

"Is she at the shop?"

"No, sir. I don't think so. I'm pretty sure not. I think she's uptown, too."

Eddie put his head in the door and Jim picked him up and kissed him. He never paid very much attention to Eddie as a rule, as he could never get over the feeling that Eddie wasn't his. He had been away when Eddie was born, and when he first saw him the kid was past two and had been fitted so smoothly into the routine of the house that he seemed like a stranger's child. But he liked Eddie, thought he was a swell little kid.

"See you at dinner, old boy," he said.

Eddie looked at him with big eyes, wondering why Jim had kissed him, then he went back into the little playroom at the side of the kitchen. It was an old pantry Marg had fixed up so Lottie could watch him and go on with her work at the same time.

Jim hurried out to the shed, got the dog out of his crate, and put a leash on him. "We'll show 'em," said Jim, and the dog looked up at him, raising his ears.

When Jim came out with the dog the brothers were

standing at the curb, waiting, anxious for a look at this super-greyhound. Jim led him up and down to show him off. Herman said:

"Nice dog. A little light-boned, but he's nice. Eh, Pete?"

Pete scratched his head.

"How old is he?"

"He's five."

"Our pups is bigger than him. We got one pup, nineteen months, weighing seventy-six pounds. His name's Kurt. He's a whale of a dog. Can run rings around a horse. Reckon Kurt can beat this dog, Herman?"

Herman didn't reply. He merely winked, then the brothers burst out laughing. Dark Hazard paid no attention to them, but stood with his body pressed against Jim's leg.

"Don't laugh yet," Jim said. "You'll have plenty of time to laugh later."

"Don't get sore," said Herman. "We just think we got the best young dog living. That's all."

The brothers got in the front seat. Jim got in the back with Dark Hazard. The dog stood staring indifferently out at the houses and the people they were passing. Herman was driving. Pete turned to look at Dark Hazard.

"He's pretty fine, that dog. Too fine for my taste. Looks like a bitch, almost."

"That's breeding," said Jim, boiling.

"It may be breeding. He may be all right in the show-ring. But give me bone and size for coursing and track."

"All right. All right. Wait."

But Jim was very uneasy. Suppose the dog wasn't

right. Suppose he hadn't hardened him up enough, walking him. Suppose he didn't have any wind. Wouldn't these Dutchmen crow?

The whole family was waiting for them. There was the father, Franz, a big man with thick gray hair and a face like Santa Claus; he looked as strong as a bull. There were four big strapping girls, ranging in age from eighteen to twenty-five. There were the two younger brothers, both red-faced, husky and tow-headed, and besides, a raft of sturdy children and the husbands of two of the girls. They all shouted and laughed as the Ford drove up. One of the girls brought Jim a stein of beer, which he drank in two gulps, keeping hold of the dog. Then they all went out beyond the barn, where the Reuterdahls had leveled off a great stretch of meadow.

Herman pointed:

"You see? We been over this place with a fine-tooth comb. No glass, no stones, no nothing. It's as fit as any coursing-park you ever saw. You don't have to worry none about your million-dollar dog."

Pete laughed loudly, then whispered something in German to Franz, who nodded and shouted with laughter. Dark Hazard looked at this crowd of loud, lusty, laughing folks with a good deal of disdain, but he was somewhat timid and worried by the noise and the rushing about, and Jim felt him trembling.

"Get that brindle dog, Albert. We'll see what he can do," called Pete, then he turned to Jim. "We'll run our second best first. We'll give you a chance."

"You better get out the best one you got," said Jim,

"because I ain't going to run this dog more than once or twice. And no jacks. We'll sprint them."

The Reuterdahls held a conference, then Herman said:

"All right. We'll run Kurt at you right away. You'll be sorry. Albert, bring Kurt out. Say, is that dog of yours a fighter?"

Jim cried vehemently:

"I should say he ain't."

"Well, don't get all excited. Our dog ain't, either. I was going to say I had a muzzle if he was. I don't want Kurt all chewed up."

Jim stamped about in his rage.

"You don't want him chewed up! Say, this dog never turned his head in his life. He don't fight, he runs. What do you think he is, a police dog!"

Albert led out a huge blue dog, one of the biggest greyhounds Jim had ever seen. He was dancing sideways and straining at the leash. He leaped playfully when he saw Dark Hazard, but the black dog stood very still, staring at him.

"Ain't he a beauty?" cried Herman.

"Nice big dog," said Jim, grudgingly. "Let's run 'em and see how good he is."

"Oh, you'll see all right," said Albert, with a smirk.

Franz laughed and shook his head. The girls capered, looking sideways at Jim. The little kids ran about, shouting with excitement.

"First," said Herman, "we'll sprint 'em a hundred yards, then if you want more, all right. Will your dog sprint without a rabbit?"

"Yes, I think so. Soon as he sees a dog running he'll try to catch him."

"Very good. Will you trust me to let him go? You want to catch him, don't you?"

"Yes. But be careful. Don't hold him too tight. He's easy to handle."

"I'll treat him like a baby."

Franz took his pipe out of his mouth.

"I'll drop the handkerchief."

Jim and Pete walked down the meadow. Pete said:

"We got it marked off. We sprint 'em a little at a time. We give 'em a longer sprint and a longer sprint till they're ready to course. Here we are."

Jim turned. He was pale and shaking with excitement. Maybe he wasn't doing the right thing at all; maybe Pat wasn't ready for anything like this. He rubbed his hands together; they were cold and clammy. A hundred yards away the whole group had gathered around the starting-mark. Albert was holding Kurt, Herman was holding Dark Hazard. A hundred yards seemed a mighty long distance when you stood and looked at it.

"Ready?" demanded Franz.

"Ready," called Pete.

Franz dropped the handkerchief. The dogs were let loose and Kurt went away with a rush. Pete was calling to him in a loud high-pitched voice. Dark Hazard seemed to hesitate. Jim jumped into the air and waved his arms, shouting. Dark Hazard overtook the blue dog in two jumps, then he flattened out and really ran, passing Kurt as if he was tied to a post. The Reuterdahls all stopped shouting and turned to look at one another.

Dark Hazard crossed the mark ten lengths ahead of the blue dog, and when Jim caught him he wasn't even panting. Three hundred feet was a mere romp for a greyhound in condition. Jim jumped up into the air and shouted "Whoopee!"

Pete stood with his mouth open, holding on to the big blue pup. Herman came on the run.

"Mr. Turner," he cried, "where did you get that dog there?"

"He got hurt in a hurdle race and I bought him for twenty-five dollars."

"Want to sell him?"

"Not a chance. Five thousand dollars wouldn't buy this dog."

The Reuterdahls stood about, stunned, for a long time, then Franz and Albert began to insist that maybe there was something wrong with Kurt. He was just a big young pup, after all, and maybe he hadn't been wormed properly or maybe he was coming down with some sickness. Finally, after a long, violent argument, Herman came over to Jim and asked him very politely if he'd consent to run his dog again. Jim was amused by the change in their attitude toward him. There was no more rollicking and winking and self-confident boasting; Dark Hazard had knocked all the cockiness out of them.

"Yes," said Jim, "I'll run him again. Make the distance a little longer this time if you want to. Two hundred yards suits me all right."

The Reuterdahls held one of their comic conferences, then Albert led out Kaiser, the brindle pup, and Pete got the old stud dog King Tut out of his crate.

Both of them were huge, gaunt dogs, high in the shoulder and powerful-looking. But the old dog was somewhat battered and had a broken tail.

"What do you say, Mr. Turner," cried Herman, "shall we run all of them? This is the best we've got. If your dog can beat all of them, why then he's all right."

"Suits me."

Jim scratched Dark Hazard's ears and talked to him soothingly, then he turned him over to Herman, who took him to the starting-mark with the others. Jim wasn't at all worried now. He knew that Dark Hazard was himself again and that all the culls in the world couldn't beat him two hundred yards even if he got left at the post. But he saw that the Reuterdahls were excited and anxious. Pete had even developed a little pallor under his sunburn.

Franz dropped the handkerchief and the dogs were off. Dark Hazard, unused to being sprinted this way, was last off again, but it didn't matter. He quickly learned what was expected of him and came toward Jim like a black arrow over the level meadow. The Reuterdahls groaned. It was no race at all. The black dog was so far ahead that the other dogs were lost in a cloud of dust. Dark Hazard slowed down at the finish line and Jim put his arms around him and hugged him. Some of the Reuterdahls caught their dogs, the others crowded round Jim, shouting and waving their arms.

"*Himmel!*" said Franz, "that's the fastest dog I ever saw. That blue pup has been a quarter of a mile in twenty-six and four-fifths seconds over the electric track."

Jim laughed.

"I thought you said them dogs had never run on a track."

Herman looked sheepish.

"Well, we wanted to fool you. Mr. Sidler was always talking and we thought we'd get the laugh on you, that's all."

Jim laughed.

"Now I'll tell you something. This dog here is the joint holder of the world's futurity record. He run the futurity at Crescent City in twenty-eight seconds flat in 1929."

"I believe you," said Herman, mopping his brow. "Turner, come on in the house. Me and Pete want to talk to you. We'll have some sandwiches and beer. Marguerite! We want good sandwiches and get Ernest to help you open that beer we got at Bellport Sunday. Albert you and Pete feed the dogs, then come in. Want to leave your dog in a crate, Turner?"

"No. I'll take him with me, if you don't mind. He's nervous in a new place."

"Mind? We don't mind. Bring him in."

They were sitting in a huge kitchen, a room bigger than the living-room in the old Mayhew house. The women had built a wood fire in a big stone fireplace; it danced on the hearth and cast big shadows over the beamed ceiling. Franz, Herman, Pete, and Jim, sitting round a huge, roughly built table, were on their third stein. The younger men hovered about, listening. The women had effaced themselves, taking the children. Dark Hazard lay on the floor, asleep, with his head on Jim's foot.

The Germans took turns at Jim, talking insistently, but he kept shaking his head. They were all excited by the chance of making a little money. Franz and his sons were prosperous farmers and they had one of the richest farms in central Ohio, where there is the best soil in the world, but since the depression things had been terrible. Prices had fallen till a farmer couldn't make a living; corn wasn't worth cutting; a man would save money by cutting his wheat and letting it rot; feeding hogs was a waste of time; cattle were a luxury. In short, the bottom had dropped out of everything. Franz explained this at great length, waving his pipe.

Then Herman took up the story. A little track was going to open at Andrewsville, just across the state line, two hundred and seventy miles away. The town had a new mayor and a new city council, all in favor of city-controlled greyhound-racing. The Andrewsville track had been closed for three years, due to the efforts of reformers. "But now," said Herman, proudly, "some good Germans are in office and things are different."

"Yes," said Pete, "people now will get a chance to see some sport and have some fun and forget all about the depression."

"Yes," Herman interposed, "and fellows with a few greyhounds can make a little money. We've got three ready to go. Kurt, Kaiser, and the old dog. We'll win a lot of races with them. There won't be much competition, because the purses ain't much. Eighty dollars for the feature race; forty-eight for the winner, twenty-four for second, and eight for third. Not good, but not bad. We can win many a race with the pups. Our expenses won't be nothing. We got our own truck."

"Yes," said Franz. "Why don't you lease us that black dog? We'll pay you good money for him."

"Why don't you sell him to us?" said Herman. "I'll give you a hundred and seventy-five dollars cash for him. That's a lot of money right now."

Marguerite, one of the big strapping girls, came in with more beer and more sandwiches; her father hugged her and said, "Good girl." Jim sat shaking his head, and kept insisting that five thousand dollars wouldn't buy Dark Hazard. After a long pause, Herman said:

"All right. I'll give you two hundred dollars for him. Ain't that fair?"

But Franz shook his head and muttered:

"Don't go too steep now, Herman."

Jim laughed. Herman turned away in despair.

"He won't sell him, he won't lease him. It's too bad. A dog like that ought to be running, not laying around the house. Will you breed him for a pup, Turner?"

"No. His stud fee is seventy-five dollars."

The Reuterdahls roared with indignation. Herman jumped up and began to walk the floor. Finally he said:

"I'd sure like to see that black dog run at Andrewsville. I'd like to see the faces on them guys 'cross the line. They think they got some pretty fair dogs. It's a shame not to run him, Turner. Listen, if you won't sell him and you won't lease him, why don't you come along with us? It's only for forty-five days. Maybe Mr. Sidler would get a man in your place till you come back. He's a sport. You could go with Pete and me. There's plenty of room in the truck. You can kennel with us and we'll take a small per cent of the winnings for carrying you

over and bringing you back. How's that for a fair
proposition?"

Jim was tempted. He drank from his stein, then
glanced down at Dark Hazard. The dog was stretched
out full length, asleep; from time to time he whined
softly and his feet twitched. Probably dreaming about
chasing a jack across a field. It would be pretty nice to
see him running on a track, breaking like a shot, hugging the rail and putting on one of his dizzy finishes
while the crowd roared and men talked in excited voices
about what a great pooch he was. Jim got up abruptly.

"Can't do it. My wife hates tracks and things like that.
I got a family to worry about. Can't be done."

The Reuterdahls finally began to understand that
Jim couldn't be persuaded, and they sighed. It was too
bad, too bad. Did Jim want Franz to speak to Mr. Sidler
just in case? Mr. Sidler and Franz were great friends.

"No," said Jim. "You going to take me back to town,
Herman?"

"Yes," said Herman; then he shook his head. "I wish
me and Pete had never brought you out here. You got
us all upset now."

Herman and Jim shook hands, then Jim took Dark
Hazard around the house and put him in his crate. He
was bursting to tell Marg all about the dog and how he
was as fit as a fiddle and how he had beaten some pretty
fair dogs so far that it was comical. He also wanted to
tell her how the Reuterdahls had tried to persuade him
to take Dark Hazard to the Andrewsville track and how
he had refused. Maybe that would show her.

He went in the back door, calling, "Marg! Marg!" but Lottie turned and put her finger to her lips.

"Eddie's taking his nap. The missus isn't here, Mr. Turner. Neither is George nor Sonny. Ain't come back yet."

Jim was very much disappointed. He wanted to talk.

"Say, Lottie, what do you think! I took my dog out and raced him against some young greyhounds and he beat them a mile."

Lottie said:

"I think maybe the missus is at the shop. I seen the girl going home about three o'clock. I know the missus would never let her shut up on Saturday afternoon. What did you say about that dog?"

"Nothing."

Jim turned away in disgust. Women were all the same. All they thought about was keeping the house in order and seeing that the baby wasn't disturbed and things like that. What did they care about sports and things that were interesting!

All the same, he was beer-warmed and exhilarated and bursting to talk, not only about Dark Hazard, but about his own strength of character in refusing to take him to the track when it would have been so easy. Just a little jaunt across the state line; forty-five days of racing; then back on the job with a lot of purse money. Jim stopped and considered. Maybe, after all . . . but no. Marg would never stand for it.

He opened the door of the shop and went in heedlessly, his mind busy with thoughts of the Andrewsville track. There was one small electric light burning above the counter. Dusk was falling and it was nearly dark in the shop. He looked about him. Funny for the door to be open like this if nobody was around. That wasn't like Marg at all. Then he heard a footstep and, turning, saw Marg coming out of the back room. He opened his mouth to tell her about Dark Hazard, but hesitated, noticing how pale she was.

"Marg! What . . ."

She interrupted:

"What are you doing home so early, Jim? It's only about five o'clock."

"I been off all afternoon. I . . ."

Jim started back as if he had been struck with a whip. Barrow came calmly out of the back room and stood looking at him.

"What's he doing here?" Then he burst out: "I guess it's not a bad idea for me to get an afternoon off once in a while and see what's going on. I got a good notion to smack you one in the jaw, you two-faced . . ."

"Come ahead," said Barrow, very pale but calm.

But Marg said:

"You're wrong, Jim. I know it looks funny, but you're wrong about us."

"Well," said Jim, with a sneer, "if you'll do it once, you'll do it again."

"What do you mean?" shouted Barrow.

"You know what I mean. Both of you."

Marg turned.

"I told him, Pres."

"Oh!"

Marg began to cry. Jim reached out and put his hand on her shoulder, but she pulled away.

"She wants to marry me, Turner," said Barrow,

sharply. "And I think you ought to be told. There's no sense in Margaret living the way she does just to . . . just to keep from hurting your feelings. That's the God's truth."

"Marg," said Jim, "is that right?"

She wouldn't look at him, but stood with her face turned away, wiping her eyes.

"Why don't you tell him, Margaret? Turner, Margaret was getting ready to get a divorce when you turned up here. But she changed her mind. At first it was all right. Now it isn't. She wants to marry me and I've wanted to marry her for years. Long before you ever came to this town and broke things up. Now you know the truth. And if you're half a man you'll know what to do about it."

Jim took two steps forward and knocked Barrow down. Barrow got up quickly and tried to fight, but Jim knocked him down again.

"Sure," said Jim, "I know what to do. I just done it."

"Oh," cried Marg, "you big tough! You race-track bum! Get out of here! Yes, it's true. Just what Pres said. And we haven't so much as kissed each other since you came home. And this is the thanks we get for it."

"Marg!"

"You might just as well know how I feel, Jim, because I'm going to get a divorce. I'm not going to live this way any longer and be laughed at by everybody in town. You don't care anything about any of us, anyway. All you care about is that dog."

Jim stood very still, looking at her. She wasn't his Marg now at all. She was just like she used to be when he was a roomer in the old Mayhew house, five or six years ago. He cleared his throat and looked from one to the other. Marg was pale as death, leaning on the counter. Barrow was standing very straight; his eyes were blazing, and a thin trickle of blood was running down his chin from a split lip.

"Well . . ." Jim said, slowly. "If that's the way you feel about it . . ."

He turned quickly and went out, closing the door softly.

Chapter III

THEY WERE PASSING THROUGH A LITTLE TOWN, A MERE string of houses and stores stretched along the broad highway. It was very late and almost all of the windows were dark. At every other corner there was a tall light-pole, curved downward at the top, from which was suspended a shaded electric bulb, casting a bright, round patch of light onto the empty road. A bluish night light was burning in the depths of the little post-office. The town slept. At the far end a red warning light flashed off and on.

"Middleboro," said Herman.

Jim turned. There was a slight grade and the road curved upward. He saw the little town lying below them, empty, quiet, melancholy under its white arc-lights.

Pete said:

"Well, we're getting along. Running into hilly country now. We'll make it by morning, sure."

"We may make it before," Herman put in, jamming on the brakes at a sharp turn. "With a little luck we'll be in 'fore dawn."

They had drunk several bottles of beer on the way and Jim had begun to feel drowsy. Herman was driving; Pete sat in the middle; Jim was squeezed up against the right side and he had one foot hanging out. The breeze was cool and steady, blowing from the southeast;

they could feel it on their faces. Jim tried to keep awake by staring out at the countryside. He smelled open country and it was good. Big farmhouses, black and sharply outlined, moved toward them rapidly, then disappeared behind. From time to time the wind carried the smell of cow-stables across their path. Herman would sniff and say: "Ah!" And Pete would laugh. "Smells like home."

Jim found himself staring at the road, white under the icy glare of the headlights; it seemed to be rushing toward them, interminably rushing toward them, and overhead, in the blackest shadow, arched the roadside trees, sometimes brushing the top of the truck with a sharp, scraping sound. They saw a pale glow over a low hill. The road climbed upward sharply, then turned, and they passed a lonely power station. They saw a brilliantly lighted interior, a lone man standing with his back to the door, and a big dynamo with a huge, black driving-wheel. For a second they caught the smell of engine heat and oil; then the wind carried it away and they were out in the dark, open country again.

Jim's eyes fell shut and he dozed. Lights exploded inside his head, then in a blurred nightmarish fashion he saw Marg, George, Eddie; they were coming toward him, then as if stopped by a sudden wind, they struggled for a moment in his direction, then turned away. He saw them in diminishing perspective till they were far, far away; gone. He began to whimper. His hair was streaked with gray. He was getting fat. Nobody had any use for him, not even the Reuterdahls; all they wanted was the dog. He was old, old, almost ready for the discard. He had pains in his legs at night from standing on his feet; Barney told him he'd better look out, maybe he had varicose veins. In the morning he couldn't get up like he used to; all the bounce was out of him; he had a bad taste in his mouth and sometimes he felt kind of dizzy till he had his morning coffee. He was getting to the place where a man likes a pipe and a fire and a dog dozing on the hearth and a nice wife and a kid and to hell with the world outside. Hadn't he done his best? He had settled down, really settled down, and what had it got him?

Pete said:

"Hey! You'll fall out. Boy, you make a buzz-saw sound quiet."

Jim laughed shortly. After a while Herman pulled up at the side of the road.

"We better walk the dogs," he said.

Dark Hazard was lying with his head in the straw. Jim woke him gently. He got up; yawned, then shook himself. Jim put the leash on him and lifted him to the ground.

"Well, old boy, how you making it?"

The dog looked up, raising his ears.

Herman had Kaiser and the old stud dog; Pete had Kurt. They walked silently up the dark road, stopping from time to time so the dogs could empty out. Jim walked a little behind the others, thinking. The whole countryside, dark and rolling, was still as death under the stars. Far across the fields a dog began to bark, the sound carrying well and echoing in the quiet night. They were walking up a short grade. Ahead of them, at the top of a low hill, the moon was rising, very white and frosty in the sky. Jim saw a farmhouse, a barn, and a silo silhouetted against the lower rim of the moon. He had never felt so depressed in his life.

Dark Hazard walked beside him quietly, never straightening out the leash. Jim heard the dog's toe nails clicking on the hard road.

Pete began to sing:

> "Ich weiss nicht was soll es bedeuten,
> Dass ich so traurig bin;
> Ein Märchen aus alten Zeiten,
> Das kommt mir nicht aus dem Sinn . . ."

Jim hoped he would stop. There was something about the song that made him feel worse than ever. Suddenly he remembered The Great Mario with his long, sallow face and his sad eyes. He remembered the night he had put the money in the till for him so he wouldn't have to kick him out into the street. He remembered the automatic the hypnotist had put on the counter, saying: "Did you ever get that low?" And he had replied: "No. Never say die."

Pete went on singing. Jim felt like wringing his neck. Pretty soon Pete stopped. The dog was still barking far off. The moon had got clear of the hill and rose so fast now that it seemed like a big white balloon lit from the inside.

"Well," said Herman, coming back, "I guess that's enough."

The old stud dog began to bay the moon. There was something wolfish in his howls which made the hair on Jim's head quiver.

"Shut up, you!" said Herman, laughing.

They put the dogs back into the crates, drank a bottle of beer apiece, and started off again.

Jim woke with a start. The truck had jolted to a stop. Jim felt cold and clammy. The sky was getting pale directly in front of them and a white mist was rising from the fields. He heard birds chirping along the fences. The wind was chilly.

Herman got down and flashed his electric torch.

"Yep, Pete, that's it. Hey, Turner, look."

Herman had his torch turned on a heavy granite post; there was a legend on it which read: "STATE LINE."

"Whoopee!" cried Pete. "It won't be long now."

Jim got down from the truck and stamped his numb feet, cursing; then he went back to look at Dark Hazard. The dog was asleep. Jim stared at him for a long time. Then suddenly he remembered the last time he had seen him run on a track. It was at Frisco. They had assembled all the best dogs to beat him and had set the Derby at five-sixteenths, which wasn't his distance. Three dogs were favored over him, but he broke in front, led all the way, and won by a scant nose, putting on one of his dizzy finishes. Lord! how they roared. People cheered until the dogs had left the track.

"Good old boy," he said. "Good old Pat."

The sky was golden when they drove into the outskirts of Andrewsville. They passed milk-wagons and empty trucks going out on the job, and they saw a lone policeman blowing on his hands at a street corner.

"Well," said Herman, "this is it."

They drove through the downtown section, which was

deserted except for two taxicabs at a stand, and a track-welder bending over the electric-blue flame of his torch. The lights went out all over town; dawn was showing in the streets, and high overhead the windows were coppery in the first rays. They drove through a little suburban district where cats were prowling and paper-boys were riding bicycles and throwing wrapped-up newspapers up onto the porches. All the lawns glistened with dew.

Then they saw the track, all pale and misty in the morning. The grandstand rose white and tall above all the other buildings. Behind it the sky was a pearly white and a red sun was showing. Jim smelled wet turf. He expanded his lungs and breathed deeply.

They saw a man coming up the street, leading a string of greyhounds.

Jim turned.

"Pat," he cried, "here we are."

THE END